Vanessa listened a̶s̶ ̶s̶h̶e̶ ̶l̶o̶o̶ked. The wind made the only sounds she heard—the rustling of the bag, the clicking of denuded tree limbs, the swishing of fallen leaves. She moved to the grave and to the treasure it offered. Her fingers reached down and clasped the chilly, crinkly plastic. She pulled it toward her, not wanting to step on the soft, muddy earth beneath the mass of funeral flowers.

Behind her, the shadow rose from behind a wide headstone. His feet moved soundlessly across the wet grass, just as they had many years ago in the jungles and rice paddies outside Saigon. In his right hand, the man she was to meet carried a small .25 caliber automatic.

His arm came around her throat. The gun jammed into a crack between her ribs. . . .

Also by Dave Pedneau
Published by Ballantine Books:

A.P.B.

D.O.A.

Dave Pedneau

BALLANTINE BOOKS • NEW YORK

Library of Congress Catalog Card Number: 87-91391

ISBN 0-345-34677-7

Manufactured in the United States of America

First Edition: March 1988

FOR MOM AND DAD . . .

PROLOGUE

"YOU SMELL IT, don't ya?" The old black woman, bent and withered, glared down from her porch at the young man in the blue cop's uniform.

"Well, don't ya?" she repeated.

"Yes, ma'am. I smell it." The young cop's gaze drifted over the peaceful residential landscape. Frame houses, the majority a single story and boxlike, lined the narrow street. Many of the homes needed some sort of repair, but the neighborhood wasn't a slum. There were no streetpeople sifting through the garbage—no clusters of idle men on the street corners. Maples, still clinging to their dying foliage, decorated the unlittered yards. The people of the community, many of whom were retired, looked to be the kind of folks who had worked very hard but received very little for it. It was the kind of neighborhood of which most towns wanted more.

The officer's attention settled on a white two-story home just west of the old woman's.

"Who lives there?"

"Mary Hairston and Jenny."

"Jenny?"

"Her daughter."

"What about her husband?"

"She's a widow lady, like me. Kinda young for it, and I don't have no notion what happened to her husband. Don't know a lot about her at all. She keeps to herself."

The breeze quickened; the stench intensified. The old woman screwed up her face. "You best get over there. I know that stink, young fella. I'm ninety-four—be ninety-five next month—and it's been tagging along behind me for a lotta years."

Old people had such a casual attitude about death. Patrolman Cole Surface had seen the quality in his grandmother. Doomed by a cancer raging in her belly, Granny Surface had maintained an optimism that strengthened the rest of the family.

On the far side of the Hairston home, an autumn-colored blanket of trees marked the beginning of a generous expanse of Appalachian forest. The street itself ended abruptly in a graveled turnaround a few yards west of the Hairston property. So, too, did the city limits of Milbrook. Cole's authority ended at that invisible jurisdictional fiction.

The odor, its pungent presence varying with the wind, made the rookie officer wish his authority ended where he stood. How nice it would be to call the Raven County Sheriff's Department to say, "Hey, guys. Ya'll got a ripe body somewhere out here." Specifically, that "somewhere" had to be in or about the Hairston house. It wasn't something Cole wanted to face on a Monday morning—or any morning, for that matter.

"Have you observed any activity over there?" he asked.

"Yessirree. Just this morning. I seen Mary—Missus Hairston—peeking out her window. Funny 'bout that, too. She works during the daytime."

The officer sagged with relief. "At least it sounds like she's okay. Where does she work?"

"Down at the newspaper."

Cole stiffened. "She a reporter?"

"Don't think so. Mary's just a plain old gal. She's got somethin' to do with putting the paper together."

"I'll go over and talk to her." The breeze had faded for the moment, and Cole felt much more at ease. The odor wasn't nearly as strong, and, if the old woman had seen Mary Hairston that morning, then there wasn't much of a chance that the same woman was in there dead and rotten—at least, not rotten.

He stepped off the old woman's porch and hesitated at the bottom. "It's probably just a dead animal. Last month, we had a dead horse in someone's backyard. Never did find out where it came from, but it raised a he—uh, heck of a smell, too. Thanks for calling in the complaint."

He turned toward the Hairston home.

"I ain't seen the little girl, though—"

Her words stopped him cold.

"—not for several days," she said.

"The little girl?" The anxiety coalesced in his gut.

"Yep. And that's a mighty odd thing, too. Jenny's out playin' all the time. Her momma keeps to herself. It's Jenny that's got the sociable turn in the family. A fine young 'un, always wanting to help me. Always wantin' to run down to the corner market for me and never wantin' so much as a penny for it. Even my kinfolk wanna charge me for a car ride. Jenny ain't like that. Polite as she can be, too."

A gust of wind delivered a mighty dose of the smell to them. The old woman gagged and covered her nose. "Lord A'mighty!"

Cole wanted to do the same thing, but he restrained himself. It wasn't professional. He hitched up his gun belt and held his breath. "I'll go check it out."

"I'm prayin' nothing's wrong."

Me, too, Cole thought.

Ten yards of overgrown lawn separated the two homes. At first blush, the Hairston residence appeared ill-kept, but a closer examination revealed recently trimmed pine shrub and a fresh coat of white housepaint. He covered the distance quickly but paused at the bottom of the steps leading to the front door. A wide porch wrapped around two sides of the two-story frame—the kind of porch that was made for a row of wicker rocking chairs.

At the point where he stood, the air, even the breeze, was scented only with the smell of freshly cut pine and the drying leaves of fall. Maybe, too, there was the hint of smoke odor from someone burning a pile of brush. Autumn always had a special aroma, and for the moment it was all that Cole Surface could detect.

He inhaled deeply, wondering what in the hell he was doing there. A lot of the guys on the Milbrook force boasted that they always wanted to be cops—ever since they had watched *Dragnet* on television. Not Cole. The lanky young man had never even thought of it as he grew up. His favorite television show had been *Mr. Wizard*. He had always wanted to be a rocket scientist. Trouble was, he didn't come up with four when he added two and two, at least not with the consistency demanded of an engineer or a nuclear physicist. He'd dropped out of college not long after his marriage.

Milbrook, as was the case in most of southern West Virginia, wasn't the best place to find a job. He wanted to own and operate a greenhouse, but a reasonable man pursued a more substantial career in a small, drab place such as Milbrook, especially if the man had a wife with no marketable skills and two ever-hungry kids. His job search had been an ego-bruising experience. Interviewer after interviewer noted his lack of skill and training. He'd left each interview feeling a little more down on himself. Then his wife had noticed the ad for a city policeman. She had also pointed out that Cole fulfilled the advertised requirements—top physical conditioning, good health, and a high school education. Finally, she had noted the starting pay of thirteen thousand dollars a year, not bad for depressed Milbrook. The clincher had been the generous health insurance. Cole's wife tended toward hypochondria and was intent upon instilling that same sense of physical gloom-and-doom in their children.

So he'd applied, suffered through the required physical and written tests and the medical examination, and, to his surprise, been hired. As of that Columbus Day morning, he'd been a cop for six months. The chief had promised to send Cole to the state police academy for training before the end of his probationary year. He'd also promised to send him out with the range officer so he could learn to use the gun he carried. In the meantime, they'd fitted him with a uniform, strapped the heavy gun on him, and assigned him to a veteran who'd spent three months telling him how to get around the "stupid-ass laws." It didn't do a lot for Cole's respect for cops.

As he looked up at the big house, glaring white in the morning sun, he felt inadequate. Cole sniffed the air again. It smelled like October, nothing else. Had the old woman been imagining the odor? Maybe she had spooked him into imagining it? Not all that unlikely, his mind playing that kind of trick with his nose. After all, the complaint was kind of déjà vu for Cole. Of squeamish nature, he suffered regular night horrors over dead bodies, especially since he'd become a cop. Spilled blood and guts turned him cold and dizzy and made him want to puke. When a fellow officer boldly brandished photos of an accident or homicide victim, Cole only pretended to look. He'd made the grievous mistake of actually looking at photos of decomposing remains in a book on homicide investigation in the department's small library. Of late the actors in his nightmares had come from the glossy photos in those books. Was he about to meet, face-to-face, his first real "live" decaying corpse?

Cole gave himself the luxury of another deep breath and then mounted the steps to the front porch. The doorbell button was covered with electrical tape, so he opened the screen and rapped gently on the door. He heard—actually felt—footsteps from inside the house. Someone was home. The porch vibrated ever so slightly as the person approached the front door. A white curtain covering one of the door's glass panes parted. Cole smiled to show that the visit was friendly.

The southeastern quadrant of Milbrook was predominantly black. While black families were gradually settling in other areas of Milbrook, the process wasn't very advanced. Cultural change penetrated the Appalachians slowly, if at all. In his short six months, Cole had discovered that police officers usually received something less than a warm welcome in the black area of town. Since the Milbrook PD wasn't, in Cole's opinion, ripe with racial tolerance, the black community's cool attitude toward the cops didn't surprise the rookie officer.

He braced himself as the door opened. The aroma that wafted from the house wasn't the heavy miasma of human rot, but it wasn't pleasant, either. It was the fruity smell of unwashed flesh, of rancid fermentation, flavored by a coppery odor that Cole did not immediately recognize.

A woman—Mary Hairston, Cole assumed—glared at him with a face so intense that he placed his hand on the butt of his revolver. She had wild, hungry eyes that belonged in an overacted B-grade horror flick. He couldn't sever the eye contact. The woman—she had a pretty face—gave the appearance of madness, of stark lunacy. When he did manage to pull his eyes from hers, he noted the circles around her eyes—flesh bruised so darkly that it contrasted with the deep, rich bronze of her skin. Her long black hair glistened with accumulated grease. The grimy robe she wore was flecked with a pattern of crusty brown stains.

"Mrs. Hairston? Is everything all right?"

She stared.

"Mrs. Hairston, I asked if everything was okay."

Slowly, she nodded.

He tried to look beyond her. Deep shadows filled the area behind her.

"Are you sure? May I come in?"

He didn't hope to receive permission and was shocked when the woman backed away from the door in a lackluster gesture of consent. Keeping a hand on the holster's hammer guard, he eased into the house.

Drawn curtains blocked the sunlight, and he paused so his eyes could adjust to the gray gloom. The smell, rich and revolting, continued to taunt his memory. The two of them stood in a narrow hallway. Wide doors opened to a living room on his right and a dining room on his left. The hall extended back to the kitchen. Cole could see the corner of a copper-tone refrigerator.

Stairs, situated in front of him, climbed to the second story. Jagged, ominous streaks of the stain paralleled the handrail up the stair wall. He looked back at her robe, then to the floor. The same discoloration darkened huge portions of the hardwood flooring.

Blood! That's what I smell . . . old blood. He remembered its taste—the same as its smell—lingering in his mouth for several days following a tooth extraction.

Cole didn't want to believe that they were bloodstains—

they were so . . . so everywhere! But that accounted for the coppery odor. He tried to clear his thickening throat. Anxiety produced a raging drought in his mouth.

"Mrs. Hairston, where's your daughter?"

She spoke for the first time. "Upstairs. Asleep, I think. Maybe she's playing."

He allowed his gaze to rise up the steps. "Maybe we'd better go check on her."

"If you want."

No smile from the woman. No frown. Just a cool submissive consent punctuated by her untamed eyes. She turned to the steps. Cole followed, feeling the cold sweat break out on his face. His attention was locked on the copious display of stains. By then the stale musk of old blood was all that he could smell, the same musk that hung for days inside a mangled car after a really gory road accident.

"What's this?" he finally dared to ask as he mounted the steps behind her. His hand indicated the wide smear just above the railing.

The woman, by then at the top, wheeled on Cole. Her dark eyes flared. He unsnapped the leather hammer guard on his .357.

But the woman only asked, "What's what?"

"This!" He tapped the crusty slash of brown.

"It's a wall." She pointed to her left, his right. "Jenny's in here."

What the hell's going on here? Cole's fear became a cramp in his gut. He climbed slowly to the top, keeping his eyes on the woman.

"She may be sleeping, mister."

He trembled a little, shaken by the prospect of what was on the other side. *A child sleeping? Playing? Probably that . . . nothing more.*

Mrs. Hairston appeared to be waiting for him to open it.

"She's in there?" he asked.

"I said she was."

"Maybe you'd better open it. I might frighten her, being a stranger and all."

Without pause, she placed a hand on the knob, clicked it open, and stood there, waiting for the officer to look inside.

But Cole Surface was reeling away, driven back by the billowing, infernal stench rushing out of the child's room. He fought it as if it were a swarm of angry wasps.

"Dear God!" he cried.

The woman cocked her head at him, puzzled by his behavior.

His stomach revolted. He managed to project the vomitus over the railing. It splattered somewhere below as Cole draped himself over the railing, gasping for breath, trying to clear his nose and throat. His feet, possessed by terror and revulsion, started of their own volition toward the steps. Something deep within him compelled him to flee, but he opposed it. He had a duty.

Suck it up, guy.

Do your fucking job!

"What the hell's happened?" he managed to ask.

"My daughter's in there." Mrs. Hairston peeked into the room. "She's playing with her doll."

He jerked a white handkerchief from his hip pocket and used it to wipe the perspiration from his face. Then, he covered his mouth and nose with it. Slowly, dutifully, he inched toward the open door. Mrs. Hairston stood just outside, smiling into the room. Cole peeked inside. Even as his anguished cries filled the house and spilled out into the neighborhood, Jenny Hairston's mother never stopped smiling.

ONE

ACROSS TOWN, as the cries of Cole Surface drifted from a partially open window of Jenny Hairston's bedroom, Anna Tyree read words composed, it seemed, by a stranger—some woman writing under the ostentatious pen name of Annie Tyson-Tyree.

The longer Anna used the pseudonym, the more disassociated she felt. The pen name—like bad breath—had preceded her throughout her career. In the newspaper game, job applications and resumés didn't warrant an editor's attention until he or she had read the applicant's clippings. Anna's very first article, and every bylined piece since, had appeared under the name Annie Tyson-Tyree. It hadn't even been her idea. Anna could live with her own mistakes—if not comfortably, at least with some dignity. She abhorred, however, suffering a lifetime because of someone else's perverse judgment.

That "someone" had been her very first editor, a desperate little man who had owned an anemic weekly in God Forsaken, Kentucky, or whatever the hell its name had really been. Why the little weasel had even noticed the middle name of Tyson on her application remained an unsolved mystery. He had garnished the alliterative combo of her middle and last names with a hyphen—"to give it class," he'd said.

10

Years later, it still made Anna quiver with old, fermented rage. The obnoxious little rodent wouldn't have known ''class'' if it had pissed on his shoes.

Anna hadn't been told about the glitzy pen name. She saw the name when it appeared at the top of her very first feature story—on the front page yet! Even if she had liked the pseudonym, it wouldn't have gone very well with a backwoods publication that printed cornbread recipes on page one along with the news. When she had challenged him about the liberty taken, he'd had the nerve to boast about it.

The name—and the writer—had stayed only a short time at the Kentucky weekly. From there, she had gone to her first daily. The pen name had followed, or preceded, her. The sequence didn't really matter. Of one thing she was certain. The *Milbrook Daily Journal* would be Annie Tyson-Tyree's last stand—maybe even the last stand for the writer herself. Small-town journalism no longer excited Anna. Not even the court and police beat—Anna's specialty—could arouse her dying interest.

Anna, seated at the small table in her kitchen, lifted her sleepy eyes from that day's front-page feature on the president of the local chapter of Mothers Against Drunk Driving. The story had started as a kind of puff piece on the woman, who had more than enough puff for three stories. In addition to her stewardship of MADD, she had also organized an anti-abortion group.

During Anna's research, she had happened to mention the MADD group to Raven County Prosecutor Tony Danton. He'd called it ''Mothers Against Cops, Judges, and Prosecutors.'' She had requested and—to her surprise—received consent to quote him. Little devil that she was, Annie Tyson-Tyree had promptly phoned the MADD president for a comment on Danton's quote. The woman had been incensed, saying that Danton had "a track record of being soft on baby killers." Annie Tyson-Tyree decided the woman had her crusades confused, but she used it anyway. That's how Annie is, Anna thought.

Her amusement had been fleeting. For one thing, Anna wondered if she was developing a kind of split personality. It just didn't seem healthy, thinking of herself as two separate individuals, but there was more to her disillusionment than that. The societal noise level, even in a small city like Milbrook, grated on Anna's nerves. No one could debate in a civil fashion anymore, not even dowdy old women like the president of MADD. Every issue became a temperamental crusade. The emotion of hate was becoming a tangible factor in the political process.

She closed her eyes and pressed her knuckles against her forehead. *Why do I want to scream right now? Surely not because of the surly national mood.*

For weeks, a gnawing discomfort had shadowed her. She was weary of trying to outdistance it. At first, she had ignored the feeling—then tried to deny it. More particularly, she tried to deny its source, but the truth was there, unwilling to be ignored or denied. Her mounting irritation came from an absence of certainty—from the constant instability of a romantic relationship. She loved a man who exasperated her, who confused her, who robbed her of the one thing she valued most—her independence.

Anna lowered her chin to her chest. "God help me, I love him." She was alone in her apartment. There was no one to hear what amounted to a confession of guilt. Her rollercoaster emotions confirmed a theory she had long held; love is a mental disorder, an addiction as debilitating as a crack habit.

Their relationship was into its fourth month—a hundred-plus days of hurt and satisfaction, of spitting anger and soaring passion, of giggly joy and hapless frustration. He relished the inconstant nature of their affair. It drained her. Never before had she met a man like him, and she never, ever wanted to meet another. She never, ever wanted to let him slip away, either, even though she knew he would never be the "settled" man she wanted him to be.

Anna glanced at the phone. Just a few melodic touch tones, and she could hear his dry voice, curt with anger because he so hated the intrusion of phone calls. He marked the privacy of his territory with the fierce resolve of a jungle cat. It was Monday, her customary day off but a holiday for him, Columbus Day. Anna hadn't talked with him since Friday night. She stared at the phone, chewing on her lower lip and struggling mightily against her urge to go to it.

He had said that he wanted to spend the weekend alone. It wasn't the first time he had demanded the seclusion of his home. Although Anna spent most nights in his bed, she knew it was too soon to give up her own new town house.

If she hadn't known him so well, she might have suspected him of infidelity. Not him, though. It wasn't another woman. That challenge she might have handled, perhaps not with grace but forcefully. Her adversary, however, was some perverse inner demon within the man that exercised a Machiavellian control over his moods. At this particular time of year, the demon surfaced as he mourned the death of summer, the coming of winter.

Anna laughed to quell her tears. The morning sun streamed into the kitchen window, twinkling as it caressed her auburn hair. She wore no makeup at all, but, other than the sleepy droop of her eyes, she looked as if she had just stepped from the cover of *Glamour* or *Vogue*. Her sleek, wraparound robe snuggled against her curvaceous figure. At thirty-one she was aging well physically—some said looking better with each passing year. Mentally, she was a disaster—a breakdown just waiting to happen.

She stood to gaze out the window. A pallet of gold and red, sprinkled with splashes of plum, covered the slopes of Tabernacle Mountain. If it hadn't been for him, the view would have been beautiful. He had robbed the season of its joy. Several weeks before, they had taken a Sunday drive south into Virginia, and she had noticed a single tree starting to yellow. "That's the first I've seen," she had quipped. "I can't wait to see the mountains when the leaves turn."

He had been in a good humor, but her comment had produced a Jekyll-to-Hyde transformation.

"Spare me your observations on the beauty of the season," he'd said through clinched teeth. "It's dying time."

She'd laughed, which had been the wrong thing to do, and said, "When something dies, my dear, it stays dead. Next spring, the trees will be bright and green."

He hadn't even given her the courtesy of a response. With jaw set and a rage in his eyes, he'd turned his car around at the next convenient place and said nothing else on their return trip home. That had been the first hint of his autumn depression. Then, in late September, they'd spent a week together vacationing in a cottage on the South Carolina coast. Anna had dreaded the trip because of his mood, but her anxiety had been unfounded. The warm subtropical climate cured the affliction of his mood. The two of them had frolicked in the warm surf under cloudless blue skies. They had shagged away the nights to the rolling rhythm of beach music. Day and night, whenever the mood struck, they made sweet, impassioned love.

On the Saturday before they were to leave, his mood swung. He had vanished around noon for a final walk on the

beach. He didn't return until after five P.M. The sun had
blistered the skin on his shoulders. The bottom of his feet
were raw. God knows how far he had walked. The following
day, a gray Sunday, the return trip to West Virginia had been
silent torture.

He had been an irritated bear ever since. She glanced once
again at the phone. "What the hell," she declared aloud.
Suffering the shame of an addict, Anna Tyree went to it and
dialed his number.

It rang fifteen times with no answer.

She slammed the handset into its cradle. "Dammit, Whit
Pynchon! I know you're home."

Cal Burton, his arms clasped behind his back, marched a
tight preordained circle in the center of the cramped inter-
rogation room. His feet kept within a well-worn path in the
waxed finish of the floor. Fluorescent lights, covered by yel-
lowing light-diffusers, illuminated the institutional green of
the walls. On one of the walls, a small calendar suffered a
lonely existence on a huge bulletin board.

By rank, Cal was a lieutenant. Just that—a lieutenant. But
he introduced himself as Detective Lieutenant Calvin O.
Burton. In his mind, the enhancement added something. It
distinguished him from all other lieutenants everywhere. The
position of detective lieutenant had never existed formally in
the Milbrook Police Department's chain of command and
would cease to exist upon Cal's departure. It was a purely
personal honor that Cal Burton bestowed upon himself.

A woman sat in a chair in the center of the circle. Her
shoulders were stooped by the burden of her ordeal.

The detective continued to circle her as he fired his questions. "For the umpteenth time, lady, what happened to your
kid?"

Mary Hairston's head twitched in a fashion that gave Cal the chills. He'd been questioning "perps"—Cal had liked that name since he had heard it on *Hill Street Blues*—for a lot of years. Never before had he encountered one who behaved as strangely as this woman. The twitch was bad enough. It was one-sided . . . kinda. When she spoke, which wasn't often, the words came from the left side of her mouth, along with strings of drool. The left side of her blouse was dark and glistening with the moisture.

"Juh . . . Juh . . . Jenny's fuh . . . fine," she said.

Cal stopped in front of her. Ignoring her rank body odor, he leaned into her face. "Jesus, lady. Your kid's been dead for days. She was about to pop open like a ripe tomato. Who in the hell shot her?"

The woman's eyes darted back and forth. The saliva continued to flow. "I juh . . . juh . . . just bathed her th . . . this muh . . . morning."

As bizarre as it was, that much was true. There was plenty of evidence indicating that the putrescent body had been bathed, not the least offensive of which were the maggots crawling all over the goddamn bathroom. It had given Cal the willies; it took something really gross to do that.

He sighed. "What'd she do? Get under your skin maybe? That why you shot her? You're a pretty good-lookin' woman, I guess. Maybe it was your boyfriend who did it?"

The woman's head jerked. Her eyes swiveled back and forth in their bruised sockets. Saliva dripped from her chin. "Where's Jenny?"

The veteran cop squinted his eyes. "What the shit is with you, lady? You trying to make me think you're loony?"

Not expecting an answer, Cal began again to stalk his suspect. He'd questioned hundreds of perps, but this petite black woman topped the list of cold-bloods—either that or she really was a cracked nut—or maybe just smart enough to start building an insanity defense. Killers were a special breed of perp. The closest you found among other criminals was the rapist. All the others—the check artists, the house burglars, the auto thiefs—were just greedy scum.

"Look, lady, I got all day. We're gonna go through this until you get it right—"

He stopped in midsentence. The door to the interview room was inching open.

"No interruptions, goddammit!"

A young uniformed officer dared to ease his head inside.

"Dammit to hell!" Cal bellowed. "Can't no one follow orders—"

The young man's face flushed. "Sorry, sir. I told them—"

"Told who?"

"The prosecutor and Pynchon."

"Mother of friggin God! Are they here?"

"Yes, sir."

Cal exploded, hammering a fist against the metal door. The detective lieutenant was a short, slight man, his round head topped by wispy strings of dark hair. His display of anger would have been amusing had it not been for his reputation. He was small of stature, often small of mind, but you didn't cross him, not if you worked for him.

"Who in the fuck called them? Did you do it?"

"No, sir. Maybe it was the chief. It's policy on homicides. We're supposed to call the prosecutor."

"Hell, man. That doesn't mean immediately."

"The policy says immediately."

Cal pirouetted in a gesture of helpless frustration. "Christ, I don't need this."

"They're demanding to see Mrs. Hairston."

"Send them to my office, kid."

"But they said—"

Cal shushed him with a rough, calloused finger placed against the young officer's lips. "Make it easy on yourself. Do like I say. You gotta spend a lot more time with me than them. Take 'em to my office, so I can fill them in before they talk to her."

"Yes, sir." The officer vanished.

Cal collected the initial report. He started to warn the woman to stay put, but her head twitched before he could issue the caution. Her left arm rose high in the air, then dropped to her side. At that moment, the detective decided she was putting on, smart bitch that she was. She was angling to make herself look crazy.

He closed the door on her and hurried back to the smelly bathroom where he intended to spend a few minutes on the throne. *Let Tony Danton and his asshole buddy cool their heels for a while.* They'd kept him waiting enough times. On grand jury days every other law enforcement agency in the county presented their cases ahead of the Milbrook PD. He and his men were left warming the goddamn benches until late in the day.

He settled down to read the scribbled, incoherent report in his hand. The young rookie who had discovered the crime hadn't even been able to prepare a report. In fact, he hadn't notified the department. Some old woman had performed that duty after she'd heard the Surface kid screaming. *A cop screaming and bawling, for God's sakes.* It was sickening to Cal—the snotty-nosed weaklings they hired these days as cops. Back when he had joined the force, you earned yourself a suspension if you puked all over a murder scene. If a fella had to puke, he caught it in his mouth until he could make it to a john or outside. If that wasn't possible, he swallowed it.

Cal turned his soured thoughts to the Prosecutor of Raven County. In the cop's estimation, a good prosecuting attorney invented those judicial sleights of hand that sanitized an officer's shortcuts. There wasn't a damned thing wrong with shortcuts, not when you were dealing with vermin. After all, nobody advises a cockroach or a rat about their rights before zapping them. You just get rid of them. Cal especially liked those electric bugwhackers, the kind that sizzled mosquitoes and flies and bees. He equated the devices with the electric chair.

Tony Danton, who raved at cops that took shortcuts, didn't fit Cal's notion of a good prosecutor. Danton had even been known to throw officers to the legal wolves right in court. Law officers and prosecutors were supposed to be a team sharing a common purpose—to rid the world of perps.

Then there was Whit Pynchon, Danton's investigator. Assholes didn't come any wider or any deeper, not even among the lawyers. Pynchon kept his nose in other cops' business. Some maggot cries that a cop got too rough with him, and Pynchon shows up to check it out.

The local fraternal order of police maintained a list of Whit Pynchon's victims, cops who had been suspended or discharged or worse because of the meddling of the prosecutor's investigator. When Pynchon wasn't investigating officers, he was commandeering their cases, especially the homicides. The real police did the legwork; Pynchon grabbed the headlines and the glory.

According to the local scuttlebutt, Pynchon had been on the verge of leaving, taking an early retirement or something. Danton, so the rumors went, had talked him out of it. Cal suspected it was all bullshit. Pynchon was younger than he, forty or so, and no way could anyone retire on a local government's pension at that age, not by legal means anyway.

Cal, sensing that he was about to lose this case to Whit Pynchon, abandoned his toilet session and started toward his office. As he walked by the interview room, he heard voices inside. He shoved open the door.

"Jesus fucking Christ!"

Danton and Pynchon stood over *his* suspect.

"Who the hell let you in here?"

Tony Danton, as short as Cal Burton but much stockier, and looking more Italian than he really was, continued his visual examination of Mary Hairston's face. "Cool down, Cal. She's a witness in a homicide. I'm the prosecutor. I don't need permission to talk to her."

But the detective lieutenant was livid. "A witness! She's a goddamned suspect! *My* goddamned suspect!"

For the first time, Tony looked up at the furious officer. "I assume, then, that you've been questioning her."

Cal threw up his hands. "Now, just what the hell do you think?"

Tony shrugged. "I wasn't sure, Cal. I don't see a rights form around here. You have mirandized her, I hope?"

"Not in writing—yet."

"You did say she was a suspect?" Tony asked.

"Look, I just haven't got to that point."

The prosecutor abandoned his examination of the woman. "And you're never going to, Cal—reach that point, I mean."

The cop looked from Tony to Whit Pynchon. The investigator loomed in a corner now, his arms crossed, his deep brown eyes heavy on Cal.

"What the hell do you mean?" the detective asked, returning his attention to the prosecutor.

"She needs medical attention," Tony said.

"What she needs, Mr. Prosecutor, is to be interrogated."

But Tony ignored him. "Whit, go tell the dispatcher to phone an ambulance."

Cal stepped to block the investigator's path to the door. "An ambulance? Mother weep for me. Lookee here, Danton. There ain't a damned thing wrong with that woman 'cept a raging case of guilt."

Tony rolled his eyes at Whit Pynchon. "I'd say she has a concussion, Burton."

The cop laughed. "Where the fuck did you get your medical degree?"

Cal fished inside his jacket pocket and withdrew a stack of photos. He shoved them under Tony Danton's nose. "Glance at them, Counselor. The poor kid smelled one hell of a lot worse'n she looked. 'Course you and your ass-kisser here missed the stinkin' part—as usual."

Danton ignored the offering, but Whit Pynchon abandoned his vantage point in the corner and snatched the photos from the detective's hand.

There's something cheap and degrading about instant photography. Although it made quick mug shots a reality, it was also the kind of technology that allowed dirty old men to take discreet porno photos of young kids. The true photographer battles with light and his subject to capture that one moment of visual perfection. By the time he sees his art, the moment is lost to the past—hours or days behind him. Not so with the instant cameras. Its technology stole the magic from an art form whose charm was its delayed reward.

And when the subject of the lens was the bloated, decomposing remains of a child, dignity lost all meaning. Whit Pynchon choked back his bile as he turned the photo in his hand. Mrs. Hairston, presumably, had arranged her daughter in a comfortable position. The child sat on the floor, her back propped against a bed covered with a pink frilly comforter. Her elephantine arms, swollen by the fumes of decomposition, were locked around a rag doll. She appeared to be sticking out her tongue at the photographer. Whit knew better. The insolence wasn't intended. Rather, the gaseous buildup inside the body had made the lips protrude and forced the tongue from her mouth.

In a purely pathological sense, Whit had seen more revolting sights, but this was a child. It didn't get any worse. He struggled with his tears. According to the preliminary examination by the local coroner, the child had died instantly as a result of a bullet wound to the forehead. The postmortem bloat had concealed the small hole from the undiscerning eyes of the cops.

Whit's damp eyes swiveled over to the mother. *Poor woman.* According to the report, she'd been bathing her daughter's body daily. He looked back at the snapshot. If that wasn't love, Whit didn't know what it was.

Men kill wives. Wives kill husbands. Fathers slay their offspring, and sometimes kids even take the lives of their parents. Rarely, though, does a mother kill the issue of her womb.

Whit, too, had a daughter. Maybe he had no conception of the depths of a mother's love, but he knew too well the depths of his own. If someone had done this thing to Tressa . . . to his daughter—

Whit Pynchon slammed the brakes on his thoughts. No way did he want to conjure that kind of hurt.

"She's a cold-blooded black bitch," Cal Burton was saying, oblivious of her presence.

The plasticized photos—at one minute in Whit's hand— smacked flat against the tile floor as his fingers latched onto the small, wiry cop. The assault caught the lieutenant off guard. He squealed as his feet cleared the floor. The wall exploded against his shoulder blades. The back of his balding head clunked against the plaster with such force that it chipped off some green paint.

Tony rushed toward Whit. "Jesus, man. Put him down."

Fear flashed across Cal Burton's face. His feet shot out as he tried to kick Whit. The big, bulky investigator avoided the cop's awkward retaliation and hoisted him even higher in the air.

"Goddammit! Put me down!"

Whit pushed him more snugly against the wall. "You're an asshole, Burton. You make me sick."

He pushed his angry face so close to Cal's that he smelled last night's stale beer. "You're an animal. You don't give a shit about that dead kid. You just want an excuse to roust someone—anyone. Even that poor lady there."

Cal squirmed. "You're . . . you're under . . . under arrest . . . assaulting an officer."

Tony had his hands on Whit, pulling on him, when Cal made the official pronouncement. It sounded so damned whimsical, the threat spoken by the little cop as he flopped high in the air. Tony laughed. Whit turned to stare at his boss. Then he, too, saw the humor, and Pynchon started to laugh.

Cal flew into a vain rage, his dark eyes ripe with humiliated fury. "Put me down, motherfucker! Now!"

Tony patted Whit's hand. "Come on, Tarzan. Return the poor lieutenant to terra firma. Let's get this lady to the hospital."

Whit opened his hands. Cal's feet slapped down on the floor.

"Before I go," Whit said, "I'd better make sure I'm not

in this pipsqueak's offical custody. I wouldn't wanna add an escape charge to my list of crimes.''

Tony, still grinning, looked at the detective lieutenant. "What about it, Cal? You got the balls to file a formal complaint?"

Cal was rearranging his coat. "No way. I'm not like your headhunter there, Danton. I don't have other cops arrested, no matter what kinda pus bags they are, but it ain't forgotten. It'll never be forgotten.''

Two

AN EMERGENCY ROOM NURSE cursed as she struggled to insert an IV needle into a male patient's arm. The man was gasping for breath, clutching his chest. Whit didn't want to watch, but he couldn't help himself. Here was human drama—maybe the life and death kind—being played out in front of his eyes. The fellow, not much older than Whit, was suffering a heart attack. Anyone could see that. At forty-one, heart attacks were something Whit thought about a lot. He smoked. He seldom exercised. He ate foods loaded with cholesterol. Until recently, it hadn't made a damn. Now, Whit could see himself sitting on that emergency room gurney, hooked up to a machine that was prepared—almost anxious—to herald the arrival of Mister Death.

"Got it!" the nurse shouted.

One of the doctors was in an extension of the emergency room, examining Mary Hairston. "Administer morphine first," he ordered in a voice loud enough to carry to the hospital's front lobby.

"His B.P.'s dropping," she said.

The doctor abandoned Mary Hairston and went to the man's aid. Whit turned away from the scene as the man moaned in pain and dropped back to the elevated surface of the cot.

25

The ER at the Milbrook hospital was a large room filled with flat carts. When the personnel wanted privacy, they pulled flowery curtains around the area in question. Mary Hairston occupied the only separate room in the emergency facility. It opened into the main ER through two wide doors. Her room, large enough to accommodate two patients, was loaded with monitors, panels of buttons, lights, and tubing. Orderlies were quickly moving the man having the heart attack into the room with Mrs. Hairston. The nurse held his hand.

One cell in the main ER was enclosed by the curtains. Whit could see another nurse's feet moving around the bed. A second pair of feet, clad in dingy tennis shoes, shifted back and forth at the foot of the invisible bed. He heard the sound of someone retching.

"Serves ya right," he heard an old woman say. "Taking all them pills."

Danton stood beside Whit, flirting with a young X-ray technician who was flattered by the attentions of the county's prosecuting attorney. Mary Hairston had already been visited by a mobile X-ray machine.

Whit shifted his weight from one foot to the other. His fingers sounded an impatient tattoo on the counter of the main desk. He didn't react well to waiting, even when he knew there was no way to avoid it. With a mindless hand, he reached into his jacket pocket and pulled out a pack of cigarettes. The filtered tip had hardly reached his lips when a second doctor appeared.

"I hope you know better than to light that," the physician said.

Whit closed his eyes. "Sorry, force of habit. I'll go out in the waiting area."

The stern face of the doctor softened not a bit. "Please do. I dislike people committing suicide in my presence."

The investigator for the Raven County prosecutor had planned to remain polite. After all, he hadn't really meant to smoke in the ER, but the comment from the doctor rubbed raw nerves. He brandished the one hundred-millimeter menthol in the little man's waxy face. "Tell me something, medicine man. If I toss this one away, and all the rest, too, will I live forever?"

The ER physician wasn't long out of school. He wore his new mantle with a pride bordering on arrogance. "Don't be ridiculous. You'll live longer probably, and you'll be much healthier. And so will everyone who has to breathe the same air you breathe."

Tony had ceased his repartee with the young, shapely technician. All too familiar with his employee's fiery temperament, he put a cautious hand on Whit's shoulder. "Let's go on out in the lobby and wait."

Whit shrugged it off. "In a sec."

The doctor had started to turn away.

"Got a question for ya, Doc."

The young man stopped. "Yes?"

"You divorced?"

The doctor's face still had some of its baby fat, but his eyebrows were dark and thick, just like his hair. He knitted them. "Why do you ask?"

Tony grabbed Whit's arm. "Don't start it, Whit."

Whit ignored his employer's warning. "I get a little nauseated with you holier-than-thou witch doctors who lecture the rest of us about our bad habits. Doctors don't have much longer life spans than human beings."

The X-ray technician gasped.

Whit went on. "Most of you are divorced four or five

times. You spread kids like they were some disease. You drink like Irishmen. Then you have the friggin' gall to harass those of us who smoke cigarettes.''

The young man seemed taken aback. ''It's your life, mister. If I offended you, I apologize. You're more than welcome to smoke out in the lobby. I'll let you know something about Mrs. Hairston as soon as I can.''

Whit glared. ''We'll be waiting.''

Tony practically shoved Whit out into the bustling lobby. ''Jesus Christ, Whit. You've been a real bastard lately.''

The investigator lit his cigarette, inhaled deeply, and exhaled a double column of smoke from his nostrils. ''Doctors gripe me.''

''Hell, everyone gripes you, and that's disgusting.''

Whit frowned. ''What?''

''Snorting that smoke out of your nose.''

''Don't you start on me, too.''

Tony slumped into one of the worn plastic chairs. ''That man was giving you good advice.''

Whit settled down beside him. ''So, I die a few years sooner than the devil intended. From what I've seen of old age, I'd be doing myself and my daughter a favor.''

''So, why do you keep telling Tressa you're going to quit?''

''She thinks I have.''

Tony chuckled. ''Hell, she knows you lie.''

''It's this damned job, Tony. I'm tired of the bullshit. I shoulda quit this summer. I shouldn't have let you con me into staying.''

Tony shook his head. ''No way, my friend. I'm not taking the rap for that any longer. Nobody—except maybe Tressa—can talk Whit Pynchon into, or out of, anything. If you had wanted to retire, you would have. I just asked you to stay so you could save face.''

Hell would suffer three Ice Ages before Whit would admit the truth aloud—the same was true about the smoking—but Tony was right. For a decade at least, Whit had wanted to retire to a small inlet on the South Carolina coast. Then the past summer he had met Anna Tyree. His life had been changed. Already, the regrets were beginning to compound themselves as he faced another dismal West Virginia winter. For damn sure, it would be his last.

He watched the ribbon of smoke from his cigarette drift all the way across the waiting area toward a woman whose frown seemed to be directed at him. He moved the cigarette to the other hand, but the drifting smoke followed the same path. For the moment, his mind drifted, too. It had been Anna, not Tressa, whose words had persuaded him to postpone his retirement. Her words, though, had been spoken on behalf of Tressa.

"Wait until Tressa graduates," Anna had said. "I know it's not the case, but it looks to her as if you don't care. These are some of the most important months in her life."

Almost as an afterthought, she had added, "Besides, it'll give me a chance to find a job."

Whit had stayed because of Tressa alone, or so he tried to tell himself. There had been a hundred common sense reasons to stay anyway, but, before he'd met Anna, Whit Pynchon would have said the hell with them all.

"Whadaya think?" Tony was asking.

"About what?"

"Did she kill the kid or not?"

The woman across the room coughed and wafted away Whit's cigarette smoke. He sighed, stubbing the cigarette out in an ashtray. He wasn't enjoying it anyway. Nowadays, when you smoked in public, you were made to feel like some kind of pariah. America was marching back toward puritanism with crusades against smoking, drinking, and casual sex. All the little sins now carried such grave punishments. Murderers and rapists walked free. Smokers and gays and alcoholics, free of other sins, died terrible deaths. It made Whit wonder.

The woman smiled in victory.

"I don't think so, Tony. It doesn't fit. Where did the mother get her injuries? What happened to the murder weapon?"

"She might have gotten rid of it. She had several days, you know."

Whit shook his head. "No way. She didn't do it."

The prosecutor shrugged. "For what it's worth, I agree, but for now she's our prime suspect."

The large waiting area faced the main entrance to the hospital. Through the front doors, Tony noticed the chief of the Milbrook Police Department as soon as he stepped from the unmarked cruiser. "Here comes trouble."

Chief Tom Wampler blustered through the doors. Save for those frequent times when he was on the golf course, the chief was an ever-sad man who believed, and not without cause, that his department "sucked hind teat"—his words—in the hierarchy of Raven County law enforcement.

"Looks pissed to me," Whit said.

Tony nodded. "Yeah, think you had anything to do with it?"

"Me? Naw!"

Wampler came straight for Whit, his forefinger brandished as a weapon. "My department's off-limits to you, Pynchon. If it was up to me, you'd be under arrest for assaulting an officer."

Whit stared up into the chief's livid face. "If you need that finger to play golf, Chief, then you'd best get it out of my face."

Tony was on his feet, trying to wedge himself between Wampler and his investigator. "Ease up, Chief."

Wampler wasn't about to be calmed. "You hear me, too, Danton. If that son'bitch even lets his shadow fall on the front door at City Hall, he's bought and paid for."

The others in the room shrunk away from the heated confrontation. A nurse came out from the ER to investigate the commotion. When she recognized the participants, she eased back out of sight.

Whit slouched in his chair. "I've been tossed out of better places, Chief."

Tom Wampler's body tensed. Tony recognized the imminent likelihood of a public fight. It wasn't the first time he'd had to defend Whit. Usually, as the saying went, the best defense was a quick offense.

"While we're raising hell, Chief, your damned detective's already screwed up the case. He didn't bother to get a search warrant for the woman's house. He didn't bother to obtain a written waiver of her rights, and I doubt he even bothered to verbally mirandize her. Even worse, Chief, he kept her at the station when she badly needed medical attention."

Wampler, though, continued to vent his rage at Whit. "That doesn't give that asshole the right—"

"Stow it!" Tony commanded.

The prosecutor looked around the waiting room. Some of the people were pretending to be interested in magazines. Others openly gawked at the loud debate. He lowered his voice. "From now on, Chief, Burton doesn't handle any more state investigations. He can investigate your shoplifting cases and your building code violations, but he's not welcome in state court."

"Like hell," Wampler said, not concerned about the attention the three of them were receiving. "That's one reason

I'm here. This damned murder investigation is ours, and we're gonna handle it. We're tired of Pynchon stepping into our jurisdiction.''

Tony shook his head. ''Didn't you hear what I just said?''

''It's our case, Danton, pure and simple.''

Tony looked back at Whit, who was smiling. Then he stuck his own finger against Wampler's thick chest. ''It's not *your* case, Chief. It's the *State's* case. And in case you've forgotten, *I'm* the State.''

The chief's voice dropped several decibels. ''Damn, Tony, Cal Burton's the best man for this case. He knows how to handle them people.''

Whit, still seated, hiked his eyebrows. ''Them people? What the hell does that mean?''

''Colored people,'' Wampler retorted, sincerely shocked that Whit even needed to ask.

''You're full of shit,'' Whit said.

The red in Wampler's face deepened, but the sudden and excited appearance of one of the ER physicians forestalled another verbal explosion. It was the younger of two, the one Whit had challenged. ''Come,'' the doctor was saying. ''I have the most amazing thing to show you.''

The three men, distracted from their anger by the physician's enthusiasm, followed him into a small private lounge adjacent to the ER. A negative already hung on the face of a lit viewing screen. The profile of a human skull was apparent to all of them.

''That's Mrs. Hairston,'' the doctor said.

Whit noticed the bright spot first. ''Jesus, Doc, that looks like—''

''It is! It is!'' The doctor was gleeful at Whit's observation.

''Enlighten us dummies,'' Tony said.

The doctor used a tongue depressor to tap the bright spot. "That's a missile."

Wampler frowned. "A missile."

Tony squinted at the negative. "You mean a bullet? Inside her head?"

"It's a bullet all right," the doctor said. "But it's not in her head . . . not exactly."

He traced a light shadow from the bright spot on the X ray to the forehead and again tapped on the screen. "The bullet entered here. Rather than penetrating the skull, it was deflected and traveled beneath the skin, lodged there at the base of the skull."

Tony moved closer to the X ray. "I'll be damned."

"So, she shot herself," the chief said.

The doctor gaped at the chief's ignorance. For the moment he abandoned his professional presentation. "Not too damned likely. There were no powder burns. The angle of entry isn't consistent with a self-inflicted wound. The entry hole was concealed in the edge of her hairline. Damn, she must have bled buckets."

"It's a wonder she's still alive," Whit said.

The doctor nodded. "Yes, it is. She's not out of the woods yet, not by a long way. I've seen this sort of thing before—I mean, a missile that fails to penetrate the skull. It was while I was interning in Baltimore. There are reasons for its failure to breach the skull. The bullet might have been old. Or it didn't carry a full load. Usually, it isn't fatal. This case, though, is unique. She went so long with the bullet insulated there that she's developed a raging infection. I'm surprised she's even conscious at this point. There's a seventy-five percent chance she won't make it."

"Can we talk to her?" Whit asked.

"She's not lucid. If she survives, she may be capable of a

coherent conversation in a week or so, but I wouldn't count on it. The infection has become quite advanced.''

Tony wheeled on Chief Wampler. ''And your damned detective was ready to jail her. If we hadn't intervened, there'd be a woman in a jail cell with a bullet in her head.''

The doctor was shaking his head. ''She would have died within twelve hours.''

THREE

THE GOSSIP MILL in a small town grinds, if not exceedingly fine, then at least with hell-bent speed. By early afternoon, the news about Mary and Jenny Hairston had reached most of Milbrook. By 2:24 P.M., deputies in a sheriff's department 120 miles north of Milbrook were talking about the woman with a bullet in her head who had bathed her putrescent child. Over the next few days the story would spread to neighboring states. It was the sort of tale cops loved to pass on—a true mystery, replete with blood and gore and a uniqueness that distinguished it from run-of-the-mill Saturday night killings.

Even Whit Pynchon wasn't immune from its singularity. For the moment, he'd put aside his pre-winter depression. Over the years, his work had become routine, haunted always by the same faces—an incessant cycle of bad check authors, B&E artists, wife beaters who became killers, and zealous or ignorant and, too often, zealously ignorant police officers. Even a recent series of murders involving cops' wives hadn't rekindled his dedication. That particular case had been too personal to be anything more than a horrid memory he yearned to forget.

But the child's slaying and the botched effort to execute Jenny Hairston's mother—as darkly revolting as they were—stimulated his juices. His enthusiasm surprised even Whit.

If the mother survived and was able to remember and communicate those memories, then surely she could put the mystery to rest. Until then it offered itself as a classic puzzle begging to be solved.

On the hope that the culprit had left some signature at the Hairston home, Whit drove his car in that direction. Burton's crew had already rummaged through the home, probably corrupting any evidence that might have been there, but Whit figured it was worth a few minutes of his time to look over the scene. Besides, there was no place else to start.

He turned onto the dead-end street where Mrs. Hairston lived. When he saw the familiar car—a little red Audi— parked in front of his destination, he cursed and slammed on his brakes. His tires squealed. Then, as astonishment escalated into fury, he jammed the accelerator to the floor, leaving burnt rubber on the street's surface as he closed the distance to the house. His car screeched to a stop behind the small import.

The door to the house stood partially ajar. Whit used his foot to shove it open. Before his eyes had time to focus, a flashbulb exploded in his eyes.

"Good God almighty!" he cried, blinded by the assault of the sharp light.

"Great action shot," Anna Tyree exclaimed. "The determined detective framed in the door of the murder house, looking as though he wants to crack someone's head wide open. Whose head would that be, Whit? Mine, I suspect. You want to thrash me within an inch of my life."

"What the hell are you doing here? This is a secured crime scene."

Anna smiled. "Not according to the Milbrook police chief. Someone tipped my editor. He called Wampler and received permission for me to shoot some photos. The chief and the editor are golfing buddies, you know.''

''Screw golf! And screw Wampler. It's not his case, Anna. It's my case, and I didn't give you permission.''

Anna rolled her azure eyes. ''You sound just like a kid, Whit—mad 'cause somebody ripped off your marbles.''

''Dammit, Anna! That's your problem, not mine. You think this is all some kind of game. Smell, Anna. Take a deep breath. That's the stink of a seven-year-old girl who will never see her eighth birthday. It reeks, huh? You wanna see the photos the cops made?''

''Ease up, Whit. This is big news, and I still work for the newspaper, you know. By the way, were you aware that Mary Hairston is an employee of the paper?''

Whit hadn't known that. ''It doesn't matter. You've got no business here.''

Anna advanced the film in the small thirty-five-millimeter camera. ''We've had this conversation before.''

''Yeah, we have.''

Whit scanned the hallway. He remembered the doctor's observation that Mary Hairston must have bled a lot. He grimaced at the slashing stains of blood, at the wide discolorations on the hardwood floor. Murder scenes became hallowed places to Whit. It was more than the evidence they offered. A few days before, this house had witnessed several moments of absolute horror. It must have seemed an eternity to the victims. Hollywood—for all its splattered ketchup and special effects—could never capture the true face of violent death. The impact was more than just a visual experience. It touched all the senses. Beyond that was the emotion, the mind-stopping fear that had to become a palpable presence in the household during those moments of death and horror.

Had the mother watched as her child was shot to death?

Had she seen her child's lifeblood spew forth from the hole in her little head? Or had the child looked on as someone aimed a gun at her mother's forehead and pulled the trigger? There had been shrieking, begging, the smell of fresh blood, and pain . . . always pain.

Whit chilled at the image.

Fingers snapped at his face. "Earth to Whit," Anna was saying.

"So, what the hell have you touched?" he asked.

"Nothing, as it turns out, but the chief did tell my editor that the technical people were finished here."

"The technical people? Wampler's crew might be many things, but 'technical' isn't one of the words I'd use. They screwed with as much as they could, then they left. You're not going to believe this, Anna, but Tony just spent three thousand dollars of his budget on a fancy video cam and recorder so we could videotape murder scenes such as this. No one bothered to call Tony, though. I'm going to see if the state police lab will send a crime scene crew down. Maybe we can salvage something. If we can type the blood, it might give us some idea of the pattern of movement during the commission of the crime."

Anna reached for her notepad. "Good. I can use that."

"Anna!"

She was busy making notes.

"Seriously," Whit said, "have you touched anything here?"

Anna finished writing and looked around. "No, nothing. Well, maybe, the doorknob and the desktop there. I just got here—"

"Fine," Whit said, cutting her off. "When you leave here, go by the sheriff's department so they can fingerprint you."

"Me? Why?"

"So we can separate your prints from others we may find."

"Like hell," Anna snapped. "I'm not going to be finger-printed."

Whit shrugged. "I'll get a court order."

Anna gaped. "You'd do that?"

"You bet your pretty little ass I would."

He would, too; Anna knew it. "Okay . . . okay. I'll do it."

"Now scram." Whit moved toward a desk in the hallway, the one Anna had indicated she might have touched.

Anna's pen remained poised on the notebook. "Before I go, give me some details. Is the mother a suspect? I hear she is."

Whit turned and pointed down to the notepad. "Write down 'no comment.' Then when you think of another nuisance question, refer back to that answer."

She stalked him as he perused the hallway. "You don't want me to print some of the wild tales I've heard."

He pulled a pen from his pocket and used it to sort through a pile of blood-soaked letters on the desktop. "Frankly, my dear, I don't give a damn what you print."

"Rhett Butler you're not. I bet Tony cares what I print."

"So, go talk to Tony."

"Come on, Whit!"

He wheeled on her. "You said it a few minutes ago. We've had this conversation before. Why do you put me in this position? You know me better than anyone other than Tressa. I don't wanna go through a hassle with you, but I'm not going to give you any information."

"I've got a job to do, Whit."

"A fact of life I'm finding it difficult to live with."

She moved to him and slipped an arm around his thick, muscular neck. She was tall at 5'7'', but he towered above her. His thatch of gray hair was slightly ruffled. From his appearance, she knew he'd left his house in a hurry that morning. So, maybe he hadn't really been home when she had called. It made her feel a little better.

"Make it easy on yourself," she purred. "Give me a few facts. That's all I ask. Do you know how hard it is to invent details when some stubborn cop won't give 'em to you?" She pressed tightly against him, feeling the broad expanse of his chest against her own.

"Anna, please." But he didn't push her away.

She kissed him. He returned the pressure of her lips. Their tongues touched. His big hands dropped to cup her full buttocks. She was lifted from the floor. When they parted, he said, "If someone walked in and found us necking at a murder scene . . ."

Whit left the sentence unfinished but smiled at the image, then lovingly patted her butt. "I missed you this weekend."

To Anna those words meant a lot. He hadn't said much of a loving, kind nature since their return from the beach. "I missed you, too, Whit."

"Now beat it, before I have you arrested for obstructing a police investigation."

"If you did that, I'd have to tell my fellow inmates that big, tough Whit Pynchon likes—"

He hushed her with a kiss, then said, "Now leave. I mean it. I have work to do."

"At least let me hang around while you search."

Whit pointed to the door.

"Please," she begged. "No more photos, I promise. I'd like to be with you a little while. Something tells me you're going to throw yourself into this case, and I won't get to see much of you."

He sighed. "You're conning me."

"I am not."

"No more photos?"

Anna nodded, smiling up at him.

"And no more questions?"

She hesitated. "You drive a hard bargain."

"Take it or leave it."

"Okay, you miserable jerk, no more questions, either."

"Cross your heart."

"And hope to—" She stopped before she said "die." The setting was inappropriate. "No more photos or questions, but I might sneak another kiss."

"Try to behave."

Whit returned his attention to the papers on the desk. Anna ambled into the living room. Whit had been right about the lingering odor. It had been ghastly at first. That's one reason she had left the door partially ajar. A cool breeze blew through it and eased the must of body rot. It seemed even stronger in the living room, which was below the child's bedroom.

A file folder, resting on a cluttered coffee table, caught her eye, but Whit stuck his head in the room before she could pick it up.

"I'm going upstairs," he said.

"I'll be up in a sec."

Whit narrowed his eyes. "What the hell are you doing?"

Anna noticed several framed photos on top of a small bookcase. "I wanna look at these photos." Just a small lie.

"Don't touch."

"I know . . . I know."

She heard him clomping up the steps and waited until distance muffled the sounds before she turned to the manila folder. It rested beneath three unwashed coffee cups. From the appearance of the house, Mary Hairston had subsisted

on coffee and cola. She used her pen to roll the cups off the
folder. With one of her long fingernails, she opened the folder
and saw a stack of recent newspaper clippings. Several were
editorials, others straight news articles. Anna sorted through
them with her fingers. No way could they lift prints from
newspaper pages.

The articles followed a theme. One criticized the government of South Africa for apartheid. Another challenged the
current Republican administration on its civil rights record.
A third took the Milbrook Council to task for its lack of
attention to the streets and other public works in Milbrook's
black community. The street in front of Mary Hairston's
home did have an inordinate number of potholes. By the end
of the winter, they would be gaping threats to the best of
shock absorbers. Anna wasn't a faithful reader of the *Journal*'s editorial page, and she didn't remember the editorial
about the city streets.

There were also several national and local columns from
the editorial page of the Milbrook paper. In fact, every one
of the clippings came from the pages of the *Journal*. Mary
Hairston obviously possessed an elevated sense of racial con-
sciousness.

Good for her, Anna thought.

The folder itself carried no label nor any other identifying
marks. All of the articles appeared to be recent.

"Anna!"

She jumped, certain that Whit had caught her. Then she
realized that he was still upstairs and was calling her. Closing
the folder, she hurried into the hall.

He stood at the top of the steps. "Come up here. There's
something I want you to see."

Anna obeyed. He led her into a neat, uncorrupted bedroom at the rear of the home. A four-poster bed was well

made and covered by a frilly canopy. The atmosphere in the room was refreshingly clean. It smelled of perfume and scented talc. Bright sunlight flowed into a sparkling, clear window, and the bedroom furniture gleamed with a fresh polish. Mary Hairston had been a good homemaker.

Whit went to a bureau and pointed to a large jewelry box, the lid of which was open. "Is that stuff real?"

She peeked inside. Diamonds winked back at her. "Can I touch them?"

"Absolutely not."

"Well, hell, Whit. How can I tell? They look real, but they're so large."

"What did Mary Hairston do at the paper?"

"She worked in production. To answer your next question, she wouldn't have earned enough money to buy those kind of rocks—if they're real."

"They look real enough to me."

Another framed portrait, this one resting on the nightstand by the bed, attracted Anna's eyes. She hadn't had the opportunity to look at the ones downstairs. She went to it and reached down to pick it up.

"Dammit, woman! Don't touch."

She yelped and jerked her hand away. "Jesus! Don't shout! You scared me."

"Then keep your hands off things."

Anna was looking at a small three-by-five portrait of a petite black child. Her hair hung in two braids, and her smile revealed white, even teeth with a toothsize gap in the center. There was a certain mischief in her eyes. "Is that Jenny Hairston?"

"I guess." Whit was waiting at the door.

"Have you even looked at it?" Anna asked.

"No, I've seen enough photos of Jenny Hairston today. If I look at that one, I'll cry."

The editor of the *Milbrook Daily Journal* frowned at the lengthy sheet of copy thrust under his face. He glared over the top of his glasses at Anna. "Why bring it to me? Leave it out there with the desk editor."

"Since Mary worked for the *Journal*, I thought you might like to review it now."

Tom Bukowsky, more interested in retirement than anything else, returned his attention to the work on his cluttered desk. "You didn't say anything derogatory about the *Journal*, I trust?"

"Of course not."

"Then, take it to the desk editor."

Bukowsky's haircut mirrored his personality. Anna had known him for only a few months, but veterans of the paper told her he'd always worn the military flattop. According to rumor, he and Will Binder, son of Billy Binder, the founder and publisher of the *Milbrook Daily Journal*, had served together in Vietnam, supposedly in some elite intelligence outfit. Binder's son had secured Bukowsky a job with the paper after the war. The son had elected to remain in California, where he managed a string of small dailies for another company. After the death of Billy Binder a year ago, Will Binder had returned to West Virginia and his inheritance, the bulk of which was the *Milbrook Daily Journal*.

"I have a question," Anna said.

"For me?" Bukowsky was much more comfortable asking questions than answering them.

"The police think the child had been dead at least five days—maybe even longer."

Bukowsky shrugged. "So?"

"It follows that Mary Hairston hadn't been to work in five days. Who would know about that?"

"Know about what?"

"If she phoned in sick or whatever, for God's sakes. If I were absent for five days, you'd want to know why, wouldn't you?"

"Obviously, you mistake me for someone who gives a damn." The lack of a smile on his face made Anna doubt that he was joking.

"Besides," he added, "what's that got to do with anything?"

"I'm curious."

"Jack Arnold's the guy to talk to."

"He's the business manager, right?"

"Yeah, he supervises all the departments except this one."

Anna gathered up her copy and started toward the door. She stopped when she remembered the clippings in Mary Hairston's home. "For what it's worth, Tom, Mary must have been a fan of yours."

Bukowsky hiked his eyebrows. With his rugged, acne-pitted face, he still looked more the part of a commando than a newspaper editor. Anna could easily visualize him standing Rambo-like in a steamy, Asian jungle, his rough hands gripping a machine gun and his coarse face darkened by jungle mud.

"Why do you say that?"

"She'd clipped several of your editorials. I saw them at her house."

"My editorials?"

"There was one about apartheid, another about the President's insensitivity to racial issues—"

Bukowsky's interest faded. "Will Binder wrote those.

Picked up those liberal notions in California, I guess. He never thought that way in Nam.''

"Oh, you didn't agree with them?" Anna had thought that Bukowsky wrote all the editorials.

"Like I said, Anna, you mistake me for someone who cares. By the way, check with personnel if you're headed that way. See if they have a photo of Mary Hairston. Too bad we don't have one of the kid.''

Jack Arnold's frumpy secretary was perusing a thick mail order catalog when Anna entered the office of the *Journal*'s business manager.

"May I see Mr. Arnold for a moment?" Anna asked.

The secretary traced an imaginary line across a page and made a face over the price she found at the tip of her pudgy finger. "He's preparing to leave for the day.''

Anna had little occasion to venture beyond the *Journal* newsroom into the more traditional corporate regions of the building. She wasn't familiar with the inner workings of the paper's other departments. As far as she was concerned, Jack Arnold had no more to do with her work or her job security than the night janitor.

"Look, lady, I need to talk with Mr. Arnold. Either you announce me, or I'll return to my desk and buzz him on the intercom.''

That brought the secretary's face up from the catalog. "Who are you?''

"Anna Tyree." Maybe that was the problem. The woman didn't know who she was.

The secretary snapped up the phone. "Mr. Arnold, one of our employees—a reporter, I think—demands to see you.'' She had spoken the word "reporter'' as if it were synonymous with "leper.''

"You're so kind," Anna quipped as she passed the woman's desk.

The name of Jack Arnold wasn't totally unfamiliar to Anna. She knew him as one of those mythical corporate beings whose name appeared on vacuous memos about such things as health insurance and tax withholding. His signature, or a stamped semblance thereof, appeared on the paychecks she received.

If Anna had ever laid eyes on the man before, she couldn't remember him. Surely she wouldn't have forgotten such an odd-looking sort. He was shorter even than she and wore a three-piece suit, the vest of which accentuated a rotund belly. A gold chain dangled on the vest. A uniform bronze cast, purporting to be a suntan, colored his skin and reached to the summit of his shining, very bald head. A sparse ring of dark hair circled his head just above his ears. The slight odor of sulfur hanging in the air suggested to Anna that its too-dark hair tone came from one of those gradual hair colorings that oxidized on contact with the air. It smelled like rotten eggs. The tan appeared to come from a bottle, too, or a tube—a bronzer probably. Here was a man who wasn't about to let his age catch him, no matter how badly he wore his youth.

Arnold stood behind his desk, a lint-free, navy blue cashmere coat draped over his arm. "You're?"

"Anna Tyree."

"Anna Tyree." He repeated the name in a fashion designed to imply it meant nothing to him. "Do you have a problem Bukowsky can't handle?"

She waited for him to ask her to have a seat. When he didn't—and even though he remained standing, she lowered herself into a plush chair in front of his polished desk. The

nostrils of Arnold's prominent nose flared, and Anna braced
for a tongue lashing.

Instead, he threw his coat onto the desk and sat down in
the huge high-backed desk chair. "Make yourself comfortable, Miss Tyree. I'll do the same."

"I'm not here on a personal matter, at least not one involving me. It's about a story I'm covering."

"Oh!" The stained face of Jack Arnold beamed a new
message of welcome. The icy block between them was shattered as the focus of his eyes dropped to the swell of Anna's
breasts. "I'm so accustomed to employee grievances that I
was prepared for another. You can understand. The news
department deals with its share of malcontents, too, I'm
sure."

Malcontents? Was that how the business manager per-
ceived the employees of the *Journal*?

The weight of his gaze was heavy on her chest. "I like the
byline you use. It's endearing."

"Personally, I hate it, Mr. Arnold. I'm here to inquire
about Mary Hairston."

The salacious good humor evaporated from his face.
"What about her? What kind of lies has she been telling
you?"

"Telling me? Mr. Arnold, you obviously haven't heard.
Mrs. Hairston is in the critical care ward with a bullet in her
head. Her daughter is dead."

A paleness blushed through the artificial coloring of the
man's skin. "I hadn't heard."

The business manager slipped a finger inside the collar of
the white shirt he wore and pulled it away from his neck.
Anna thought she could see a tan discoloration around the
inner edge of the collar. It brought back high school memories. Since she had no musical talent, Anna had been one

of the band's majorettes. The entire corps had darkened the skin of their legs with something they called "leg makeup." It rubbed off on anything it touched. Was that what Jack Arnold used?

"Ms. Tyree, I don't feel compelled to discuss the internal personnel affairs of the *Journal* with you."

"With all due respect, sir, the woman was off work for several days. Was it an excused absence? If not, did anyone from here call to check on her?"

"I've made my position clear, Ms. Tyree." He stood. "I must be leaving. You've kept me long enough."

Anna's shock was sincere. "Mr. Arnold, the police are going to be asking these same questions."

"And I'll cooperate with the appropriate authorities."

"But not a reporter for this paper?"

"That's it in a nutshell."

Anna rose. "That's bullshit in a nutshell."

He stabbed a finger at her. Even the palms of his hands were bronzed.

"Young lady, I occupy a position of authority with this company. I don't intend to suffer that kind of gutter language from an employee. I strongly suggest that you remember your place. What you request isn't of relevant editorial concern."

"That's a decision for Bukowsky."

Arnold leaned over the desk. Beads of perspiration had formed on the smooth skin of his forehead. They hung suspended, resembling drops of thick gelatin. "It may come as a shock to you, but I exercise as much authority over the news department as I choose."

"Then, I'll say you have no comment."

A bead of sweat broke loose and rolled off his head. She

stared and tried not to laugh as it dribbled down his face, leaving behind a white streak.

"No, you will not, Ms. Tyree. You won't write anything about me—or the status of Mary Hairston's absence from work."

FOUR

A ROUGH HAND jammed against Vanessa Andrews's side.

"Get up, girl. Now!"

The young black woman struggled to pull the heavy bedcovers over her pretty face. "Go away, Momma."

The sheet, blanket, and comforter were ripped from the bed. The bedroom air, not really all that chilly so late in the day, still shocked the toasty body of the sleeper.

"For God's sakes, Momma!" Vanessa raised her head just enough to see that her mother had flung the bedcovers to the other side of the room. "What's gotten into you?"

'You got a call, child."

"So, I'll call whoever it is back."

Mattie Andrews was shaking her head and reaching for Vanessa at the same time. "Not this time. You haul those lazy bones outa bed now."

Vanessa rubbed the sleep from her eyes. "Who the he—uh, heck . . . is it?"

"Cindy."

"Cindy! God, Momma, I can call her anytime. She probably wants somethin' flaky anyway."

Mrs. Andrews wrapped a rough hand around her daughter's arm. "You're gonna talk to her now."

51

The young woman's mind was slowly beginning to find its proper pace. "What's wrong, Momma?"

"That's for Cindy to tell you. It won't keep. Hurry on into my room and talk to her."

Vanessa forgot her goose bumps and pulled herself from the bed. She wore a silky blue nightgown that clung to her full breasts and tented her otherwise lean frame. "This better be important," she said as she fumbled with a pair of worn fuzzy blue bedroom shoes.

Her mother was waiting at the door. "It's nearly noon. Time you was outa bed. If it was up to you, you'd sleep the rest of your life away."

"I was out late last night."

"I know," her mother said.

She finally conquered the slippers. "A person's gotta have some relaxation," she said as she stepped by her mother and out into the hall.

"Just go talk to Cindy—if she hasn't hung up already."

The phone in her mother's room rested on the nightstand. The handset was lying on the pillow. Vanessa snatched it up. "Cindy Jackson! This had better be something important—"

"Something awful's happened," the voice cried. "Mary's been shot!"

"Mary? Mary Hairston?"

"Yes, and, Vanessa, Jenny was shot, too. She was killed."

"Jenny?"

"Yes, Jenny."

Vanessa plopped down on her mother's bed. "They're both dead?"

"No, not Mary. She's in the hospital. She's still got a bullet in her head."

Vanessa's mind raced. Mary Hairston was her closest

friend. The other young black woman on the phone, Cindy Jackson, had been her second best friend during school days. All three of them—Mary, Cindy, and herself—had been a kind of exclusive club since grade school. In recent years, they only saw one another at Mary's home.

"I'm dreaming," Vanessa said.

"It's true!" Cindy blubbered. "It's terrible."

"What happened?"

"I can't find out. I don't think no one knows."

Mattie Andrews had come into her bedroom. She sat down beside Vanessa and put a hand around her daughter's trembling shoulders.

"You mean they haven't arrested anybody?" Vanessa asked.

"They arrested Mary. I heard—" Cindy choked her words.

Vanessa clenched her fist. "Talk to me, Cindy. Why did they arrest Mary?"

"They thought she shot Jenny."

"Shit," Vanessa said.

Mrs. Andrews hiked her eyebrows but decided to ignore what she considered an obscenity.

"Where is Mary?"

"In the hospital."

"And that's all you know?"

"Un huh . . . that's all."

The two talked for a few more minutes before Vanessa hung up the phone. She sat there, staring at the worn carpet that covered the floor of her mother's bedroom.

"Tamantha doesn't know yet," her mother was saying. "It'll kill her." Tamantha was Vanessa's younger sister. Everyone but their mother called her Tams. In the last few years she had spent more time with Mary and Jenny Hairston than Vanessa had.

Vanessa was shaking her head. "I can't believe it."

"Would you go to the school and get Tams? I don't want her finding out about this from anybody else."

Vanessa turned her face to her mother. "Me? You want me to tell her?"

Mrs. Andrews eased back in shock. "If you don't want to, just bring her home. I'll tell her."

"She probably won't hear about it until she gets home, Momma."

Mrs. Andrews stood. "Vanessa Andrews, without a doubt you're the most useless one person." Her mother strutted from the room.

Though twenty-six, Vanessa lived with her mother as an arrangement of convenience, Vanessa's especially. She had left the nest at twenty. She remembered the very night itself. It had been an icy February evening, and Vanessa had come in at three A.M. Her father had been waiting up for her. He had struck her twice that night. The argument wasn't unusual. Since she had reached puberty, there had been a constant rift between them. After his death she had returned. So, she'd walked out—gone to Mary's, in fact. Eventually she'd moved to Charleston.

Vanessa hadn't fared well away from home. She'd spent more than a few nights in jail—once on a drug possession charge. She'd lost her job, too, and that, more than anything else, had forced her to return home. She'd stopped looking for a job as soon as she came home, telling her mother that she would stay home instead to take care of her. Mattie Andrews, Vanessa's mother, somehow ended up doing most of the work around the house.

Her mother's round, pudgy face peered back into the room. "Are you gonna go get Tamantha at least? You think you can do that much for me?"

Vanessa really didn't want to go after her younger sister. "Momma, she's gonna know something's wrong."

"I know that. Just do like I ask this one time. For your sister's sake. You know how much she loved the little Hairston girl."

Vanessa sighed. "Okay, but I'm gonna dress and go now so I can get back."

"Afraid you gonna miss one of them soap operas?" Mrs. Andrews asked, a sharp edge to her voice.

"No, Momma. I wanna try to find out about Mary—maybe try to go see her."

"Good. I'm sure Tamantha will want to go with you."

"No way, Mama. Mary won't need some kid bawling and cryin'."

Mrs. Andrews threw up her hands. "You'd argue with a stop sign, child. Just go get your sister."

"But I'm not gonna take her to the hospital," Vanessa said.

Her mother turned to leave. "I'll be surprised if you even git yourself there."

As Mrs. Andrews vanished, Vanessa hoisted her middle finger in an unobserved response.

Whit was surprised to receive the call from West Virginia's Chief Medical Examiner so soon after Jenny Hairston's body had been sent to him.

"How's the weather down there?" the pathologist asked.

"Warm for October."

"Even hotter up here," Dr. Merrill Barucha said, referring to Charleston. "Christ, I wish it would cool off. I was hoping for an early ski season."

Whit gladly suffered his small talk. Barucha had several assistants, not a one of whom could match his forensic ability or his talent on a witness stand. Every law enforcement agency in the state had a favorite tale about a smart-aleck defense lawyer humiliated in front of a jury by the diminutive Dr. Barucha. His courtroom demeanor was as sharp as his postmortem knives.

"I didn't know you were a skier, Doc."

"I try. To be honest, Whitley"—he always used the investigator's proper first name—"I also like to ogle the young girls who frequent the ski lodges."

Whit laughed. "I go to the beach for that. You can see more of them that way."

"Perhaps it's an occupational prejudice," Barucha said, "but I see them naked—and dead—all the time. I have a fetish for fully clothed women."

"You must lead a boring sex life, Doc, but to each his own."

"I don't know about that, Whitley. It's decidedly erotic to try to make love fully clothed."

"I did enough of that in school, Doc."

"About the Hairston subject you sent, Whitley, I have a preliminary report. The full postmortem won't reach you for several weeks. We've had a rash of homicides, unusual for this time of the year. Usually, the rush doesn't start until closer to Christmas—'peace on earth, good will toward men' notwithstanding."

Whit chuckled as Barucha launched into his report. "The postmortem interval is five days, meaning she died last Wednesday within a six-hour tolerance. I would establish a bracket between nine P.M. Tuesday and three A.M. Thursday. That's as close as I can come."

"That's close enough for government work. It helps."

"As you know, Whitley, certain types of bacteria characterize certain stages of decomposition. You might imagine the little buggers as actors in a play, each appearing on the scene at specific points in the chronology of the script.''

Whit appreciated the pathologist's analogies. So, too, did Tony, who claimed that Barucha was a master of morbid oratory, especially before a jury. No matter how white or green jurors' faces turned, they absorbed the gore. It made them feel a part of the criminal justice process, as if they were privy to dark secrets customarily reserved for a small and morally superior elite.

Barucha was still lecturing about his microbes. ''The presence of *Micrococcus albus* and *Bacillus mesentericus* determined the time of death with substantial precision. When we augment the fact of their presence with the absence of rigor, we can surmise she expired from ninety-six to one hundred twenty hours before discovery.''

''You amaze me, Doc. I was afraid the baths the mother had given the child might have interfered with your results.''

Barucha laughed as only an ME can over such things. ''It prejudiced the gross examination, but even a daily bath, absent chemical preservation or refrigeration, won't stop the human body's inexorable journey back to dust. As to the cause of death, she expired as the consequence of a contact gunshot wound. The missile entered the right parietal region. The entry wound is three-fourths of an inch in greatest diameter and shows stellate lacerations and powder residue about the wound, within the underlying musculature and soft tissue, and upon the outer and inner periosteum. The missile transversed both cerebral hemispheres, from left to right of the decedent and on a track slightly upward and slightly from front to back. The missile lodged in the left superior parietal skull. I recovered what I estimate to be a .32 caliber—perhaps a nine millimeter—slug.''

"In other words," Whit said, "the bastard jammed the gun against her right temple and *bam*!"

"Succinctly put, Whitley. I'd say she was reclining at the time. However, my examination also suggests that she was manhandled prior to death. Not much, mind you, but there does appear to be some bruising. I found no evidence of sexual assault. I've forwarded the missile to the ballistics lab. If you recover the weapon, I'd say you'll find traces of blood from the blow back on it."

"Any skin under the nails? Any other extraneous evidence?"

"None. However, if the remains were bathed several times, I wouldn't expect to find such evidence. Besides, those who removed the body were not especially cautious to preserve that kind of evidence."

"Thanks, Doc. I hope it snows real soon, but only north of Charleston."

"That's kind of you, but, if people keep slaughtering one another at the current rate, I'll never get to the ski lodge. I understand the child's mother walked around five days with a slug lodged against her skull."

"You heard right."

"And she's still alive?"

"So far, but it's touch and go."

"I'll be damned. Do me a favor, Whitley?"

Whit was surprised. "Sure, Doc. If I can."

"When you locate the bastard, forward him on to me—dead or alive."

Anna's confrontation with Jack Arnold left her shaken. Not that she was intimidated, but he had caught her unprepared. Will Binder, the publisher, had interviewed her for the job. He didn't appear the type to tolerate an overbearing asshole like Arnold. In fact, Anna had found herself a little infatuated with Binder, who brought to the *Journal* a liberal editorial persuasion that received a dubious welcome in Milbrook.

Binder impressed her with his apparent youth, his intelligence, and his grace. In today's jargon, most women would call him a "hunk." He stood well over six feet, possessed a light and natural tan and clean-cut good looks that reeked of sensitivity. She had heard several female staffers refer to him as "the Greek God," which was probably a class or so above a hunk. It was apt, though a little gushing for Anna's style.

Jack Arnold just didn't seem like Will Binder's kind of person. They were complete opposites. She wondered just how much authority Arnold had. Bukowsky could tell her what to write, as could Binder, of course, but Arnold could go straight to hell without passing GO and without collecting two hundred dollars. Her interest in Mary Hairston's absence had become something of a crusade—and a point of professional pride—as she marched into the paper's production department, where Mary had worked.

While most people were heading home for dinner and a quiet evening before the television, the *Journal* was just beginning its main day's work. A handful of bored women leaned over slanting tables, busily trimming and designing full-page grocery ads. Anna had learned in her first week of a newspaper career that advertising always took precedence over news. The cream of the composing room staff pasted up the grocery ads, the meat of the advertising. The composing room rookies put together the news pages. Reporters' errors could be corrected, but an incorrect price on a jar of peanut butter or a pound of chicken breasts was a mistake badly tolerated.

The production department foreman stood over a glasstop

table. A bright light burned beneath the table as he studied a full-page negative that rested upon the frosted glass top. The light revealed flaws in the negative that he blacked out with smelly ink.

Windy—that was the foreman's name—might have been the prototype for the "good ol' boy." Black ink always streaked his rough beer-reddened face. He daily wore a dark blue work uniform with the word FOREMAN in blue on a white patch just above his shirt pocket, which itself was crammed full of pens and small knives that he used to trim paper. One cheek or the other concealed an ever-shifting tumor that Anna knew to be a huge plug of tobacco.

"Hiya, Windy." God knew how he'd earned his nickname. He grunted more often than he spoke. "You've heard about Mary Hairston?"

"Yep—a cryin' shame." He shifted the wad from one cheek to another. Rich brown flecks of it clung to the whiskers below his lips, and the juices gathered in the corner of his mouth.

"I understand Mary hadn't been to work for several days."

Windy dabbed black goo on the negative. The substance reeked of alcohol. "Thass right."

"How come?"

"Got me, Miss Tyree. I checked with the front office. They tol' me to hire a new girl."

"Already? Arnold didn't even know what had happened to her."

"No, last week, I mean."

Anna scratched her head. "Wait a minute. Are you saying they were going to replace her before this happened?"

"I guess so."

"Why?"

The foreman straightened up, then leaned back so far that his back popped. It made Anna cringe.

He screwed the cap on the bottle of touch-up ink. "Mary was a sweet girl, but she was a fighter."

"What does that mean?"

The foreman's deep eyes took time to scan the department. His staff were busy at their tables, paying him and Anna no mind. "I think Mary thought she was being done wrong. Thought she was being mistreated 'cause she was colored."

He spat a dark brown gob into a white foam cup. " 'Tween you and me, she had cause to think what she thought."

"Damn, Windy, don't make me pull it out of you a word at a time—between spits. What the devil was going on?"

"Don't rightly know, Miss Tyree. A few weeks back, we needed a girl for second shift. Arnold came and tol' me to move Mary off dayside."

"And?"

"See, we kinda work on an informal seniority system. Ain't no union. No contract. Nothing like that. Mary, though, she'd been here about as long as any of the girls. It shoulda been her choice about moving. That's kinda the way I've always run this department. Arnold, now, he didn't give her— or me—no choice."

"Is that unusual?"

Windy's face squinched up. "Yeah, but it happens sometimes. Arnold said it was 'cause Mary messed up an ad for Buy-Mart, but, hell, she didn't mess it up that bad. No price mistakes or anything like that. One of the product names was misspelled. Hell, Miss Tyree, they misspelled it when they named it. You know what I mean. They came up with some cockeyed, cutesy way to spell it. Mary just spelled it like she found it in the dictionary."

"Did she move to the night shift?"

"Nope. When I give her the news, she gets mighty steamed and goes to talk to somebody. Arnold, I guess." Windy waved an arm around the expanse of his department. "You kin see, we got several blacks working here. I tried to tell Mary it wasn't because she was colored, but she wouldn't even talk to me. She was really p.o.'ed. She was s'posed to go on second shift last week, but she didn't show."

Anna was making mental notes of the conversation. "Is that all?"

"Lordy, gimme time." He expectorated again. Anna tried not to gag as he continued.

"Anyways, I tol' Mary to cool it. I tol' her I thought I could work it out, just give me a little time, but she was pissed. She went and filed one of them complaints with the equal rights people."

"The Human Rights Commission?"

"I guess."

"So, what happened?"

"Nothin'. Some investigator was going to come down this week and check it out."

"Do you think Arnold fired her?"

"Got me," Windy said. He lifted the negative from the table and slid it into a huge paper folder.

"Tell me, Windy. Does Arnold treat the black employees all right? Does he discriminate?"

Windy laughed so hard that Anna backed away, fearful that some of his stained saliva might shower her. "Hell, girl! Jack Arnold don't need a reason to be a son of a bitch. It just comes natural to him—kinda like it does to a rattlesnake. You don't need to be colored to be on his list, neither. You cross 'im and he gets even. It's that simple."

"Was Mary close to any other employees here?"

Windy thought about it. "She and Cindy Jackson went to lunch together. I'd say she and Cindy were close."

"Is she working today?"

"Yep. That's her—way down at the end of the composing room. I did my damnedest to send her home. She's been spillin' tears all over the page layouts."

Anna was gazing down at a short, chunky black woman who was dabbing at her eyes with a tissue as she leaned over a slanted worktable. "She looks upset. I gather they were very close."

Windy shrugged. "Folks that cry in public a lotta times laugh in private."

"That's a harsh thought," Anna retorted.

"But true—leastways I think so."

"Mind if I talk to her?" Anna asked.

"Nope, but he might." Windy nodded towards the door. Jack Arnold glared from the doorway at her.

"Don't look none too pleased to me." Windy muttered.

"Don't worry. I'm gone, Windy. I'll talk to Cindy later."

She walked by Arnold without even looking at him. It didn't work.

"Miss Tyree!"

Anna halted. The business manager waited for her to return to him, but Anna stood her ground. He yielded first, moving towards her. "I gather you're out here being nosy."

"I'm out here doing what the *Journal* pays me to do."

"I see," Arnold said. He was wearing the navy cashmere coat, and dandruff dusted his shoulders. "I've discussed the matter with Bukowsky. We've reached a decision, and I wanted to be the one to give you the news."

Anna braced herself. Was she about to be fired?

"You're off the Hairston story."

Anna wouldn't have been nearly so furious had she been fired. "You can't do that!"

Faces in the production department turned at the sound of her angry words.

"Lower your voice," Arnold said.

"Like hell I will."

"Miss Tyree, I warn you. I have the authority to fire you."

Maybe he did, but Anna had been hired by the publisher. Something told her that only the publisher, Will Binder, could terminate her.

"If you had that power, Mr. Arnold, I suspect you would have already exercised it. And if you do get me fired, then I can promise you one thing, mister. Mary Hairston's protest will be a puff of wind compared to the storm I'll stir."

Anna pranced off toward what she hoped was the sanctuary of the newsroom.

Dusk comes to Milbrook long before other places on the same longitude. Tabernacle Mountain, rising to nearly five thousand feet to the west of the small city, boasts a double summit that casts a distant shadow. Milbrook occupies the mountain's early evening shade. In the heat of summer, the nights cool off a little more quickly. In the harsh Appalachian winter, the bitter winds from the west are blocked by its towering presence. But the effects of its looming mass are mixed. In the early fall, it also means an earlier killing frost.

As warm as the October day had been, the night promised a chill, perhaps even a frost. Vanessa Andrews wrapped herself in a thick sweater as she sat in a rocker on her mother's front porch. The odor of frying pork drifted thought the screen door. Her mother was preparing dinner.

Down deep, Vanessa wanted to escape shadowy Milbrook. She wanted to go to Hollywood and get into show business. With each passing day, her desperation mounted. If she waited much longer, she'd lose her looks and have no chance at modeling and maybe even acting.

Now maybe it wasn't such an impossible dream after all. Vanessa enjoyed conniving. It was one of the few things at which she excelled. As she rocked gently on the porch, shivering a little in the late afternoon chill, she thought about the phone call earlier that day. Besides going to school together, they had dated together, told each other their deepest secrets. Vanessa knew things about Mary that other people didn't know—not even Cindy Jackson and certainly not Tams.

The mountain-thrown shadow deepened as Vanessa plotted. Mattie Andrews came to the screen door. "Come help me with the table, girl."

Vanessa stared into the gathering dusk. She had more than an idea who Jenny Hairston's killer was. If her suspicions were right, it guaranteed her a ticket out of Milbrook. Even if she was wrong, she still might have that same ticket. Mary Hairston had confided a last magnificent secret to Vanessa a month or so before. It was a bombshell.

"Vanessa!"

"What?"

"Come help me."

"Get Tams," Vanessa said.

"You know she's upstairs cryin' her eyes out over the little Hairston girl."

Vanessa threw up her hands. "And you don't think I'm upset, too, Momma?"

"Not so upset that you can't lay down a few knives and forks."

"I don't even like pork, Momma."

Anna couldn't wait to get home to vent her fury. She had

planned to stop at Kroger's for a bottle of Asti Spumante and a take-out dinner, but by the time she left the paper she'd forgotten all about a romantic evening. She stormed into Whit's house.

"That bastard!" she said, coming through the door.

Whit sat in front of the television, trying to beat *Jeopardy!* contestants to the right question. Her furious entrance startled him. "What the hell's the matter?"

"I got yanked off the Hairston story." She threw her pocketbook across the room and collapsed in a chair. "Can you believe it? I asked the wrong questions, stepped on the wrong toes, and they gave the story to that wimp Harold Jones."

"So, what's wrong with Harold Jones?" Whit asked, trying to lighten her mood.

"That son of a bitch is the obituary writer, for God's sakes."

"Appropriate," Whit mused.

"Go to hell."

"Ease up, lady." Whit turned down the television. "Who did you offend this time?"

"That's a hell of thing for you—of all people—to say."

"Touché."

"Anyway, I found out something they didn't want me to know. Mary Hairston had filed a human rights complaint against the *Journal*. Get this. I think they canned her last week."

"Fired her?" Whit leaned forward. Anna's discovery was becoming relevant to his own investigation. People are usually fired because they make someone mad, and Whit was desperate for a motive—anything with which to initiate his investigation. The killing of Jennifer Hairston and the shooting of her mother had some reason—some motive—behind them. This wasn't New York or L.A.

"They wouldn't come right out and say it, but that's the scuttlebutt. Hell, the business manager wouldn't say anything to me. He practically tossed me out of his office."

She explained it all to him.

"Sounds like you drilled into a nerve, but then that's your strong suit, Anna."

"Gee, Whit! That's what I need tonight—more bullshit."

Whit eased back in his chair. "I'm sorry, Anna. I don't know about you, but I've had about all the furor I can stand for one day. I thought you were bringing dinner."

Anna's hands flew to her mouth. "I forgot. I drove right by the store. Jeez, I'm sorry. I'll go back."

Whit shook his head. "Forget it. There's beer in the fridge. We can have sandwiches."

Anna turned up her nose. "No, thanks. I'm famished. Besides, I might want to get drunk tonight. I have a hankering for some good wine. The way things are going I might be fired, too, before long."

"That *would* be worth a toast or two."

"Whit!"

"Just a thought."

She rose and headed for the door. "I do have a favor to ask."

Whit eyed her. "What might that be?"

"First thing tomorrow, visit Jack Arnold, the business manager, and find out what actually did happen to Mary. Brutalize him if you have to."

He laughed. "If I promise to do that, just visit him, I mean, do you promise not to talk about your job anymore tonight?"

She pondered the proposition. "I don't know if I can make that promise. If I drink too much Asti Spumante, I tend to lose control."

Whit leered. "That's what I had in mind."

"Oh, funny!" Anna had been so wrapped up in her own turmoil that she hadn't noticed the improvement in Whit's mood. "You're jovial tonight. Are the autumn blues behind us?"

"For now."

"Jesus, Whit. Does it take a murder to get you in a good mood?"

"Just go get the food."

Whit was in a good mood. Perhaps it was the challenge of the mystery. After Anna was gone, he rose from his chair and ambled to the back door of his small home. A wedge of moon cast an inadequate glow over his yard. He flipped on a pair of bright spotlights that were mounted on the corners of his house and stepped out onto the spacious deck. The beauty of his yard—his subtropical oasis—was fading. To make his life in West Virginia more palatable, he'd recreated a little of his beloved Carolina low country in the flat landscape that reached from his deck to the edge of the forest. It required a heroic effort to maintain it against the bitter winters.

Fall was taking its toll. The lush ferns, planted in the spaces between his rhododendron, were turning brown, many of their fronds having already collapsed on the thick pine bark mulch. The leaves of his deciduous azalea were leprous, ready to drop. The potted evergreen azaleas, a new addition, had been carted down to a makeshift greenhouse in his basement.

A chilly breeze wrapped its unwelcome arms around him and then tittered as it danced over the drying leaves of the forest that swept up the slope of Tabernacle Mountain. Long strands of Spanish moss, collected during an early spring visit to the Carolinas, dangled like witches' fingers from the limbs of his oak and maple. By January, the moss would be freeze-dried.

Whit saw no beauty in fall's onslaught, but he refused to let it darken his mood, at least not on this night. He wanted to cuddle in the warmth of Anna's arms. Since his divorce many years before, Whit had avoided the company of other people in his private life, especially women. Then Anna had come into his life.

A ringing phone interrupted his fantasy. Whit dropped his head, repressing his rage. He let it ring several times before he went to answer it.

"Daddy, I heard about the little Hairston girl." It was Tressa, his daughter. His mood lifted.

"Yeah, it was bad, hon."

"I knew her, Daddy."

The bane of small-town living. Whit detested the familiarity. Big-city cops could maintain a healthy emotional distance between themselves and their victims. Not so in a place like Milbrook. The dead inevitably became friends and relatives to those he knew, and the case became "personal." It meant that cops attended victims' funerals for reasons not just professional.

"Tams knew her real well. She baby-sat for Mrs. Hairston."

Tams—short for Tamantha—was a young black girl who attended school with Tressa. Whit's daughter, lacking her father's antisocial bent, had many friends, but Tamantha Andrews was special. She was the friend who really wasn't quite welcome at the home of Julia Pynchon, Whit's ex. So, Tressa often brought Tams to Whit's. He found the petite black girl delightful—so happy and straightforward, no pretense to her at all. She was one of Whit's favorite people, and that was no small claim to fame. Besides, Tams held a very impressionable Tressa down to earth.

Tressa was still chattering. "Tams called me and said you all think Mrs. Hairston did it."

"Not true, hon. Call Tams right back and tell her we know Mrs. Hairston didn't do it."

"She also said Mrs. Hairston's in the hospital."

Whit sagged a little. "That's right. She's hurt very bad, Tress. She was shot, too. The bullet didn't penetrate the skull, but—"

Whit stopped his clinical explanation. Tressa didn't need to know the grisly details. "Anyway, hon, it doesn't look good for her."

"Who did it?"

"We don't know."

"I saw Jenny at Tams's a lot. She was a doll baby. Tams dearly loved her. I feel so sorry for her, Daddy."

"You know—and you can tell Tams this—I'll do my best to find whoever did this. That won't help the little girl or her mother, but it's all I can do."

"I know, Daddy. G'night."

She was hanging up to cry. Whit could hear the emotion in her voice. Tressa shared her friend's pain. That meant that Whit shared it, too.

Anna was just coming in the door when the phone rang again. If anything could foul Whit's mood, it was the phone. His manners on the phone were, in Anna's word, "cannibalistic." Anna dropped the bags and beat him to it.

He was sniffing the aromatic bags of food when she offered him the phone.

"Who the hell is it?"

"A doctor."

"What?"

"A doctor, Whit. Be nice. He is—nice, I mean."

Whit snatched the phone. "Yeah."

Anna cringed, waiting for him to say something crude and unkind. If there was anything he despised more than phone calls, it was doctors. Instead, she saw a strange look cross his face. "You're sure?" he was saying.

Whit gave Anna a look of weary frustration. "Can you do that?" he was asking of the doctor.

Anna eased down into a chair, aware that the conversation was something extra special.

"What was that about?" she asked once he hung up.

Whit stood there. "Mary Hairston suffered some kind of . . . well, a cerebral incident. That's what the doctor called it. She's lapsed into a coma. They think she's brain-dead."

Anna moaned. "Dear God."

"It gets worse," Whit said.

Anna looked up, puzzled.

"Mary Hairston's pregnant, Anna."

"Pregnant?"

"That doctor was an obstetrician. He says there's a chance they can keep her alive until the baby comes."

Anna whistled. "What a story!"

FIVE

THE LIGHTS of Tressa Pynchon's battered Toyota struggled against the thick morning fog that often settled along the foothills of Tabernacle Mountain during season's change. Fog or no fog, Tressa could have reached her destination blindfolded. She drove it every morning. This morning, though, a knot of anxiety throbbed in Tressa's stomach. She was going to pick up Tams, and she dreaded to face her grieving friend. The Toyota eased to a stop in front of the Andrews home. The large house sat high on a hill. A long flight of steps reached from the deteriorating sidewalk to the house itself. Tressa mounted them slowly, her own breath white and heavy in the chilly morning air.

Mrs. Andrews answered the door. "Come in, child. It's a dreary morning."

"How's Tams?"

"Lord God, child. She cried herself to sleep last night. I thought I was gonna have to call our doctor to get something to calm her down. She loved that little Hairston girl like a sister—maybe more'n her own sister, but don't tell Vanessa I said so."

Tressa smiled. "I know. Where is she?"

"Upstairs, but I don't think she's going to school."

Tressa started for the steps, but Tams came bounding

down. She wrapped her arms around Tressa, who felt the warm dampness of tears on her cheek and neck.''

"It's not right," Tams said, her voice quivering with emotion. "If there *was* a God, he wouldn't let this happen."

Mattie Andrews gasped. "Tamantha! Don't say things like that."

Tams wheeled on her mother. "It's true, Momma!"

Tressa saw her best friend's red, ragged eyes. "Tams, God just took Jenny to heaven."

Tressa shocked herself with her words. That's what adults always said when children died. It made no sense to Tressa, but she'd said it anyway, just because she had to say something.

Tams, her hands upraised and clinched, cried, "There's not any heaven!"

Mattie Andrews struck with the speed of a lightweight fighter. Her palm smacked against Tams's face. The teenager's eyes betrayed her disbelief.

"I know you're grievin', girl, but you don't never say things like that, not in my house."

Tams turned and fled up the steps, tripping several times before she reached the top. Once Tams was out of sight, Tressa heard loud, angry voices above. In a moment, Vanessa Andrews appeared at the top of the steps.

"Hi, Vanessa."

But Vanessa wasn't smiling. "Can't you all hold it down? I'm trying to sleep."

Mrs. Andrews went to the bottom of the steps. "Time you got your lazy behind outa bed. You'd think you'd be down here tryin' to comfort your sister."

Vanessa rolled her eyes and vanished.

Mrs. Andrews turned to Tressa. "I don't know what's

gotten into Vanessa. She's more of a child than Tamantha is. Mary Hairston was just about her only friend in the world, and she ain't as much as shed a tear—not that I've seen anyway.''

"I'm worried about Tams.''

The aging black woman lowered her head. "I shouldn't have hit her like that. Young 'uns just can't understand death. Come have some coffee."

Tressa wasn't concerned about being late for school. Somehow, outside events seemed more important. Mrs. Andrews sat her at the table and poured her a cup of coffee.

"You know, Mrs. Andrews, it does make you think. If there is God, and he is good, then why would he let something like that happen to a small child? I guess I don't understand either.''

Mrs. Andrews joined her at the table. "I don't have them kinda answers, child.''

The coffee warmed Tressa. Nobody made it like Mrs. Andrews. "Maybe I oughta go up and see Tams.''

Tams's mother reached over and put a hand on Tressa's. "I wish you would. I really shouldn't have hit her.''

Upstairs, Tressa tapped lightly on Tams's door.

"Go away," a voice said from inside.

"Tams. It's me.''

She heard movement. The door opened. Tears streaked the rich tan skin of Tams's face. Her eyes were puffy and weak.

"*Can* I come in?''

Tams opened the door and closed it behind Tressa. They sat beside each other on the bed.

"Your mother's down there worrying about you. She's sorry she hit you.''

Tams sniffed back mucus. "I shouldn't have said those things."

Tressa put an arm around her friend. "You were thinking them. There's no difference in saying. I guess it's the way you said them."

"I'm not going to school today."

Tressa looked at her wristwatch. "And I'm going to be late. Will you be okay today?"

Tams nodded. "I have something to do today."

"What's that?"

Someone knocked on Tams's door. Tressa went to open it. Tams's mother poked her head inside. "I'm sorry Tamantha."

The young black girl nodded. "Me, too."

"Tams was just telling me that she had something to do today," Tressa said.

Mrs. Andrews sat down beside her daughter. "What is it, child?"

Tams looked at Tressa first, then at her mother. "Someone needs to see about a funeral for Jenny."

"Lord, child, we can't do that. We can't afford it, I mean."

"I know that, Momma, but maybe Mrs. Hairston has something. I just know someone has to do something. They have to." The tears filled her eyes again. "Mrs. Hairston didn't have any other family."

Mrs. Andrews sighed. "There has to be someone. It's not your place."

"But there's not, Momma! There's not anyone."

"What can you do?" Tressa asked.

Tams gave her friend a look of defiant determination. "If I don't do something, no one will."

* * *

Whit paid no attention to the people crowding the physician's waiting room as he approached the receptionist's desk. "I'd like to see the doctor for a few minutes."

"Are you a drug salesman?" she asked.

"God, no. Do I look like one?"

The receptionist looked at a second woman totaling figures on an adding machine and smiled. She turned back to Whit. "Uh, Dr. Fragliano is an obstetrician. He restricts his practice to prenatal care and delivery."

"Don't I look pregnant?" Whit asked.

The receptionist giggled.

Whit hated flashing his ID. It made him feel too much like Kojak. Nonetheless, he withdrew it from his coat pocket and showed it to the young woman. He spoke just above a whisper. "Dr. Fragliano phoned me at home last night about Mary Hairston. I believe he's treating her at the hospital."

"Ohhhh! Yes, sir. I'm sorry. We have a lotta men come in here thinking Dr. Fragliano is a general practitioner. Have a seat."

Whit turned to the roomful of women, all of whom appeared to be suffering from varying degrees of pregnancies. Their faces were turned on him, some with smiles on their faces. Others glared with the same kind of hostility Whit felt when he visited the cells of the Milbrook jail. There were several vacant chairs, each one wedged between intimidatingly over-sized women. Whit chose the closest, stopping on his way to grab a magazine. When he got to his chair, he saw that it was titled *Modern Mother*. It was three years old. The magazines in doctors' offices were always several years old. No way did he want to draw attention to himself again just to get a four-year-old *Time*, so he thumbed through it. He stopped at an article called "Breast Feeding and the Working Mother."

The woman beside him snickered. Whit didn't dare look at her. Instead, he quickly dropped the magazine to the floor and then took a clandestine look to his left. If Whit was any judge, the woman who had snickered, presumably at the article he had started to read, was ready to deliver at any moment. The woman on his right was much older and not quite so pregnant. He had settled between a conversation.

The snickerer leaned forward a little. "I can't believe how hard he's kicking."

"When he stops, he's ready to be born."

Or he's dead, Whit thought. The irreverence of the idea made Whit shake his head at himself.

Whit detested waiting. It brought out his evil self. He avoided movie houses because it meant standing in lines. He neglected his own health because it meant waiting in places just like this. He didn't eat at cafeterias and never went to concerts.

"Have you decided on a name?" the older woman was asking.

"Joshua Bernard."

Poor kid, Whit thought.

"Mr. Pynchon." It was the receptionist. She stood just outside the door to what turned out to be a suite of examination rooms.

Thank God! He jumped to his feet.

"Dr. Fragliano will see you now."

"Some of us have been waiting for a long time," an unhappy woman said to Whit as he strode toward the receptionist.

Whit smiled down at the complaining woman. "The doctor gives priority to pregnant men."

He hurried to catch up to the receptionist, leaving the woman to sputter. Others in the waiting room were laughing.

"Good for you," the receptionist whispered. "She's a real pain."

"Men don't care who they get pregnant, do they?"

By then, they were away from the waiting area. The receptionist continued to laugh as she guided Whit into a small magazine-cluttered office. "The doctor has two more patients he wants to finish with, but you'll be more comfortable in here. He'll be with you shortly."

"Many thanks." Whit meant it.

"Shortly" turned out to be fifteen minutes, most of which time Whit spent staring at a life-size medical reproduction of a baby cradled in a woman's womb and wondering if all the medical journals scattered around were three and four years old, too. Dr. Fragliano, a short man of Oriental persuasion, bustled into the office. He plopped into a huge desk chair that threatened to swallow him and began to turn back and forth in it.

"Good to see you, Officer." His English was practiced and perfect. "I have reviewed Mrs. Hairston's situation this morning and discussed the matter with my colleagues. In the light of day, so to speak, I am less inclined toward optimism."

"Meaning?" Whit asked.

"I have doubts as to the feasibility—or wisdom, for that matter—of keeping the young woman alive throughout the duration of a pregnancy."

"That's kind of up to her, isn't it, Doc? I mean, she might remain as she is for months."

Dr. Fragliano shook his head. "At this point, she's on life support. We have inserted a ventilator. If we remove that, she might continue to breathe of her own accord, but, given the area of the brain that's damaged, we doubt it."

"What's the policy on that?"

Fragliano shrugged. "I don't know. It's not my area of expertise. Another physician is responsible for that aspect of her treatment. I was brought in to consult with regard to the obstetrical issue. Frankly, Officer, none of us think we would be doing that child any favors. The risk of a birth defect is unusually high. I gather Mrs. Hairston has no other family—no one to care for the child following birth. A heroic effort in this instance might be a misguided kindness."

"So, what's to happen, Doc?"

The little man adjusted himself in his big chair. "I cannot say at this point. The woman's primary physician and the hospital will make the decision. If it is decided to maintain her on life support, then I will reluctantly initiate the proper procedures for prenatal care."

"You sounded—" Whit stopped, uncertain of the right words to use. "You gave me the impression last night that the prospect challenged you."

"A rash first impression," he answered. "Then, as you Americans say, I slept on it."

Whit didn't know what to say. "Do you think anyone will move quickly on this? I mean, will they pull the plug right away?"

Fragliano shrugged. "Who can say?"

"Has anyone been to visit her, any male friend?"

"I would not know that, Officer."

Whit inhaled. The obstetrician's offices smelled of Lysol

and alcohol. His eyes roamed over a book-lined wall on one end of the small office. Rarely did Whit feel as though he was floundering, but at the moment that described his condition.

Fragliano stood. "I have patients."

"Hold it a sec," Whit said. "Lemme get this straight. Are you telling me that the hospital might pull the plug on Mary Hairston at any time? Has that decision been made?"

The man offered a smile that Whit considered inscrutable. "I do not know what they intend to do."

Anna looked at the wall clock in the office of Will Binder's secretary and saw that it was 10:30 A.M. She crossed her legs and sighed. The movement caught the attention of the young woman, which had been Anna's intent.

"What time does he usually come in?" Anna asked.

"Usually ten, but sometimes he's late. As I told you, Anna, I'd be glad to phone you in the newsroom when he arrives."

Anna shook her head. "I'll wait."

"Suit yourself."

"Does he come through here?"

"He has a private entrance."

"Maybe he's in there," Anna suggested.

The secretary laughed. "The first thing he'll do, even before he removes his coat, is buzz me for some coffee. He's a man of rather precise habits."

At that point, as if to prove a point, the intercom buzzed. Anna tensed as the secretary answered it.

"My coffee, please." The voice belonged to Will Binder.

Anna started to stand.

"It'll be a few more minutes," the secretary said quickly, as if to head Anna off.

Anna wanted to say something sarcastic, but she had to keep in mind that this was the publisher she was waiting to see. "I was just stretching."

Another ten minutes passed before Anna was granted her audience. As she was ushered in to his presence, he came around from behind his desk to greet her. "Anna, I understand I've kept you waiting. I apologize. I got away from home rather late this morning. The wife had a chore or two that needed to be done."

Somehow, Will Binder just didn't seem the type of man to be sidetracked by household chores.

"I have a complaint to register," Anna said, coming quickly to the point.

"Ah, I see. Please, have a seat. Would you care for some coffee?"

"No, thanks."

Tall and lean, tanned just right, with sun-touched blond hair, he reminded her of a surfer who had aged with cultured grace. She imagined him in skimpy swimming trunks and was embarrassed that the vision threatened to arouse her—"make my kitty hop," her mother often said with particular regard to Tom Selleck.

Binder didn't go back around his desk. Instead, he sat beside her in a chair in front of his desk. Anna had once taken a course in interviewing techniques. Binder must have taken the same course. Sharp interviewers knew that it disarmed most people to lose the buffer provided by a desk or table.

"Now, Anna, what's the problem?"

"You know about Mary Hairston?"

The publisher slowly nodded. He crossed his legs and steepled his fingers.

"I was working on the story yesterday, and I went to see Mr. Arnold to inquire about the status of Mary Hairston's absence from work."

"I'm aware of that, also."

Anna chuckled. "I bet you are. Anyway, we had a few words. After our conversation, I gather that Mr. Arnold went to see Tom, and as a result I was pulled from the story."

She found herself unable to match his gaze. His eyes were so interested, so intense. She ended up studying the expertly pressed white shirt and the navy blue tie he wore. They both seemed crispy-new.

"Anyway, sir, I don't think it was fair." God, what a lousy job she was doing. Even to her own ears, she sounded like some schoolgirl protesting some minor breach of etiquette. Her eyes drifted to a photo behind him. It showed five soldiers with their arms around one another, their faces streaked with dirt and their fatigues stained with sweat. They stood in a field backed by tall palms. She surmised that it had been taken in Vietnam. Anna found herself trying to pick Will Binder from the group, an almost impossible task at such a distance.

The publisher hadn't altered his physical position. "I can see how it might appear that way to you. Be assured, Anna, that you were not removed from the story because of your little confrontation with Mr. Arnold. He can sometimes seem a bit self-important, and your inquiries were relevant."

"So, what's the problem, Mr. Binder? I don't understand."

He finally shifted in the chair, leaning even closer to her. She felt a moistness underneath her arms.

"If you hadn't come to talk with me, Anna, I was going to arrange an appointment. We've had some complaints about your work, and I think it fair to confront you with them. Understand, please, that I have no opinion myself. In fact, I have no facts upon which to form an opinion."

"Complaints? About me?"

"I fear so, Anna."

"What?"

"We've received several calls from police officers, Anna, who claim that your stories are biased. I, as much as anyone, respect your right to a private life. I'm not a judgmental sort of individual in that regard, but I gather you're involved with a gentleman by the name of Whitley Pynchon, an investigator for the county attorney?"

"For the prosecuting attorney."

"I stand corrected. Nonetheless, the callers allege that your coverage of police and court activities is influenced by your relationship with this individual."

Anna shook her head. "I can't believe this."

"As I say, Anna, I have no facts upon which to base an opinion."

She climbed to her feet. "Well, it's untrue. They're lying."

Will Binder kept his seat. "About the relationship?"

"No, about it influencing my work."

"As they say in the legal realm, sometimes the appearance of impropriety is as serious as impropriety itself."

Anna paced his office. "I can't believe this, Mr. Binder. Did they cite any examples of prejudiced reporting? It's easy to say things, but where are the facts to support such a nonsensical charge?"

Binder stood and went behind his desk. "Let's not over-react, Anna. For right now, you'll be placed on a general assignment beat—"

"I'm losing my beat?"

"Hear me out, Anna. In a few weeks, I plan a major change here. I plan to discontinue what we have tradition-ally called the society pages and replace it with a distinct section known as 'Lifestyles.' I want to broaden our cov-erage of the arts and literature. I want to see local review-ers of books and movies. We even plan to budget some funds to buy freelance work. I was hoping that you might be interested in editing that section of the paper. You have the ability and motivation and, I think, the discretion to make the new section a success. It will mean a substantial salary increase, of course, not to mention prestige."

" 'Lifestyles'?"

"Yes, I have some great hopes for it."

Anna's head spun. She was losing grip on herself. "I like the police beat, sir."

"Think over the promotion, Anna."

"Your decision is final?"

Binder smiled. "For now, Anna, but nothing's ever fi-nal. Bear that in mind."

Detective Lieutenant Cal Burton cursed the phone on his desk when it rang. "Whadaya want?"

The department secretary wasn't cowered by Cal Bur-ton. Some said it was because they had been "a thing" in their younger days. Others suspected that she and the chief were currently "a thing." Whatever the reason for her independence, it frustrated Cal.

"Magistrate Bud Holder's on the phone," the secretary announced.

"Tell him I'm busy."

The secretary snorted. "Like hell I will."

She hung up, which put Holder on the other end of Cal's line. He cursed the secretary to himself and said aloud, "Mornin', Judge."

"Greetings, Cal. How goes it?"

"Rough, Bud. Damned rough."

"I have some information I thought you might find interesting."

Cal rolled his eyes. "I'm all ears."

"I read about that colored woman and her kid. Tough deal."

Cal started to tell the magistrate that it wasn't his case, but he decided to hold off. "Yeah, it was one of those messy ones."

"I don't know whether it means anything or not, but about six months ago that Hairston woman—leastways I think it was her—came to the court and filed a complaint about some buck that was threatening her life. A lovers' spat kinda thing."

Holder, who'd been a court bailiff before becoming a magistrate, paused in his tale. Cal could hear him stuffing a wad of tobacco in his mouth.

"Anyway," Holder said, his words muffled by the plug, "she had grounds."

"We arrest him?"

"Naw. She dropped it. Fact is, Cal, I never even typed the warrant. I know how them people are. I just left it laying. I got a special pile for complaints between spouses and lovers. You might say, I let 'em fester a little while. Just like I figured, a couple of days later she waltzed in and wanted to withdraw the complaint."

"You don't happen to remember they guy's name, do you?"

"Better'n that, Cal. I got a copy of her complaint. Had my girl dig it out of the pile."

Cal tried to conceal his excitement. "Wanna give me the name, Bud?"

The detective heard papers rattling.

"His name's Lewis Luther. She claims he threatened her over the phone. Hell, he probably threatened her in person, too, but that ain't against the law. Hell of a world, ain't it, Cal?"

The detective lieutenant forced a laugh as he jotted down notes. "What was the date on that?"

The magistrate gave it to him. "Don't know if that'll help a bit, but I wanted to let ya know."

"Thanks, Bud. You never know what's important in a case like this till you check it out."

"You decide to get a warrant for the guy, you come to me," the magistrate said. "Don't matter what time, day or night. With the election next year, I need all the publicity I can get. Murder cases are always good for publicity."

"You got my word on it, Bud."

As soon as the conversation ended, Cal hurried into the jail control room. All criminal records were stored in battered filed cabinets that lined one wall. He gave the dispatcher Luther's name. "Pull that file for me. Pronto."

The dispatcher went to a Rolodex and located the name. The card told him the number of the file. He pulled it from the drawer and handed it to Cal. "He's been here before."

Cal withdrew the rap sheet. "Let's see here. Three arrests for misdemeanor assault. Three arrests for battery. A shoplifting charge. This bird's lived a charmed life.''

"Big black guy," the dispatcher said. "You remember him?''

"Shit, are you kidding?'' Cal whistled. "Look at this. His most recent conviction was a felony assault. He's on probation.''

Only then did Cal pull the mug shot out of the file. He squinted at the huge round face. "Hell, they all look the same to me.''

"What's he done?''

Cal narrowed his eyes. "Not a goddamned thing I know of, but I want the street units to see this photo and file. Tell 'em if anyone sees Luther to pick him up and get a hold of me right then.''

"Yes, sir.''

"Now listen to me. Make sure you understand me. I mean *right then*, and they're not to call anyone else. I'm the only person they notify. You understand?''

"I gotcha.''

Cal started to leave, but he thought of something else. "I don't wanna a word about this to go beyond this department. Make that clear, too. If it leaks, I'll have your ass first.''

Six

TONY MET WHIT at Hardee's for lunch. The young pimply-faced boy who took their orders probably wished the two men had gone to one of the other fast-food houses. Both Whit and Tony disrupted the flow of the noonday rush by ordering hamburgers without cheese.

"That'll take a few minutes," the red-faced kid stammered.

Whit leaned across the counter. "I thought this was a fast-food restaurant. Not everyone in this country wants cheese drooping on a hamburger."

"Yes, sir." He turned and called out the order to the people in the back.

"Just tell your cooks to shake a leg," Tony said.

"Yes, sir. If you want, go find a seat. I'll have your burgers sent out."

"We'll wait here," Tony said. "That way you won't forget about us."

Someone behind them grumbled about the holdup. The two men ignored it.

"You sounded disturbed when you called me," Tony said as they waited.

"They're talking about pulling the plug on Mary Hairston," Whit said.

"Who's talking about it?"

"The hospital, I guess. The doctor I talked to this morning wasn't nearly as enthusiastic about the situation as he was last night."

"Maybe they checked out her health insurance," Tony said.

An elderly man behind them, perhaps the one who had fussed about the delay, inched closer, his attention obviously tuned to their conversation. Whit noticed it. "Gettin' your ears full, mister?"

The man blushed and took several steps back. In the process, he stepped on the toes of a young woman, who cried out in pain.

"Let's wait until we get our food," the prosecutor suggested. "I can't believe you picked this place anyway. I thought you hated these places."

"A moment's weakness."

The young man behind the register was saying, "Excuse me."

"What is it?" Whit asked.

He told them the price of their meals.

"When we get the food, kid, you get the money."

The young man looked behind him for some backup. There was no one there. At that moment, the reedy voice of a girl, hidden from view back in the kitchen, announced, "Burgers up—no cheese." It solved his dilemma.

They located a small booth and wedged themselves into it. "Can you believe that these joints represent the height of American popular culture?" Tony said as he unwrapped the burger.

Whit chuckled. "I wouldn't complain a bit if I could just get a friggin' hamburger without cheese. What should we do about the Hairston woman?"

"Did you get the impression they were going to remove the life support soon?"

"I asked that question. Fragliano just shrugged and said it was the hospital's decision or something to that effect."

Tony chomped off a huge hunk of the sandwich. "When I get back to the office," he said, his mouth full, "I'll call the attorney for the hospital and advise him that I object to the removal of life support."

Whit seemed surprised. "Can you do that?"

Tony grinned. "I don't know. I do know, though, that an argument can be made that it's murder, if not of the mother, then at least of the unborn child. That's what the pro-lifers say anyway. I suspect the call will eliminate the possibility of any immediate action."

"What then?" Whit asked. His sandwich remained untouched on his tray.

"Aren't you gonna eat?"

Whit made a face. "You're enjoying yours enough for the both of us."

"Go to hell," Tony mumbled. "As for Mary Hairston, I guess I could ask for a circuit court hearing and suggest that the court appoint a guardian *ad litem* for the mother and the child, maybe a separate one for each. If the lady had no family, then she at least deserves to have someone arguing her right to try to give birth to that child. Surely, the child deserves to have someone arguing for its right to be born."

"Sounds good to me." Only then did Whit pick up the sandwich.

Tony was swallowing the last bite of his. "Why the concern, Whit?"

"Whadaya mean?"

"You didn't know the lady. Don't get me wrong. I'm concerned, too, but you seem extraordinarily upset over it. It's not in character.''

Whit shrugged. ''I think we have a better chance of catching this bastard if the woman's alive. She's four months pregnant, and, the Christmas story notwithstanding, she didn't get that way by herself. No lover or fiancé or whatever has shown up at the hospital. I got a hunch that the killer may be the man who got her pregnant. It finally gives the case a focus.''

Tony shook his head. ''I shoulda known it wasn't because of your humanitarianism.''

''Jesus, Tony. I care about that, too.''

''Just kidding you, Whit. Damn, you're like a powder keg these days. You have no sense of humor whatsoever.''

''I'll try to do better. I do have a favor to ask.''

Tony started to crunch on the ice from his soft drink. ''Should I brace myself? This sounds like something big.''

''Not that big. I'd like to have the state police send a crime scene crew to Mary Hairston's house.''

Tony's eyes widened. ''Hell, Whit, the crime scene's lost its integrity. You know that?''

''If we can't get any admissible evidence, maybe we can at least find a lead or two, anything to point us in the right direction. I want them to do a blood pattern analysis, too.''

''I'll ask, but they'll probably laugh me off the phone. What are you going to be doing?''

Whit started to gather up the debris of his lunch. ''I'm gonna start talking to her friends and coworkers. I need to find out who she's been fucking.''

''You're such a tactful man, Whit.''

Anna stared at the blank screen of her terminal. She had absolutely nothing to do—no stories to write, no calls to make. Following her dismal conversation with Will Binder, she had returned to the newsroom. As was his custom, Bukowsky hadn't arrived at work until after lunch. She had stopped him as he passed her desk.

"So, what do I do?" she'd asked.

"Sit tight. I'll let you know."

That had been two hours ago. During that time, she had polished her nails in full view of the entire newsroom. She had read several stories in a trade journal. As a last resort, she had cleaned the dark muck from the screen of her terminal. The little green blip that marked the entry point of text continuously winked at her—a mocking reminder of her plight.

"Anna."

The sound of someone speaking her named startled her. She turned. Tressa Pynchon and Tamantha Andrews stood behind her. The woman the foreman had identified as Cindy Jackson loomed behind them.

"My goodness, what are you two doing here?"

"We need help," Tressa said.

Before they had gone to bed the night before, Whit had told her about Tressa's call. She knew how close the Andrews girl had been to the Hairstons.

"I'm so sorry, Tams." Anna reached out and took the young girl's hand. "If there's anything I can do—"

A tear dribbled down Tams's cheek.

"Tams is concerned about Jenny's funeral," Tressa said.

"Her funeral?"

Tams nodded. "Who's going to arrange it? Who's going to pay for it?" She turned to the chunky young woman who had been keeping a distance from the conversation. "You know Cindy, don't you? She works here, too. She and Mary were friends."

Cindy inched forward.

Anna smiled and nodded at her. "Yes, I'd like to chat with Cindy about Mary, but let's talk about the funeral right now. What about family? I'm sure there must be family—"

"There's no one," Tressa said.

A few other reporters were in the newsroom. They were casting curious or bothered glances at the two girls.

Bukowsky strolled from his office. Anna suspected it was no coincidence. He stared indiscreetly at the unusual gathering around Anna's desk.

"Uh, let's go down to the lounge. We can get a Coke or something," Anna said. "Can you come with us, Cindy?"

"Yes, ma'am. Windy said I could try to help Tams, but I don't rightly know what to do."

Anna got up from her desk. "Let's go talk about it."

The two newspaper employees guided the teenagers down a flight of steps to a room filled with small tables, brightly colored plastic chairs, and an array of vending machines. Anna bought them all colas, and they settled down at one of the tables. Other than the four of them, the lounge was empty. It was just a little too early for the full evening crew to arrive.

"How come you two aren't in school?"

Tressa offered the explanation. "We took the day off. Tams is really worried about the funeral. We went to a funeral home, but the guy there didn't even want to talk to us. He told us that the county would probably bury Jenny. It was terrible, Anna. The way he said it, I mean."

Tams was sullen, her eyes red and weak from emotion. "Nobody cares."

Anna's mind raced. If there was no family, as the girls contended, and with Mary Hairston in a coma, what would become of Jenny? Who would make the arrangements? All very good questions, and it shocked—and impressed—Anna that a caring teenager like Tams had been the first to think of it.

"I have an idea," she said. "Obviously, there are some legal issues here, and I'm sure Tony will be more than willing to help with those."

Tams frowned. "Tony?"

"The prosecutor," Tressa explained. "You know, the guy my dad works for."

"Oh," Tams said. "I forgot about him."

"As for the cost of the funeral," Anna said, "maybe Mary had insurance here. They have family life insurance and health insurance plans. I tell you what. Let's go talk to the publisher, Mr. Binder. Maybe Mary had a life insurance policy on her daughter?"

Tams's eyes brightened. "Do you think so?"

Anna reached over and took the young girl's hand. "I suspect she had some, but what kind I don't know. Let's go see."

Cindy spoke up. "Maybe I'd best get back to work."

"No," Anna protested. "You come with us. After all, you were a friend of Mary's. I really didn't know her."

"To see Mr. Binder," Cindy said, obviously uncomfortable with the idea. "I'd better not, Miss Tyree."

"For God's sakes, call me Anna. He won't bite."

"I don't know."

"Well, I do, Cindy."

This time, Anna wasn't kept waiting. She and the others were immediately escorted into his office. Tressa gawked at the plush carpeting and dark wood furniture as she was led into the presence of the publisher.

Binder came around to the desk and shook both their hands. "I'm always impressed by young people who show an interest in the press," he said. "Has Ms. Tyree given you a tour?"

Tressa and Tams exchanged glances.

Anna jumped in with an explanation. "Mr. Binder, Tams here"—she tapped the black girl on the shoulder—"was a very close friend of Mary Hairston and her daughter. Tressa is the daughter of Whit Pynchon."

"And this," Anna said, "is Cindy Jackson. She works in composing and was a good friend of Miss Hairston." Cindy hung back in the shadows of the cavernous office.

Binder raised his eyebrows. "I see. Have a seat, ladies. What can I do for you?" He sat on the edge of his desk. The two girls accepted his offer and sat down, but Anna and Cindy both remained standing.

Cindy drifted back toward the door while Anna did the talking. "It seems, sir, that Mary Hairston has absolutely no other relatives. I haven't verified that information, but Tams and Cindy were close enough to the Hairstons to know. Anyway, they're very concerned that arrangements be made for services for Jenny Hairston."

Binder was nodding. "Hmmm. That's thoughtful of all of you."

Tams was wiping a tear from her eye but didn't offer to speak.

Anna went on. "We were wondering if Mary carried any life insurance on the child through the company."

The publisher's gaze was affixed on Anna. He always maintained eye contact, and it continued to be disarming. "I don't know myself, but I'll make a phone call and find out."

He started to pick up the phone but replaced it. "Better yet, let me walk over to the personnel office and see. Make yourselves comfortable. I won't be a minute. And, Anna, feel free to sit on the couch."

"I'm fine, sir. I'll stand."

Binder exited the office, smiling at Cindy as he walked by her.

"He's nice," Tressa said.

"By that, you mean handsome," Anna said.

Tressa giggled. "That, too."

Tams just sat there, one hand clenched in the other.

Whit went first to the elementary school Jenny Hairston had attended. The door of the school opened into an empty hallway lined with closed classroom doors. Why did schools, even relatively new ones such as this, have to smell so bad? It was a kind of composite stench of gym dressing rooms, institutional cleaners, floor wax, and grease.

A small boy exited one of the classrooms. He walked with his legs pinched together.

Whit leaned down to him. "Can you tell me where the office is?"

"I gotta go to the bathroom, mister."

"I can tell. Just point me in the right direction."

"Thataway." The boy pointed down the hall and waddled on toward his destination.

"Gee, thanks," Whit mumbled.

The office turned out to be on the far end of the building. He had wandered most of the halls before he found it. A middle-aged woman, her face soured by too many years of bureaucracy and kids, gave Whit one quick look and then went back to her work.

"Can I help you?" she asked, her mind concentrating on the form in her typewriter.

Whit identified himself. "I'd like to ask some questions about Jenny Hairston."

That snagged her attention. In fact, she started to weep.

The change was so dramatic that Whit felt guilty. "Uh, I'm sorry. I didn't mean to upset you."

"She was such a sweet, sweet child," the woman said through her tears. "During lunch, she'd come and help me. You know, a lot of kids these days are pure hellions. Not Jenny. I just can't stand to think of it."

Whit kept quiet, hoping the woman might regain her composure. When she did, Whit asked, "What was the last contact you had with her?"

The woman answered quickly. "Last Wednesday. Her mother called to say Jenny was sick. Jenny's not sick often. She's not like a lotta these kids that call in sick once a week."

"But you didn't talk to Jenny herself?"

The woman nodded. "Oh, yes. I did. I was worried about her and was asking Mrs. Hairston how bad she was. Jenny got on the phone, just to say hello. She's that kind of child."

"Did she sound sick?"

"Yes, in a way. Her mother said she had a bug of some kind, and Jenny was coughing a little."

Whit was making notes. "What time was that?"

The woman had a tissue in her hands. "Lemme think." While she thought, she blew her nose.

"It was around nine A.M.," she finally said.

Whit leaned over the office counter. "Did Jenny ever mention anything about home?"

The woman's eyes turned hostile. "What on earth do you mean?"

Whit shrugged. "Did she talk about her mother's friends? Maybe her mother's boyfriends? Anything like that."

"Not a word. Listen, mister, I didn't know Jenny's mother too well, but she was a good mother. I can tell. When you've been around kids as long as I have, you know these things. Jenny came to school clean. Her clothes were always well kept and laundered. Mrs. Hairston always came to Parents' Night."

So what, Whit thought. "I didn't mean to upset you with the question, but Jenny was murdered. I do have to ask these questions."

"I understand, but Jenny never said much about home. I never heard her once talk about her daddy. I guess she didn't remember him."

"Did she have close friends here at the school?"

"Not that I know of, mister. She was kinda young to have close friends like that."

Whit sighed. "Think about it for a moment. Were there any other children whom she might have walked home with? Or talked to?"

She answered without thinking. "None that I know of."

Whit pulled out one of his cards. "If you think of anything, call me."

She accepted it. "Is this gonna be another one of those times when some killer gets a slap on the wrist?"

"We don't even know who it is yet," Whit said.

"They oughta fry the guy," the secretary said. "How's Mrs. Hairston?"

"Not good," Whit said.

"Do you know anything about the funeral services? The paper didn't say anything about it."

Whit remembered that the story had been turned over to the paper's obit writer. "It'll be in there tomorrow. You can bet on it."

Will Binder entered his office shaking his head. Jack Arnold, the business manager, came back with him. "I have bad news, ladies. Mr. Arnold will give you the details."

Anna dropped her head.

Arnold cleared his throat. "Mrs. Hairston had taken out a twenty-five thousand dollar life insurance policy on herself, but she had opted not to take coverage for her daughter."

Tams covered her face with her hands.

The publisher went to the young girl and placed a hand on her head. "I suggest you let Anna here talk to an attorney. Mary may have sufficient assets herself to pay for a nice service. Someone, of course, would have to be named to handle her affairs."

His hand comforted Tams, but his words were addressed to Anna.

Cindy shifted back and forth, anxious to escape the offices of the *Journal* publisher. "I'd best be getting back to work 'fore Windy comes to fetch me."

Binder's eyes settled upon the composing room employee. He chuckled at her choice of words. "Don't worry about that for a moment, Cindy."

The four of them rose to leave.

Binder walked them to the door. Arnold simply moved out of the way.

The publisher was still talking. "In fact, Anna, you—and Cindy, too—take whatever time you need to help the young ladies. That's the least the *Journal* can do."

Once outside of Binder's office, Cindy started to hurry back to the composing room.

"Can you stay with me a second?" Anna asked.

"I'd best get back."

"Okay, but I would like to get some information from you, Cindy."

"For the paper? To print, I mean."

"Well, maybe, but mostly just some background data." Cindy Jackson probably didn't know Anna was no longer covering the story, but, even at that, it wasn't a big lie.

"I don't know," Cindy said.

"You go back to work, Cindy. We'll chat later."

"Maybe," the chunky young woman said. She vanished around the corner.

Anna walked with Tams and Tressa to the front door of the office. "I'll talk with Whit tonight. Maybe he'll call Tony. Something will work itself out."

Tams shook her head. "It isn't right, Anna."

"I know. Before you and Tressa go, let me ask you a question."

"What?"

"Was Mary Hairston acting all right? Did you notice anything unusual?"

Tams looked at Tressa before she answered. "I don't know. She was sorta quiet lately, like she wasn't real happy. Mary was always happy."

"Did she say anything about why she wasn't happy?"

"No, not to me. I kinda figured it had something to do with work."

Tressa put an arm around Tams's shoulders. "I'll come over to Dad's tonight."

"Fine. And Tams, don't worry. We'll manage to do something. I promise."

After leaving the school he headed toward the offices of the *Milbrook Daily Journal*. On his way there Whit decided to stop by Mary Hairston's residence. He wanted to talk to some of the neighbors. Most of the people he had interviewed had noticed nothing in or around the Hairston home. Of course, none appeared too anxious to become involved, so Whit wasn't confident that they were being honest. He saved the old woman who had called in the original complaint for last. Her name was Mrs. Olivia Howard.

He had to wait a long time for her to answer the door. When she did, he told her who he was.

"You here about that mess next door?" she asked at once.

"I am."

"Come in."

She led him into her living room. The furniture was old, some of it worn threadbare, but the housekeeping was faultless. He did notice the aroma of a medicinal arthritis cream. He knew from the report that the woman was well into her nineties. For that reason alone, he didn't expect much. He turned out to be wrong.

"I wondered when you folks would git 'round to me," she said as she lowered herself into a rocking chair.

"Do you have something that might help us?"

"Don't rightly know. What is it you're looking for?"

"A killer, Mrs. Howard."

Mrs. Howard trembled. "Gives me goose bumps . . . thinkin' about what went on over there."

"Did you notice anything unusual, say from last Wednesday until yesterday?"

"That's a fool question. I called you people 'cause the whole neighborhood smelled like rotten meat. I tol' that young officer yesterday that I ain't seen Jenny for several days and that I ain't seen Mary goin' to work."

Whit smiled. "Yes, I have that. I mean, did you see any strangers hanging around the house?"

"Nope."

"Did Mrs. Hairston have many visitors?"

"Nope. Not many. There was them Andrews sisters, not the singin' ones neither." She laughed at her joke. "The youngest of 'em sat with Jenny a lot."

"How about boyfriends?"

"Oh, she had 'em."

Whit sat up. "She did?"

"Lordy, yes. She was a young woman. And she wasn't hard on men's eyes. You can't fault her none for that."

"I'm not faulting her, Mrs. Howard. I just need to know who they are—if you know, that is."

"I 'member one in particular." She rocked slowly in her chair as she spoke. "Now, I'd bet he's a no-account man. Big, burly fella. Kinda mean-lookin'. That was back durin' the winter. Last winter. I don't know his name."

"Would you recognize him again?"

"Yessirree. I may be old, but I ain't blind."

"Were there others?"

Mrs. Howard nodded. "This latest one, he was a lawyer, I think. Leastways, that's what Jenny tol' me. He looked like one. Dressed fine in them suits with vests. He kinda stopped coming around about mid-summer though. Ain't seen no one around much since then."

"Any others?"

"Mighta been some a long ways back, but I can't 'member 'em."

"Can you describe these two?"

"I just did!"

"Well, you said one was big and heavy. The other you mentioned wore a suit and vest."

"See, I described 'em."

"Can you be a little more specific?"

"Nope. I didn't meet either one of 'em."

At least it was something—a lot more than Whit had expected. "Can I borrow your phone?"

"You ain't gonna call long-distance?"

"No, ma'am."

"It's there."

Milbrook had only one black lawyer. That didn't mean he

was the man who had been seeing Mary Hairston, but it was a place for Whit to start. Mrs. Howard kept her phone book under the phone. Whit looked up the number of attorney Cullen Brown and dialed it. Mrs. Howard was paying close attention to him.

"Is Mr. Brown in?"

The secretary said that he was not.

Whit told her who he was. "I need to talk with him rather urgently."

He was told that Cullen Brown was in a neighboring county trying a personal injury case.

When he hung up the phone, Mrs. Howard laughed and slapped her leg. "That's who I figured it was, too."

"Why didn't you tell me?" Whit asked.

"That's your job, mister, 'Sides, just 'cause he's the only colored lawyer hereabouts don't mean he's the one Jenny tol' me about. I never seen lawyer Brown befo' so I can't swear it was him—not by name anyways."

"Mrs. Howard, I hope I'm as sharp as you are when I get to be your age."

"Sonny, you'll be damned lucky to ever be my age."

The prosecutor of Raven County had been attempting to reach Ben Shanklin most of the afternoon.

On the fourth try, Shanklin came on the line. "You're a hard man to find," Tony told his fellow lawyer.

"Busy . . . busy . . . busy," Shanklin quipped.

Ben Shanklin was attorney for Milbrook Community Hospital. He had earned the job, not because of any great legal expertise in malpractice law, but rather because he was well versed in debt collection. The insurance companies provided the hospital with the former. The hospital, however, had needed a local lawyer who didn't have any qualms about going after the life savings of old folks. Shanklin was such a lawyer.

"What can I do for you?" Shanklin asked.

"Has the hospital talked with you about a patient by the name of Mary Hairston?"

"The woman involved in the shooting?"

"That's her."

"No, why?"

"According to my information, she's currently on life support, and there's some talk that the hospital might pull the plug."

"So?"

Tony laughed. "So, my friend, I just wanted to advise you as counsel for the hospital that the State has an interest in Mrs. Hairston. As it turns out, she's pregnant."

"Pregnant?"

"That's what I said, Counselor. I don't want anything done to her that might harm her or the baby until we can have someone appointed to represent her interests. Do I make myself clear?"

Shanklin was out of his depths. "Uh, I'll have to get back to you on this, Tony. I . . . No one's contacted me."

"You're stammering, Shanklin."

"Look, Danton, don't try to bully me or the hospital. I said I'd get back to you. That's the best I can do right now."

"Right away, Ben. Get back to me right away. And you'd better hope that no one down at that hospital has done anything cute already."

Shanklin was trying to find some ground on which he might stand. "Are you threatening my client?"

"You could say that, Ben. I do have the power to present matters with possible criminal implications to the grand jury. Now, I don't want any trouble. Nor, I'm sure, does Milbrook

Community Hospital. Just advise your clients to be cool for the moment. Advise them not to turn off any machines or pull any plugs out of the wall.''

Shanklin was silent for a moment. ''What legal authority do you have for all of this?''

Tony's voice became deadly serious. ''Let's just say, Shanklin, that we want a second or third opinion before we allow your client to kill one and maybe two people.''

SEVEN

ANNA, STILL WITHOUT AN ASSIGNMENT, was gazing out the newsroom window when she saw Whit park his car on the street and head toward the newspaper offices. She hurried from the newsroom to intercept him in the lobby.

"It took you long enough to get here," she said.

Whit was surprised. "Whadaya mean?"

"You promised me last night that you'd be here early to harass Arnold."

Whit shook his head. "You're a vindictive lady, Anna. I've had a busy day. I've been working my way here since early this morning."

"Any breaks yet?"

"Not a one. Where's this Mr. Arnold's office?"

She cocked her head at him. "Why do I get the feeling that you're lying through your teeth?"

"Because you're as suspicious as you are vindictive."

"Did you know that Tressa didn't go to school today?"

"Is she sick?"

"No, she's with Tams. They're trying to make arrangements for Jenny Hairston's funeral."

"What?"

Anna shrugged. "Have you even bothered to think about that—Jenny Hairston's funeral, I mean? There's no one to take care of it. I hadn't thought about it until Tressa and the Andrews girl stopped by here this afternoon.''

A small couch sat in the newspaper lobby. Whit moved to it and sat down. "I hadn't thought about it, either. Of course, you know how I feel about funerals anyway.''

She sat beside him. "Most people don't share your odd-ball opinion. Nonetheless, I told her that you might ask Tony to give them some legal guidance. If Mary Hairston has some funds, then maybe there's some way to use that money for the services.''

Whit was thinking. "This is going to get complicated. Dammit, Anna, I don't need all this personal involvement. I've got a crime to solve. I know that makes me sound like a horse's ass—''

"It's a little late in your life for you to worry about that.''

"I was going to say that the personal involvements distract me from the case.''

"Well, you're involved. Or at least Tressa is, and that's about the same thing. The Andrews girl is beside herself with grief. I gather the funeral's become something of an obsession to her. She feels personally responsible.''

Whit's fingers moved back and forth over a rip in the vinyl covering of the couch. "I'll talk to Tony.''

He stood. "Now, if you'll kindly direct me to where I need to go—''

"One more thing, Whit. Can I go back to Mary Hairston's house?''

"No way!''

"Look, maybe there are some papers there, bankbooks or something. We need to know something about her business affairs. Or maybe she had some relatives. If we could come up with somebody, it would sure make things easier on everyone."

Whit was shaking his head. "We still want a crime scene crew to look over the place. After that, then we'll see."

"We don't have a lot of time, Whit. You can go with me if you want."

Whit's patience was wearing thin. "Dammit, Anna, I have work to do. Let me get to it."

Anna pouted. "Jeez, Whit. You're back in foul spirits again. I knew it was too good to last. I won't be home until late tonight."

"That makes two of us. Now just tell me how to get to Arnold's office."

"You're the detective. Find it yourself." She turned back toward the newsroom.

Jack Arnold came out to escort Whit into his office. "I assume you're here about Mary Hairston."

"I do have a few questions," Whit said.

Arnold lifted a file folder from his desk. "This should answer most of them. This is Mrs. Hairston's personnel file. It's complete. As you will discover, we terminated her employment last week. She failed to report to work for several days."

Whit accepted the file. "Don't you think a bullet in the head might have constituted good cause?"

"Of course We didn't know that at the time."

"Did you make any effort to look into her absence?"

No wonder Anna had been so antagonistic toward the man. To Whit, the *Journal*'s business manager epitomized the concept of "sleazy." He imagined him as the type of man who kept pornographic photos of little girls—or maybe little boys—tucked away somewhere in his bedroom.

As Arnold leaned forward, Whit noticed the sheen of sweat on his bald head.

"Let me be candid with you, investigator Pynchon. Mrs. Hairston was a good employee, but she was overly sensitive about her race. We had transferred her from one shift to another, and she was threatening some sort of civil rights action against us. I know she's in very bad condition. If she survives, she'll be offered her job back, of course, but she would be expected to work the shift we assign her to work."

Whit smiled. "That's mighty white of you."

"That's not funny, Mr. Pynchon."

"There's very little about this case that is funny, Arnold. I don't give a damn about your personnel problems. My only interest is in apprehending the person who killed Jenny Hairston and turned her mother into a vegetable."

Arnold flopped back in his seat. "I certainly can't help you on that point."

"With your permission, I'd like to question some of her coworkers."

"I'd prefer that you do that on their time, not ours. We have a newspaper to publish."

Whit brandished the file. "We appreciate your cooperation. As for the questioning, I'm going to do it at the time most convenient for me, Mr. Arnold, and the hell with your newspaper."

Cullen Brown parked his car in his driveway. He didn't get out immediately. Instead, he sat inside, gathering his wits. He'd noticed the car in front of his house as soon as he'd turned onto his street. The lawyer had a pretty good idea who was in the darkened interior of the vehicle. As he guided his car into the driveway, a figure had exited the car. In the light of the street lamp, Brown's suspicion had been confirmed.

The attorney inhaled deeply and lifted his briefcase from the seat. Whit Pynchon stood at his front porch, waiting for him. Brown exited his vehicle.

"Hi, Whit."

"Evening, Counselor. You had a long day in court."

"Yeah, but I won. That makes it worthwhile."

They stood at the bottom of the short steps that climbed to Brown's porch.

Brown motioned toward his house. "Come on in. Pardon the mess, though. The cleaning lady comes just once a week."

Whit nodded in sympathy. "I'm a bachelor, too."

Inside, there was little mess. A dirty glass sat on a chair beside a recliner. The morning paper lay on the floor. Otherwise the spartan living room was well kept. The lawyer offered Whit a seat and a beer. Whit took the seat and passed on the beer.

"I'm going to get me one," Brown said. "Then we can talk."

The attorney vanished through a hallway.

"My secretary told me you had called," Brown shouted from the kitchen.

He returned with a can of imported beer.

"Good taste in beer," Whit said.

"I went skiing for the first time last winter. I was introduced to it up at Snowshoe. I never liked beer until I tasted this brand." Brown sat down on the couch beside Whit.

"What's important enough to have you working this late?" the lawyer asked.

"Mary Hairston."

Brown sipped the beer.

"That was tragic."

"You knew her, then?"

Brown's dark, sleek face revealed no emotion. "You already know that, Whit. That's why you're here."

"Am I correct in assuming that you were more than just friends?"

The attorney chugged the beer. "Pardon my manners, but I was dry as a bone. Look, Whit, I don't really think I have to discuss my personal life with you. Mary and I saw each other for a short time. It ended several months ago."

"How many months ago?" Whit asked.

"Five or six. It was late spring."

"What happened?"

Brown smiled. His teeth were perfect, white and straight. The contrast against his dark skin was glaring. "I thought I made myself clear, Whit. I'm not anxious to discuss it. If I thought I could shed some light on the mystery, I'd be happy to tell you about our relationship. Since I can't, I see no reason to bare my soul, so to speak."

Whit pursed his lips. "Cullen, why not let me be the judge of what you know? Unless you know a lot more than I do."

"What the hell does that mean?"

"You're an intelligent guy. You know what it means."

Brown loosened his tie. Then he slipped off his jacket. His shirt was soaked with perspiration.

"Dammit, Whit. I can't afford to get mixed up in a murder case. It's hard enough to make a living around here as it is. Mary dropped me and started to see someone else.

Before you ask, I haven't the foggiest notion as to who it was. I tried to find out, but she was seeing the bastard on the sly.''

"How do you know that?"

"Because I followed her once or twice."

"Where did she go?"

"The first time, she gave me the slip. I think she saw my car. The second time, she drove into the parking building downtown. When she didn't come out in a reasonable period of time, I went and found her car. She wasn't in it. I figured it was some kind of meeting place. After that, I gave up. Christ, I was behaving like some jealous kid. She's a good-looking woman, but I didn't need those kinda problems.''

The lawyer crunched the empty beer can. "I felt like I was about to get hooked on her, you know what I mean?''

"Yeah. I do.''

"Anyway, I cut my losses and gave Mary up for a lost cause.''

Whit's eyes turned hard. "Where were you last Wednesday night and Thursday?''

The question, so direct, stunned Brown. "Am I a suspect?''

"If you were, I'd have read you your rights.''

Brown managed a laugh. "Sure you would. Lemme think, Whit. I don't want to screw up my alibi. Last Wednesday night, I had a dinner date with a local physician. Her name's Trudy Haycraft. She works in the ER at Milbrook Community Hospital. She was called back to the ER because of a bad accident. I came home and spent the night here—by myself. On Thursday, I spent all day in depositions. I'll give you the name of the office if you wish.''

"I wish," Whit said.

He wrote the name of the law firm in his notebook, along with the name of Dr. Trudy Haycraft.

"You had those answers ready, didn't ya, Counselor?"

Brown nodded that he had. "As soon as I read about Jenny's death and the assault on Mary, I knew someone would eventually want to talk to me. We didn't keep our brief relationship any secret. Besides, you can't keep secrets in this town. It's like a fishbowl."

"You don't happen to know who she was seeing before she started seeing you?"

"Yeah, it just so happens that I do, and him I want to tell you about."

The stealthy figure kept well within the dark shadows around the base of the Hairston home. It was a cloudy night, and no lights, of course, burned inside the house. The city hadn't bothered to erect any streetlights at the end of the street. In fact, the closest source of light was the home of Olivia Howard. The prowler, climbing the steps to the front porch, was careful to stay on the side away from the lights from the Howard home.

The floorboards of the porch creaked. A gentle breeze rustled the leaves of the huge maple in the front yard. The shadow moved first to the front door and found it locked. So, too, was every accessible window. Quickly, the figure trotted down from the porch and went around to the darkest side of the house. Crumbling steps led down to a basement door. The trespasser moved down them slowly, anxious not to fall on the uncertain surface of the steps.

Rubber surgical gloves covered the hand that gripped the doorknob. It clicked and swung open. The musty, damp odor of earth came out to greet the clandestine visitor. Once inside the basement, a flashlight clicked on. The expansive basement room was cluttered with boxes and broken children's toys. A quick sweep of the flashlight beam revealed the stairs up to the main living quarters. The sleek, gloved hands swept away the dangling spider webs as the figure picked a cautious path through the basement toward the steps.

The intruder sighed with relief at the bottom of the wooden steps. They popped under the weight.

Several blocks away, at the house of lawyer Brown, Whit was gaping at the lawyer's revelation. "You know his name? The man Mary Hairston was seeing?"

"The one before me, yes. His name is Lewis Luther. He was a client of mine. That's how I met Mary."

"Can I ask what you were doing for him?"

"Defending him on a charge of malicious assault. He was placed on probation."

Whit's pen flew across the paper. Cullen Brown seemed more than willing to provide Whit with information about Luther.

"I gather you suspect this character."

"He's capable of it."

"Aren't you violating some kinda confidence?"

Brown shook his head. "I haven't told you anything you can't get from his police record . . . other than that he was seeing Mary, which has—or had—nothing to do with the case I was handling for him."

"Did she have trouble with him because of you?"

Brown fiddled with the crumpled beer can. "Not really. I gather he abused her while they were seeing each other, but he didn't seem especially upset when she discontinued the relationship. I'm not even certain he knew she was seeing me. Luther has a short attention span.''

"One more question, Counselor. Did you plan to tell us this?''

"Yeah, I didn't even know about Mary until the first break in court this morning. I didn't watch the news last night. I was too busy preparing my closing argument.''

The lawyer caught Whit staring down at the newspaper on the floor, the one that had obviously been there since early that morning.

"Okay . . . okay. I knew it early this morning. I just wanted to figure some way to tell you without disclosing my relationship with her—on the outside chance that you hadn't already known about it.''

"Tell me about the assault he was charged with?''

The lawyer shrugged. "Hell, it was the usual kinda thing. He and some guy had a fender bender. There were words, and Luther used a tire iron on the guy. He shattered the guy's arm and gave him a concussion.''

"Sounds like a real nice guy. I'll probably be seeing you again, Cullen. After I ponder this, I suspect I'll have some more questions. I'm still bothered a little by your attitude. The impression I got when we first started talking was that you had no intention of telling me anything.''

"I had no intention of getting into our relationship; the rest I wanted to tell you. Frankly, I'm impressed that you're so insistent. Sometimes, the murder of a member of an ethnic group doesn't warrant much police attention.''

Whit was on his way to the door. "I haven't figured you out yet, Brown. I'll tell you this, though. The prosecutor's office doesn't ignore any murders, and certainly not the murder of a defenseless little girl.''

"I didn't mean to imply—''

"Forget it. By the way, did you know that Mary Hairston was pregnant?"

Brown's face went slack. "Pregnant? Mary? You're shitting me."

"So, you didn't know?"

"Hell, no."

"Which means that you don't think you're the father?"

"There's no way I'm the father. Take my word for it. If you were to judge by my experience, Mary Hairston was asexual."

"You sound bitter, Counselor."

The small lamp on Mary Hairston's desk clicked on. Light filled the living room. Anna Tyree held her breath and froze, hoping that the pulled curtains would block the light. She slipped the flashlight in the hip pocket of her jeans and began to rummage through the middle drawer of the desk.

Her heart was thudding away in her chest. If Whit found out she was here . . .

The prospect gave her the shakes. Her hand trembled as she pulled out one piece of paper after another to examine it under the soft light. Besides the faint hope that she might find some clue to the identity of Mary's lover, she also wanted to locate the name of some relative, no matter how distant, who might take some interest in the tragedy of the Hairstons.

The residue of odor lingered in the house. In fact, it seemed much worse than it had the day before. Anna blamed it on the darkness and her supersensitive nerves. She spent a good hour searching the lower floor of the house. Aided by the flashlight, she entered each room and was careful to close the curtains before flipping on a light.

It was risky, but there was just no way the small flashlight could provide enough illumination for a decent search. If she was going to take such a chance as to trespass, she had decided, then it might as well be for some good purpose.

As she started up the steps, the ray of her flashlight fell upon the wide strokes of blood. It gave her the chills. Then came the sound, the sharp but soft crack of flooring. She froze. If it hadn't been so quiet, Anna would have never heard it.

"Who's there?"

Foot sounds . . . as if someone in socks were coming down the upstairs hall . . .

Anna's hand wrapped tightly around the handrail. She held her breath as her other hand lifted the flashlight so its beam reached the top of the steps.

The movement itself wrenched a piercing scream from Anna. Her muscles locked tight. By the time she realized it was a squirrel, the large gray creature had darted down the handrail, right over her hand.

"Jesus!" she gasped. It wasn't uncommon for large gray squirrels to find their way into homes, especially empty ones during the fall of the year, but Anna hadn't been prepared for it.

Her heart did flip-flops. A little urine had dampened the crotch of her jeans.

Several minutes passed before Anna was able to finish the climb. The odor of Jenny Hairston hung even heavier in the second-story atmosphere, a grim reminder of the reality of it all. Anna hurried to finish her search.

The dispatcher at the Milbrook Police Department knew Mrs. Olivia Howard. She called in complaints often. Usu-

ally, they were worth the effort. The lady was better than
a patrol car—a one-person community watch program. She
kept a concerned eye on her house and those of her neighbors.

"What exactly did you hear, Mrs. Howard?"

The elderly woman didn't like repeating herself. "I tol'
you—a scream. Sounds to me like it came from the Hairston house. You know which one I mean."

"Yes, ma'am. It's supposed to be empty."

"I know that, young 'un. That's why I'm calling."

Anna didn't spend nearly as much time upstairs as she
had on the first floor. The incident with the squirrel had
robbed her of her courage. She made a cursory search of
Mary Hairston's bedroom, careful to try to return things
as they were. As she searched, she tried to remember
where she herself put such things as addresses and letters.
The bureau drawers contained clothing, nothing else. In
the nightstand were a bottle of Rolaids, some sleeping
pills that had been prescribed and filled several years before, and a small assortment of paperback books, most of
them easy-to-read vanilla romances. There were several
boxes under the bed, but they contained old shoes and
Christmas ornaments. Where were the old family photos,
the high school diploma, the old love letters, the photos
of Mary Hairston and her deceased husband? It was as if
the woman had no past life.

She had to go to the bathroom, and she didn't want to
use the Hairstons' toilet. It was ten o'clock when she decided to abandon the search. At the bottom of the steps,
the beam of light fell upon the phone book. It rested, quite
appropriately, beneath the phone. Each time she got a new
book, she wrote her important numbers in the spaces pro-

vided in the front of the book. She lifted the phone and picked up the directory. A slip of paper marked a place in the book. She opened the book at the marker.

Black circles, made by a wide-tipped marker, surrounded several of the numbers. Anna squinted. She was able to see that they were numbers of abortion clinics, all of which were out of town. Milbrook had no such clinics. Rumor had it that the well-to-do could obtain an abortion at the Milbrook hospital, but only after they were admitted under the pretense of a routine D&C. On the same page, she noticed the scribbled numbers 9-8 and 9-15. Had Mary Hairston planned to have an abortion?

The plot thickens, Anna thought.

At that instant, the cold barrel of a gun was jammed against the base of her skull.

"Freeze, lady."

EIGHT

VANESSA ANDREWS CHEWED on her lip to divert her mind from the sharp teeth abrading her right nipple. She wanted to scream at the bastard to stop, but her common sense prevailed. At the moment, the man who was mauling her tits was the best prospect Vanessa had. Lloyd Smith owned several laundromats and a car wash. He was in the Jaycees and sat on the Board of Directors of the Chamber of Commerce. To Vanessa's mind, that made him rich and respectable.

She writhed in pain. He mistook it for passion. His sucking became more furious. Then he began to chew.

"Ooooh, gaawwwdamn," Vanessa wailed.

His teeth released her nipple. "Um. Go for it, babe. You're the hottest fucking woman I know."

He started to nurse the tender flesh as if he were a starving infant. Tears filled Vanessa's eyes. Her fists thumped against his broad back. It compounded his passion, and he worked to funnel most of the flesh of her right breast into his mouth.

"Oh, sweet Jesus," she screamed.

"Ummmmmm."

She couldn't take it any longer. She shoved him back and gasped in relief.

Lloyd Smith was grinning broadly. "You come just from a little tit-sucking?"

Vanessa managed both a smile and a lie. "I sure did."

"My God, imagine what you'll do if I get my tongue down around that hot snatch of yours." Lloyd began to fumble with the snap on her jeans.

Vanessa scooted away. "Oh, no! You've worn me out."

She felt his muscles tighten.

He pulled back from her. "What about me, woman? My balls are ready to explode."

She dropped her hand in his lap. Her tongue wet her lips. Even in the dim light of his cluttered bedroom. Lloyd saw and understood. "Oh, babe. Would you do that to me?"

"Would I do it to you," she cooed. I'll bite the goddamn little fucker off so you can have a taste of your own medicine, she thought to herself.

He flopped back on the bed.

"You still got your pants on, Lloyd!"

"Take 'em off for me. And, while you're at it, reach in that nightstand drawer. I got some good shit in there."

Vanessa frowned. "What kinda shit?"

"Well, look, hon."

Vanessa did. She pulled a hefty bag of marijuana from the drawer. "You been holding out on me, Lloyd. Hell, man, I'd like to have had a hit on that myself."

"Be my guest. Roll one for you and one for me."

She stroked the bulging mass under his tight jeans. "Can you keep it up?"

"Shit, woman. Give me a few drags off that, and I can stay hard all gawdamned night."

Like hell, Vanessa thought. That was the last thing she wanted. "I want you now, baby." She shoved the pouch of marijuana back in the drawer and put her hand on the zipper of his pants.

Lloyd laughed but pushed her hand away. "Come on, Vanessa. Lemme get a few tokes first. It makes it feel better."

"I can make it feel good without that stuff." She tried to push him back on the bed.

He resisted. "What's the matter with you? Cool off and slow down, for God's sakes. We got all fuckin' night. I'm a man with a slow hand . . . just like the song says."

The evening's good times were over with as far as Vanessa was concerned. Lloyd had taken her to dinner and a movie. He'd spent somewhere between forty and fifty dollars altogether. Now it was payback time. Vanessa didn't mind that. She accepted it. Trouble was, Lloyd didn't know what the word "gentle" meant. Sometimes, after she'd had enough vodka, she even enjoyed Lloyd. On this particular night, she didn't want to spend hour after hour being eaten alive by the bastard. She had a phone call to make.

"I gotta get home early tonight, Lloyd. Momma's not feeling too good."

"You got time for a smoke or two," he pronounced. He pulled the grass back out of the drawer.

Vanessa decided not to argue. Besides, with any luck, she wouldn't have to put up with the Lloyd Smiths of Milbrook much longer. She had a plan to land her in Tinsel Town. The man who'd knocked Mary up—he'd probably be willing to pay her a little traveling money to keep her mouth shut. If she could just get to California, with enough of his money for a few capital improvements to her body, then she knew she could make it as a model, maybe even as an actress. After all, she'd sure made Lloyd believe that her pain was pure ecstasy. For that she deserved an Oscar.

Whit burst into the door of the Milbrook Police Department. "Where is she?" he demanded to know.

The dispatcher was smiling. "Who might that be, Mr. Pynchon?"

"This goddamned female cat burglar you people apprehended."

"Oh, you mean Miss Tyree."

"Yeah, asshole."

The dispatcher lifted a phone and dialed an intercom number. "Whit Pynchon's here. He wants to see Miss Tyree."

"Now!" Whit shouted for the benefit of whoever was on the other end of the line.

"It'll be just a second," the dispatcher said after he hung up the phone.

Whit leaned down over the radio console. "Kid, you got thirty seconds."

"Well, I'll be fucked." The words came from Cal Burton, who was standing behind Whit. "Look who's come to the rescue of our female felon."

The prosecutor's investigator whirled around. "Where the hell is she, Burton?"

"In my custody, Pynchon."

"I wanna see her—now."

"We're not done processing her."

The faces of the two men were inches apart—Burton so short that he was standing on tiptoes; Whit bowing, gritting his teeth as he glared into the dark eyes of his nemesis. Other officers had filtered into the lobby and control area.

"Processing her for what?"

"Burglary, goddammit. The dumb bitch broke into Mary Hairston's house."

Whit's forearm came around, making contact with the city detective and sending him staggering down a hall. The smaller cop fought to keep his balance. Three city officers rushed to subdue Whit. He danced away from their grasps.

Somewhere in the distance, he heard the words "You're un-der arrest." Hands dug into his arms.

"Nooo!" Cal bellowed. "Let the bastard go! I want a piece of him! He'll wish you had arrested him."

"Not here, Lieutenant." It was the voice of a uniformed officer.

"Let him go, goddammit!" Cal cried. The hands released Whit's arms.

Cal inched toward him. "You wanna get it on, Pynchon? Come on."

The lieutenant hunched down in a crouch, starting to slowly circle Whit.

Suddenly, a new set of arms wrapped themselves around Whit's chest. "That's enough." Whit couldn't see the man who owned the arms, but he recognized the voice. It was Tony Danton.

Cal Burton literally exploded. "Who the fuck let 'im in? I wanna know now." He pranced like a bantam rooster.

Tony turned Whit over to some of the city policemen and went up to Cal. "Shut it up, Burton. One more outburst, and I'll have your goddamned badge."

The two men, both of them nearly the same height, traded cold stares. Cal ended the standoff by spitting on the floor, then vanishing into offices in the back.

Tony wheeled around to Whit. "Friend, you are outa your mind."

"The bastard arrested Anna."

Tony nodded. "And from what I hear, she needed it. If not for burglary, then at least for criminal trespass."

"That's not the point."

"That *is* the friggin' point, Whit. She just can't go busting into people's houses, especially houses that are secured for crime scene attention. I don't give a damn if she's a reporter or not. Frankly, I don't give a damn if she's your girlfriend. She can't do it!''

''I had to.'' Anna stood in the doorway through which Cal had vanished. ''Burton let me out just now.''

Tony slowly shook his head. ''You had to? Why the hell did you have to? Christ, you had on rubber gloves! Just like some kinda damned pro. Couldn't you have asked for permission?''

''I did,'' Anna said.

Tony looked back at Whit.

''Yeah, she did,'' Whit said.

''I see,'' Tony said, turning back to Anna. ''He said no, so you decided to do it anyway.''

Anna's face was streaked with black, the remnants of fingerprint ink from her hand. Her clothing was disheveled, her hair a mess.

Tony went up to her. ''You know something, lady. When you look like hell, you still look good.''

Anna backed away. ''What?''

Whit started to laugh.

Anna threw up her hands. ''Did I miss something?''

''The damned boat,'' Tony said. ''Anna, do you know the sentence for house burglary?''

''I didn't steal anything,'' Anna said.

Tony ignored her. ''It's one to fifteen. That's years!''

Anna eased by him to join Whit. ''I thought the lectures were over. Look, I was just trying to see if there were some relatives, anyone to help with this mess. Tams is beside herself. So is Tressa.''

Whit slipped an arm around her.

''What have those kids got to do with this?'' Tony asked.

Whit sighed. ''It's a long story. I'll tell you over a cup of coffee.''

Cal Burton appeared. "The lady's being charged, Danton."

"I just dismissed them, Burton."

"She broke into the fuckin' house, man!"

"Just one problem, Burton."

The detective leaned against a doorframe. "We caught her red-handed. What the hell kinda problem is there?"

Tony patted Cal on the cheek. "She had my permission, pal."

"That was some scene," Patrolman Cole Surface said. After his behavior upon discovery of Jenny Hairston's body, the chief had called him in the office and reassigned him to the graveyard shift.

"This isn't punishment, Cole. A man can't help some things." Those had been Chief Wampler's words, and Cole hadn't believed them for a minute.

He braked the cruiser for a cat that darted across the quiet street.

His partner, Charlie Belcher, spread his legs to avoid the hot coffee that sloshed out of his cup. "Jesus, kid. Easy, man. This shit's hot."

"So, what do you want? I'm not running over a goddamned cat."

"Damn," Belcher said, "better a pussy than my goddamned cock. If this coffee hit me, I'd be ruined for life."

Cole reached over to poke his partner's shoulder. "Hell, man. It's made for hot stuff."

"Fuck you. So, who do you think woulda walked away, Pynchon or Burton?"

"Pynchon," Cole said. "No doubt about it."

"I don't know about that, kid. Burton's a little hellcat. I've seen him take down some pretty tough customers. I remember once, back in the old days, we walked into Maudie's.

That was a beer joint downtown. Roughest goddamn place east of Cinder Bottom. This big fuckin' nigger's in there raising hell, trying to get one of the 'white pussies'—his words—to fight.''

"I've heard this one," Cole said. Since his assignment to the shift, he was trying to bolster his image.

"So, you're gonna hear it again. I'm the goddamned senior man here." Belcher balanced the coffee cup on his knee. "Anyway, Burton walks up to this big buck and says, 'Who you calling pussy?' Before the guy can say diddly shit, Burton brings a knee up in his nuts. He didn't give us no trouble at all after that.''

"He's a low-blow ballbuster. That's no great shakes in my book.''

The veteran cast an unhappy eye toward his partner. "Your book don't count.''

The main street of Milbrook was empty when the cruiser pulled onto it. Cole slowed the car and rode along close to the sidewalk. Belcher kept his eyes on the storefronts.

"Looks fine to me, kid.''

The lights of a car filled the cruiser's rearview mirror. It was coming up very fast until the driver recognized the police cruiser. Squealing brakes ruptured the post-midnight solitude.

Cole snickered. "That stupid son of a bitch almost stood his car on its fuckin' nose.''

Belcher was glaring over his shoulder at the offending vehicle.

"Wanna write him, Charlie?''

The car, a dark and battered Plymouth, eased by the parked cruiser.

"Ah, he's had a scare. We'll let him slide on this one. I just wanna finish my coffee.''

Cole, though, continued to study the car. He turned on a map light and picked up a note from the console. "Hey, Charlie—"

"Yeah, kid."

"That looks like the car Burton wanted us to look for."

"Ah, hell. Lemme see that BOLO." Belcher snatched it and read it in the glow of the map light. He looked back up at the car as it started to speed up. "You're fuckin' right, Cole."

Cole slammed the cruiser down into DRIVE. "Hit the light and sirens."

Both cops saw the dust and smoke as the driver in the Plymouth jammed down his accelerator.

"Oh, sheeet!" Cole cried. "We got us a chase!"

Charlie Belcher was trying to find something to do with the coffee. "Hey, I got my hands full."

"Throw it out the damned window. The son of a bitch's heading for Tabernacle Mountain."

Belcher managed to dodge most of the sloshed coffee until he could throw it, cup and all, out the window.

"Radio the station," Cole was saying. "Have them notify county for some assistance."

Belcher was trying to check the handwritten note. "According to this, we're s'posed to keep this to ourselves."

"Okay, forget the friggin' county. I'm gonna catch this bastard." Cole Surface saw the perfect opportunity to redeem himself in the eyes of Cal Burton and maybe Chief Wampler.

The two vehicles roared down Milbrook's main business district. The sound of their engines echoed over the entire town.

"He's going up the mountain," Belcher cried.

They rolled past the city limits of Milbrook at ninety miles an hour. At that point, the street became a road. It started to wind its way up toward the double summit of Tabernacle Mountain. Screeching tires cried for a grip on the tight curves.

In the cruiser, Cole's mind was on a single track. He slammed the steering wheel as he roared out of the curves and into the all-too-short straightaways. Belcher hung onto the dash.

"That son of a bitch can drive," Cole said.

"You're losing him."

"I'm pushing this mother as fast as she'll go."

By that time the two officers couldn't even see the two bright red taillights.

"He's gone," Belcher said.

"Maybe . . . maybe not." Cole worked himself down in his seat and began to urge his cruiser forward with body motion. "Come on, you no-good fuckin' Ford, faster . . . faster."

Belcher swallowed his hot bile. "I don't wanna die over this scumbag. Use your head, man. You don't have to prove a damned thing to me."

Cole glanced at his partner. Was that a not-too-subtle reference to his behavior at the scene of the Hairston murder? The young officer started to respond, but taillights suddenly exploded in his face. Cole locked up the brakes. The cruiser whined and screamed as it did donuts on the highway. Belcher screamed and buried his face in his hands.

Finally, the cruiser stopped. Both officers saw that the taillights belonged to the vehicle they were chasing. Its passenger-side tires were over the bank. The driver's side of the Plymouth filled only a small portion of the ascending lane.

"Damn, Cole. I thought it was dead center of the road."

Cole was gleeful. "I told ya, Charlie. The bastard lost it. He wrecked."

Belcher slowly raised his head. Perspiration glistened on his face. "God Almighty, kid. You almost made me piss in my pants."

"Sorry, Charlie, but I caught him, didn't I?"

Cole bounded out of the car. By the time Belcher got out, his partner was at the window of the Plymouth, angrily pounding on its roof.

"Whatsa matter? The guy dead?"

"Dead, hell! He's gone. Took off into the fuckin' woods, I guess. Dammit to hell!"

Belcher inched up to the edge of the berm. The mountainside dropped off immediately.

"We gonna go after him, Charlie?"

"You can if you want. I'm not. We know who the bastard is. If it was very important, we'd have a warrant or something. That's why I wasn't anxious to get killed over him."

Cole patted his senior partner on the shoulder. "Hell, man. I had it under control the whole time. Radio the station and have 'em send a tow truck out here. I got the maggot's car. That's good enough for me. He'll show up later to claim it."

Lloyd Smith sighed. "Damn, you're good."

Vanessa stood in his bathroom, scrubbing her mouth clean with his toothbrush. "I gotta git home, Lloyd."

He struggled from the bed. "Jesus, lady. Looks to me like you could curl up with me for the night. Call your mother and tell her you're spending the night with a friend. I'd like to have you for breakfast."

Still nude, she stepped back into the bedroom and dodged his hand as he reached for her jiggling breasts. "The only friend I'd do that with is in the hospital. Remember?"

"Hell, I'm that kinda friend."

"Com'on, man. Get dressed and take me home."

"Sorry, I need to spend a few minutes in the john."

Vanessa rolled her eyes and checked the digital clock on his nightstand. "Hurry up—" Then she saw the phone. "Are you gonna be long?"

"Ten minutes, at least." He was leaning against the door-frame. "Sorry, doll. Some things take priority."

"I'll give Momma a ring," Vanessa said. "Let her know I'm gonna be late."

"The good little daughter."

"Fuck ya, Lloyd."

She gathered up her clothes and left him laughing. Rather than use the phone in his bedroom, she padded barefoot into the kitchen where a phone rested on a cluttered breakfast bar. Vanessa tossed her clothes onto a stool and started searching for a phone book.

Damn! Where the hell is it?

She tiptoed back into the bedroom. The door to the bath-room was closed. Disgusting noises issued from the other side of it. She grimaced and eased open the drawer of the night-stand. A pile of color advertisements for porn flicks greeted her. Hell, the bastard was too cheap to buy the real things.

Vanessa caught herself before she slammed the drawer shut. She couldn't ask him about the book. He'd wonder why in the hell she needed to look up her own phone number.

Slipping out of the bedroom, she moved to the small living room. It contained no phone, and she had no idea where to look for a phone book. Time was slipping through her fin-gers.

Back to the kitchen where she began to go through the drawers.

The phone book was buried beneath a small pile of greasy

hot pads. She pulled it out and started searching for the number, hoping to God—or whoever—that the guy had a listed number.

She found it and grabbed the phone. Her stomach, alive with nerves, gurgled and growled. Her heart thumped, and sweat was being squeezed from the pores along her hairline. She punched each number with an anxious determination.

One ring.

"Please," she whispered.

Two rings.

Still unclothed, Vanessa used the long handset cord to prowl Lloyd's kitchen.

Three rings.

"Answer!" she demanded.

Four—

"Hello." The voice on the other end was at once sleepy and angry.

Vanessa's heart lifted into her throat. She muffled the phone with her hand and lowered her voice. "I know about you and that Hairston woman," she said. Even to Vanessa, her voice sounded so high and squeaky.

"Who the hell is this?"

"And you're gonna fetch me a little money so I can keep my mouth shut," she drawled, her courage starting to mount.

"Vanessa? You ready?" It was Lloyd.

"I'll call again," she said. She slammed the phone down just as Lloyd's smiling face peeked around the kitchen's doorfacing.

"God, you're so fucking sexy, standing there naked." He sidled up to her.

Her hand rapped hard against his face. He staggered back against the wall, as much from shock as from pain.

"Jesus! What the hell's the matter with you?"

The look on Lloyd Smith's face produced an explosion of hysterical laughter from Vanessa. The man's shock deepened. "Are you crazy, woman?"

"I'm sorry, Lloyd. You scared me. You should see the way you look."

He reached out and wrapped a tight hand around her arm. "You ever hit me again, bitch, you won't think it's so damned funny." He pulled her to him.

She let him. Suddenly, and for the first time that night, she was aroused.

His hands cupped the soft skin of her ass as he kissed her.

"Got time for a quickie?" he asked when they parted.

She licked the reddened skin of his cheek. "I guess I owe you that much."

NINE

THE PANEL OF FORTY JURORS was restless. Each of them had been sitting on the hard benches in the rear of the courtroom for almost an hour while a steady string of attorneys talked legal mumbo jumbo to Circuit Judge David O'Brien.

"We have a few unrelated matters to take up before jury selection begins." Those had been the words of Judge O'Brien at 9:30 A.M. It was now almost 10:30, and still the panel was waiting. The case scheduled for a jury trial was a felony charge involving receiving stolen property, which—to the jurors anyway—didn't seem like such a big deal. Who hadn't received some stolen property at one time or another?

The judge, barrel-bellied with an ashen face that hinted at a fading heart, lifted his voice to the impatient jurors at the rear of his courtroom. "We have one last matter before we get to the trial," he told them. They issued a collective sigh.

O'Brien looked down at Tony Danton, who had been sitting at the State's counsel table since 9:30 A.M. "Mr. Danton, I have your petition. I must say, this is rather out-of-the-ordinary."

Tony stood. "I agree, Your Honor. It's not often that a hospital wants to take a life rather than save one."

Lawyer Ben Shanklin pushed his way out of a crowd of lawyers. He set a hefty briefcase on the counsel table reserved for defendants. "Your Honor, I object to Mr. Danton's characterization. There's no cause to sensationalize this matter."

The judge peered over his wire-rimmed glasses at the prosecutor. "I agree with Ben. That was out-of-line."

Tony bowed slightly. "If the court found it so, I offer my humblest apologizes."

But Shanklin, attorney for the Milbrook hospital, wasn't finished with his objection. "If I may, Your Honor . . . before we even get into the issue here, the hospital objects to the prosecutor's appearance. We don't think he has any standing in this matter."

O'Brien closed his eyes—not even noon and already the tension was beginning to build around his temples. Both hands began a furious motioning. "Gentlemen, come up here. Approach the bench."

Once Tony and Ben Shanklin were below him, O'Brien leaned close. "What the hell is this, Tony?"

The prosecutor started to explain. "The petition—"

O'Brien patted the short document. "I haven't even had time to read it. I just skimmed it."

The other attorneys were quiet, doing their best to overhear the bench conference. None of them knew its subject matter, but they each had enough sense to realize that something unusual was going on in the courtroom. Most matters of pretrial procedure had a certain unexciting routine attached to them, but the obvious emotional antagonism between Shanklin and the Raven County prosecutor hinted at something worthy of coffee table gossip.

Shanklin had noticed his colleagues' curiosity. "Your Honor, might I suggest that we take this matter up in chambers?"

Tony nodded. "I'll agree with Ben on that."

The judge lowered his head in frustration. "I have a damned jury trial I'd like to finish today. Could this wait?"

Tony looked to the hospital's attorney. "A life might hinge in the balance."

O'Brien sighed. "Then, for God's sakes let's go talk about it, and let's be brief."

The judge stood behind his bench. "Ladies and gentlemen, after a brief conference, we'll begin jury selection. Please remain in the courtroom until I return."

There were angry murmurings from the rear of the courtroom as the judge, followed by the two lawyers, slipped from the courthouse.

Dusty law books, more decoration than necessity, filled O'Brien's cramped chambers. Thick curtains, their once-rich burgundy color subdued by still more dust, blocked the light. Tony and Shanklin sat down on a leather sofa off to the side of Judge O'Brien's desk. The judge himself paused to light a cigarette before he sat down. A few ashes settled on his shiny black robe.

"Okay, Tony. Now, what the hell is this?" He waved Tony's petition in the air.

"Dave, we've got a sticky situation. You read about the murder of that young black girl and the shooting of her mother?"

O'Brien nodded.

"The mother has lapsed into a coma. The hospital says she's brain-dead. I have reason to believe they want to discontinue life support."

"Does the woman have any family?" O'Brien asked.

"None that we know of, Your Honor, and we have gone to some lengths to research that issue."

O'Brien inhaled a lungful of smoke. "If she's brain-dead, what's the problem?"

Shanklin sat back, more than willing to permit the prosecutor to tell the judge "the problem."

"The victim," Tony said, pausing for effect, "is pregnant. At least one physician has indicated that there's a chance the victim may be able to carry the child to term even if she is brain-dead."

O'Brien's green eyes widened. "Oh, my God."

Shanklin jumped into the discussion. "Your Honor, after a great deal of review, the medical staff at the hospital is less than enamored with the idea of trying anything so far-reaching."

Tony interrupted. "They mean they don't want to foot the bill."

"That's a legitimate concern," Shanklin said.

Tony smiled at the aging lawyer. "An attitude that doesn't surprise me, coming from a lawyer whose main practice consists of collecting overdue bills."

"That's unnecessary," O'Brien snapped.

But Tony wasn't letting go. "Look, Dave, all we ask is that you temporarily restrain the hospital from doing anything that might precipitate this woman's death. Schedule a full hearing on the matter at a later date. What objection can the hospital have to that? It's reasonable."

"We object strenuously," Shanklin said. "The hospital wants to remove life support. That's all."

"That's all?" Tony exclaimed.

O'Brien pounded his desk with his fist. "Let Ben speak."

"If Mrs. Hairston survives," Shanklin went on, "and

they tell me she very well may, then so be it. If she ex-
pires, well, that's probably for the best.''

''There's another life involved here, Ben. I didn't want
to get into this in front of the court, but, if you remove
life support without proper consent, and she does die, then
I might decide to pursue a charge of involuntary manslaughter.''

''That's bullshit,'' Shanklin said.

O'Brien was measuring Tony. ''That's bluff, Tony. Pure
and simple.''

Tony set his jaw. ''I think I can get a conviction.''

The jurist inhaled deeply of the cigarette. ''Always
muddying the waters, aren't you, Tony?''

''Think about it a few minutes, Judge. Moral concerns
aside, there are some incredibly complex legal issues
here.''

The judge looked at his watch. ''I have a trial to complete today. I'll schedule a hearing on a temporary injunction for tomorrow morning at 9:30. Until that time, Ben,
your client is enjoined from removing Mrs. Hairston from
life support. Am I clear?''

Shanklin nodded.

The jurist checked a list under the glass that covered his
desk. ''And I'm going to appoint Cullen Brown as guardian *ad litem* for Mrs. Hairston.''

Jack Arnold exited the editor's office as Anna arrived.
Each passed the other without so much as a glance. Inside
the glass-encased office, Anna found Tom Bukowsky staring out a window.

''There was frost on the mountain this morning,'' Bukowsky said, his eyes directed toward the towering mass.
''I guess our mild autumn is almost over.''

Anna, her anger over the loss of her beat undiminished, settled into a chair. "You didn't call me in here to discuss the weather."

As soon as she had come to work that morning, the receptionist had told her that the editor wanted to see her. If he was in the office that early, then she was really in trouble, she had thought. She had marched straight to his office and had encountered Arnold, apparently leaving the editor's office. It had done nothing to improve her mood.

Bukowsky swiveled to face her. "You're right. I didn't. Since you want to get right to the point, I'll make it brief."

The muscles of his face were rock-hard, his eyes not exactly angry but rather icy and uncaring. "According to police reports, you were arrested last night. Is that true?"

Anna turned cold. How the hell had he found out so damned quickly? "Uh . . . yes. The charges were dropped."

"Only because you had some influence."

"Christ, Tom! It was a misunderstanding."

"Was it, Anna?"

"What on earth do you mean?"

Bukowsky lurched forward in his chair. "The way I hear it, they caught you red-handed, burglarizing Mary Hairston's home. Your boyfriend and Tony Danton pulled enough weight to set you free."

"I resent that, Tom."

Bukowsky sprung to his feet. "You resent it? Lady, we pulled you off the Hairston story. You're done with it! I don't know *how in the hell* we could make our point any more effectively."

Anna stood, too. "I wasn't working on your god-damned story."

Bukowsky gasped. "I can't believe you, Anna. You have a great many faults, but I never knew you were a liar."

Anna folded her arms on her chest. "Is that why Arnold was just in here? Did he come in to tell you to ride me about this?"

"I run the newsroom, Anna."

She marched over to the windows and looked out on the vacant room. The screens on the terminals were dark, the Teletypes silent. The few reporters who worked during the day were out on assignments. "I always thought you did, Tom. I see I was wrong."

"Be seated, Anna."

She pirouetted. "Screw you, Tom. I'm not one of your wet-tailed privates in Vietnam. For your information, my boyfriend's daughter knew the Hairston girl. Her best friend baby-sat the child. I was trying to locate the name of some relative who could bury the little girl."

"Then, why in the hell didn't your boyfriend let you in? It doesn't wash, Anna."

"Because he didn't want me there, dammit! Sometimes, he's as rock-headed as . . . never mind."

"As who, Anna?"

"Forget it. I'm telling you the truth."

Bukowsky ran a weary hand over the trimmed stubble atop his head. "Is that on the level?"

"Yes!" Anna shouted. "But if you don't believe me, I don't give a damn. And while we're on the subject, I resent like hell being pulled off the Hairston story simply because I made that pompous fart Arnold mad. I can't imagine that someone with as much intelligence as Binder would suffer an asshole like that."

Bukowsky was sitting back down. "Easy, Anna. He's second from the top in this company."

"That's the best position for ass-licking," Anna said.

Bukowsky shook his head. "Your vocabulary would make a drill sergeant blush."

"The English language is vague enough as it is. Why censor the most vivid words we have?"

"Be that as it may, Anna, I'm bound to inform you that you are now on a form of probation. The next foul-up and you're gone. That's about as straight as I can say it. If we have the slightest reason to believe that you're involving yourself in the Hairston matter, then you'll be fired."

Anna's face warmed. "If that happens, Tom, this paper will find itself facing a sex-discrimination action. I've done nothing to deserve this kind of notice."

"I'm sorry, Anna."

She realized that Bukowsky had little say in the matter. "I have some sick days accumulated," she said. "I don't feel so good. I'm going to call it a day."

She rose to leave. "One thing, Tom. I do plan to help with funeral arrangements for Jenny Hairston. I'm doing that because of a friend. I plan to continue. If you—no, if Arnold thinks that's out-of-line, then he may as well fire me now."

Bukowsky had lowered his head to read a piece of copy. "I don't plan to discuss it with Arnold," he said, without looking up. "As for how your activities will be viewed, do what you have to do. Just remember. You've been warned."

The phone call from the mother of Lewis Luther was transferred to Cal Burton. "How can I help ya, Mrs. Luther?"

"What kinda trouble is my boy in?" Her voice was weak, nervous.

Cal smiled. "Just reckless driving."

"They gonna put him in prison if they catch 'im?"

The lieutenant's fingers toyed with the twisted cord of the phone. "You know how things work, Mrs. Luther. The courts do what they want. They don't ask my opinion. If I know the judge, he ain't gonna put your boy in prison for driving too fast."

"He's on probation. Ya know that, don't ya?"

"Yes, ma'am. I surely do."

There were several seconds of silence. Then the aging black woman said, "I tol' him things would go easier for him if he turned hisself in, but he's afraid, mister. He thinks you're gonna hurt him."

"Hurt him? Just so long as he don't give us any trouble, he won't get any trouble."

"That's what I tol' him, mister, but he says he's got a whippin' comin' because he got away from them cops."

Cal was growing weary of her whining tone. "Look, lady, we're gonna find him. It's just a matter of time. Make it easy for the boy. Tell us where he is."

"Promise you won't beat him or anything like that?"

"If he gives up without any trouble, there won't be any trouble. I've said that once."

"I dunno. Maybe it's best if I just leave things as they are. Maybe I shouldn't even have called."

Damn! He was losing her. "Hold on, Mrs. Luther. Now listen to me good, lady. If your boy keeps on a runnin', I'd say there's a damned good chance the judge is going to revoke that probation and toss him in the state pen. That boy of yours has got a bad record to start with."

"That's 'cause ya'll pick on him!"

"Now, lady, you know better'n that. Just hush up for a minute and listen to what I got to say. You tell me where we can find him. I promise you we'll get him without hurting him. I'll even tell the judge that the boy turned himself in—that's assuming, of course, he don't give us any trouble.''

"I don't know what to do.''

"Course you do. That's why you called. You wanna do the right thing.''

"You promise you won't whip up on him?''

"Lady, I done told ya—''

"Okay, he's on Tabernacle Mountain. He's stayin' in a shack back on Red Oak Ridge. You turn off on a timberin' road 'bout halfways up this side.''

Cal was making notes. "Is he armed?''

"Whatcha mean?''

"Has Lewis got any guns on him?''

"Lordy, I don't know. I don't think he does. I never seen him with a gun.''

"Is he alone?''

"Course he's alone. Lookee here, mister. When you all get him, don't you say a word about me—''

At that point Cal broke the connection and buzzed the dispatcher. "Get me Sheriff Early on the phone and have all units return to station.''

Cal replaced the phone and leaned back in his chair, very satisfied with himself. The intercom interrupted his quiet celebration.

"You got the sheriff?'' Cal asked of the dispatcher.

"No, sir. This is Mrs. Luther. She says you got cut off.''

"Tell the dumb cow I'm gone.''

Cindy Jackson knew that her own misery was more than grief over Mary and her daughter. She hadn't even been so upset when her grandmother had died two years before. Cindy's grandmother had been eighty-five. She was supposed to die. Kids weren't supposed to die. Mary was the same age as Cindy, and Mary was going to die, too. Cindy knew it. If a kid could die, then Cindy could, too. That's what the young black woman found so difficult to accept.

Her eyes refused to focus on the price list for the Food-Mart ad. She stopped to rub the sleepy itch from her eyes. She had slept very little the night before. Windy, the foreman, had been watching her like a hawk all morning, and she felt him behind her.

"You okay?" he asked.

"Just tired."

"Be careful with that."

"Yes, sir."

Cindy lived alone in a small apartment in the Five Points Manor, a moderate-income housing development just inside the southeastern boundary of Milbrook. She hadn't wanted to spend the previous night by herself, so she'd gone to a movie. The movie had won a bunch of awards, and this was about the tenth time that it had played in the small theater at the Milbrook Shopping Center. Cindy, though, didn't read much, and she had no idea about the kind of movie it was. Just as soon as she realized that a young woman not much older than she was probably going to die in the movie, she'd rushed out of the theater.

Back at home, she'd taken a hot bath and brewed some hot chocolate. She'd consumed a half-pound bag of hot chips and then gone to bed. That was one reason Cindy was so chubby. When she was uptight, she ate anything. The night before, she'd paid a different price for her nervous gluttony. A fiery case of indigestion had kept her awake through most of the night.

Windy came up behind her again. She jumped at the touch of his hand on her shoulder.

"They want you in the publisher's office," he said.

Sheriff Ted Early was cautious. He'd had dealings with Cal Burton before.

"What do you want this guy for?" Early asked.

The Milbrook city detective was on the other end of the phone. "We've got several traffic warrants on him. He's on probation for a felony assault."

The alleged hideout of Lewis Luther was outside the city limits of Milbrook. Technically, city officers had a right to arrest on their warrants anywhere in Raven County, but, as a matter of policy, they always took a county deputy or state trooper along with them. This time, Cal wanted Early to send several men.

"I do expect trouble," Burton was saying.

"Why?" the sheriff asked.

"This guy's pond scum."

But Early wasn't buying it. "Come on, Cal. There's something you're not telling me. You wouldn't go to all this trouble over some minor traffic charge. Besides, you and I both know they aren't likely to jerk the guy off probation just because he was hot-rodding his vehicle."

Cal chuckled. "You're too wise, Ted. I don't want anyone gettin' wind of this, especially not Whit Pynchon. The guy's probably the one that killed that Hairston kid and shot her mother."

"No kidding?"

"He's our prime suspect. Wouldn't you like to see the look on that asshole Pynchon's face if we collar the guy?"

Early laughed, too. "Yeah, I heard he took the case away from you, Cal."

"He and Danton are both assholes."

"You'll get no argument from me."

Cal checked his watch. "How about it, Ted? Can you spare me a few men?"

"Better'n that, Cal. I'll come myself with the entire day shift."

"Great! One thing, Ted. Ya'll got any tear gas?"

Early didn't even have to think about it. "Yeah, but it's as old as Tabernacle Mountain itself. It might not be worth a tinker's damn."

"Bring it anyway."

Will Binder put aside the *Charleston Gazette* as his secretary ushered Cindy into his office. The secretary closed the door and remained in the room.

"Good morning, Cindy."

The girl mumbled "hi," taking the seat the secretary offered her.

"Cindy isn't feeling good," his secretary said.

"I can see that she's shivering. Are you coming down with something?" he asked.

Cindy shook her head. "I don't think so. I'm just still upset."

"I gather you and Mrs. Hairston were very close."

Cindy nodded, her eyes turned down to her hands, which clung to each other.

"Do you want some hot coffee?" the publisher asked.

She shook her head.

"The last time I saw somebody shake like that I was in Vietnam," he said, offering Cindy a smile. "The poor fellow had a case of malaria."

"I'm okay, sir."

Binder glanced up at his secretary. She just shrugged

and eased out of the office. Cindy jumped when the door clicked shut behind her.

The publisher lifted himself from his leather desk chair and came around to sit on the edge of the desk. "You're not frightened of me, are you, Cindy?"

"I've never been called to the publisher's office before."

"You think you're here because of something you did?"

Cindy shrugged. "I don't know."

"Goodness, I didn't meant to scare you. It's nothing like that."

The trembling seemed to ease a little. "I thought maybe it was," she said.

"No . . . no! It's about the tragedy, Cindy. Mrs. Binder and I were talking about it last night. As I said, I gather you and Mary Hairston were close friends."

"Yes, sir. We *are* close friends."

"Excuse me. It was a bad choice of words."

"That's okay. I've been thinking like that, too."

"Anyway, if you two were close, then you probably know that she had had some difficulty here at the paper, something about a shift change, I think."

Cindy shifted in her chair. "Mary didn't talk much to me about it."

"Well, be that as it may, my wife and I wanted you and Mrs. Hairston's other friends to know that we're going to take care of the child's funeral expenses."

Cindy looked up for the first time. "Really?"

"Yes. If you would, you might let the young girl know who was here with you yesterday. I planned to tell Miss Tyree this morning, but she's out today."

"That's nice of you, Mr. Binder."

"It's the least we can do. I think you should take the rest of the day off."

"I'll be okay. I feel a lot better now. And thank you and Mrs. Binder."

As soon as Cindy was out of his office, his secretary poked her head inside. "I think she was scared of you. I've been trying to get the mortician on the phone."

"So, what are you standing in here for? Go on back to your desk and keep trying."

His secretary flushed. "Yes, sir. Right away, sir."

Sometimes he was like that. She blamed it on his years in the military.

TEN

ANNA LUNCHED WITH WHIT at a local dairy bar. It wasn't quite noon yet, but the morning was warm. The frost was gone even from the top of Tabernacle Mountain, and people could be overheard talking about an Indian summer. They ate on a concrete table on the front lawn of the restaurant.

"I'd hate to see Jenny Hairston buried as a pauper," Anna was saying.

Whit's mouth was crammed full of hot dog. "She'll never know the difference."

"Whit Pynchon!"

"Funerals are a waste of time and money."

Anna toyed with her sundae. "Sometimes I wonder if you're human, Whit."

"Don't expect me to get incensed over a funeral—or lack thereof."

Anna smiled. "I know . . . I know. You've told me a hundred times. That's not the point. Funeral services are for the benefit of the living, Whit. They're a way to say good-bye—a way to purge the grief."

Whit urged the final bite of hot dog into his mouth. "Bull-shit," he mumbled.

"It means a lot to Tamantha Andrews. And to Tressa, too."

"There's nothing either of them can do about it. I like Tams, too. If there were anything I could do, I would. I can't, though, and you can't, either. Let's change the subject."

But Anna wasn't ready to change the subject. "Death bothers you, doesn't it, Whit?"

"Of course it bothers me. I'm doing my damnedest to find that kid's killer."

"You know what I mean, Whit. I'm talking about the thought of your own death. You've reached that point in life when you've started to hear footsteps. It's your own sense of mortality creeping up on you."

"Jesus, Anna. Ease up, and spare me this ice cream parlor philosophizing. Okay? That's one thing most cops have—a good sense of their own mortality."

Anna pushed the sundae away. She had no appetite. "I'm not sure I'm going to survive your midlife crisis."

"My what?"

"You heard me. You're not immune to a midlife crisis— just like you're not immune to lung cancer or heart disease. No matter how tough and irascible you may think you are, you're not Superman."

Whit threw up his hands. "Women absolutely flabbergast me. What brought all this on anyway? There's not a god- damned thing I can do about the kid's funeral. If I could, I would—just for Tams's sake."

"Go talk to the funeral home."

"And say what?" Whit snapped, his voice so loud that it turned the head of another couple at a nearby table.

"Not so loud."

"No, you tell me, Anna. What should I say to the man? He's in business to make money. Now, I may happen to think he leeches on grief and guilt, but he's not doing anything wrong or illegal. I can't make him give a funeral away for free. Come on, woman. Be reasonable.''

"The girls are willing to work something out to pay him over time, but he wants a hundred a month at least. See if you can get him down to fifty maybe. I'm no good at that kinda thing.''

Whit dropped his head into his hands. "No, I'm not gonna do it. Now, eat your ice cream. I have an investigation to continue.''

"You finish the ice cream," she snapped.

Before he could react, it splattered in his lap.

Cullen Brown had been out of his office when the circuit clerk had phoned to inform him of his appointment as guardian *ad litem* for Mary Hairston. As soon as he returned, his secretary handed him the message. Brown took one quick glance at it and hurried into his office, where he quickly dialed the number of Judge O'Brien's office.

"I'm just on my way out to lunch," the judge told Brown.

"I apologize, Your Honor, but I wanted to get back to you as soon as possible about this Mary Hairston matter. I can't handle—"

The judge laughed into the phone. "I knew you'd want to wiggle out of it. No self-respecting lawyer in his right mind would want this case. It's trouble. On the other hand, Cullen, this case is probably going to attract a lot of interest. The publicity might do you a lot of good.''

"Please, Judge. Let me plead my case. It won't take but a second.''

O'Brien's voice turned serious. "Cullen, my wife has lunch on the table precisely at twelve-fifteen every day. I'm never late. Make it quick.''

"I was romantically involved with Mary Hairston, Judge.

Frankly, it sounds like a fascinating case, but I just couldn't handle it.''

O'Brien was silent for a moment. ''Do you mean she is your girlfriend?''

Brown realized the implication. ''She *was* my girlfriend. We broke up several months ago. I'm not the father, if that's what you're thinking.''

''The possibility crossed my mind, Cullen.''

''No way,'' Brown retorted.

''I'm still not certain that your conflict is grounds for you to withdraw. I would think that your personal interest might make you an even more aggressive advocate.''

Cullen's voice cracked. ''Please, Judge. I care very much for that lady. I can't handle it emotionally.''

''I see. Well, Cullen, given the nature of your conflict, I will appoint another attorney.''

''Thanks, Judge. I'll take—''

O'Brien had hung up. Cullen Brown looked at the phone for a moment, gave it—and the irascible judge—the finger, then slumped down into his desk chair. He pulled open his middle desk drawer and pulled a portrait from beneath a pile of papers. It was a studio shot replete with autumn scenery in the background. In the foreground, both Jenny Hairston and her mother smiled up at him.

Anna had left as Whit was trying to scoop the ice cream from his lap. He'd called after her, but she had ignored him. Sometimes, he could be such a bastard. Prior to the argument, she'd planned to tell him about her theory that Mary Hairston was planning to have an abortion. *Oh, well . . . maybe later.* Snuggled deep in her purse were the numbers of the Charleston area abortion clinics that had been marked in Mary Hairston's phone book. She drove her Audi straight by the offices of the *Journal* through Milbrook, and turned north on the four-lane highway that headed toward Charleston.

Along with the numbers, she carried the street addresses of the clinics and a photo of Mary Hairston. Golden oldies blasted from the radio of her compact car. The warm midday air rushed into the open window to ruffle her thick auburn hair. The draft carried the odor of gasoline and diesel fuel along with the perfume of fall.

Despite her troubles at the *Journal* and the dispute with Whit, she was experiencing an emotional high. Some instinct compelled her to make the trip to Charleston. As did Whit, she believed that the father of Mary Hairston's child either was the killer or could provide a very definite lead to the killer's identity.

Maybe the father lived away from Milbrook? Maybe he didn't even know of the tragedy? Those were possibilities, but Anna didn't accept them. Not for a moment.

Either way, Annie Tyson-Tyree, driven by a good journalist's obsessive curiosity, wanted to know if someone had impregnated Mary Hairston and then abandoned her. If that cost her a job that she no longer wanted, then no big deal. There were worse things that could happen. *Just ask Mary and Jenny Hairston—if you could.*

"Keep your heads down," Cal Burton said in a harsh whisper.

The eight officers, five from the Raven County Sheriff's Department and three from the Milbrook PD, hunkered in the heavy shadows of a stand of pine about fifty yards from a small, weathered logging hut. Years ago it had provided shelter for timbering crews that worked the lush southern slope of the mountain. It occupied a clearing about a mile

up a small logging road that turned off the main mountain
highway. Hunting huts and logging shacks dotted the mountainside, but this structure was the only one in the area known
as Red Oak Ridge.

"I smell wood smoke," Sheriff Ted Early said.

Both the sheriff and Burton studied the small stovepipe
protruding from the top of the shack. At that moment, it was
framed by a white cloud that concealed any smoke.

"Not hot enough for a fire," one of the uniformed deputies observed.

"Maybe the guy likes a hot lunch," Cal answered.

A deputy squinted at the stovepipe. "There's a little smoke
coming out of it. Someone's home. That's for damned sure."

Early was measuring the rugged landscape. "We can circle the house—then call him out."

"Better yet," Cal offered, "let's circle the house and lob
a tear gas canister inside. Why give him the chance to take a
shot?"

The deputy with the tear gas gun inched forward. "I ain't
none too sure this fuckin' thing's gonna work, Cal. The
damned rust is rubbing off on my hands."

He offered them for Cal to see. It was true. The palms of
the cop's hands were stained a bright orange.

"Jesus fucking Christ, Sheriff. Don't you folks ever clean
your equipment?"

Early flushed. "You take care of your business, Burton.
I'll take care of mine. The damned thing'll work."

The door to the shack creaked open. The bulky form of a
black man stepped out on the porch. He carried a small pan
of steaming water. A bright white bandage circled his left
thigh.

"Down!" Cal hissed.

The squad dropped to the ground. One of the men landed

right on a dry tree limb. It cracked with a sharp report that sounded like lightning in the sylvan tranquillity of midday.

The black man's eyes swiveled toward them.

"We oughta take him now," someone said.

"Shadup!" Cal whispered.

The man at the shack studied the forest in front of his hiding place for several minutes, then shrugged and dumped the steaming liquid into the front yard. He limped back into the house.

"The guy's injured," the sheriff said.

"Probably did it running through the goddamn mountains after dark," Cal said.

A deputy eyed Cal with obvious disbelief. "Man, you just missed your chance."

"We're too far away, goddammit!"

"We coulda taken him right then," the deputy said.

Early put a hand on his subordinate's shoulder. "Cal's right. Now, let's ease around that hut. Move slow. We got all the time in the world. Remember, don't kill him unless you have to—unless he's an immediate threat to you or someone else."

The men started creeping through the edge of the forest. Cal and Sheriff Early remained squarely in front of the house. The officer with the tear gas gun stayed with them.

Other than the distant cry of a crow, the mountain silence was undisturbed—except for the cracking twigs and rustling leaves caused by the men moving through the low-growing brush around the hut.

"I wish the wind would blow or something," Early whispered. "Them guys sound like a herd of buffalo moving through there."

"Let's take 'im," Cal said, "before the bastard hears us."

They abandoned the concealment of the pine glade and

crawled belly-down through the high grass that fringed the clearing. The small porch came closer and closer.

"He's a big son of a bitch," Early said as they reached their position.

Cal pulled his revolver and checked the cylinder. "One of these'll stop him."

"I hope we don't need it," Early said.

"How are we gonna know when the men are in position?" Cal asked.

The sheriff looked at the detective lieutenant. "Christ almighty, I forgot to work out some kind of signal."

Cal checked his wristwatch. "We'll give 'em a few more minutes.

"I hope they'll wait that long."

Cal's eyes widened as he saw the subject he presumed to be Lewis Luther again step out of the house. This time he carried a shotgun in his hands. His gaze was drifting over the mountain landscape.

"He's heard us!" Early rasped.

Cal tensed. "Shhh!"

The crisp crack of a rifle exploded on their right. The black man grabbed his upper left arm and reeled back into the house. One of their men had fired.

"Dammit to hell!" Ted Early bellowed as he rose to his feet. "Who fired?"

Before he received an answer, the deep roar of a shotgun blast echoed over the face of Tabernacle Mountain. Buckshot whizzed by Early's head. The sheriff dropped to the ground. "Mother of God, I felt the breeze off them friggin' pellets."

Cal had his .357 leveled at the window from which the shotgun blast had come. He unloaded five quick shots into the cabin, but the sounds of his fire were lost in the barrage that circled the house. Mountain echoes turned the fusillade into an incessant ear-hammering roar.

"Pump a damned canister in there," Early shouted back to the officer with the tear gas gun.

The cadence of the firing escalated until it found a rhythm, punctuated only occasionally by the throaty rumble of the suspect's shotgun. In the breathless atmosphere, the gun-smoke hung low to the ground. The afternoon reeked of sulfur. The deputy with the tear gas gun rose to his knees and aimed the tear gas gun at a front window.

"Look out!" someone cried.

The shotgun belched a plume of white smoke. Dust erupted just to right of the deputy with the tear gas gun. He dived back to the ground.

"Christ!" Cal shouted. "Put a fuckin' can of that stuff in there."

The deputy was hugging the ground. "Then you keep the bastard out of the windows."

Cal and the sheriff both reloaded.

"Now!" Cal cried.

The deputy raised up and aimed again at the front window. It thumped as it launched the smoking projectile toward the house. The canister struck the house and dribbled back out into the yard. Boiling clouds of tear gas mingled with the smoke and drifted back toward the officers themselves.

Cal began to cough and gag. "You fuckin' moron!" he cried, not even knowing if the officer who had missed the window could hear him.

"That's why I . . . I hate that shit," Early was saying.

The firing had dropped off as the tear gas stymied the side it was to have helped. Officers covered their noses and eyes with handkerchiefs.

Cal stumbled around in teary confusion, hoping he didn't

catch a load of buckshot. Finally, he located the deputy with the tear gas. "Fire another one, goddammit."

"I can't even see!"

The thunder of the shotgun sent everyone to their knees.

"We're sitting ducks," a panicky voice cried.

The officer with the launcher wiped the tear gas from his eyes and tried to sight the gun. Cal stood behind him, gauging the elevation. "By God, you'd best do it right this time."

"Go fuck yourself," the deputy growled.

The firing gradually increased, but the suspect's shotgun was silent.

. . . *Thruummmpp* . . .

The small canister clunked against the window facing and bounced into the house, its weight ripping away the grimy curtains that covered the window.

Smoke could be seen filling the house, but there was something else there, too—something that brought several officers to their feet.

"Fire!" a voice cried.

Cal tried to wipe the tears from his tortured eyes. It was one of those things that happened with tear gas every now and then. The canister was so hot that it had ignited the dry-rotted curtains.

"Get ready!" Cal shouted. "The bastard'll be coming out."

The men within the sound of the lieutenant's voice tried to regain their composure. White handkerchiefs and shirt-sleeves wiped tears out of eyes. They trembled with both fear and anticipation as they waited for the suspect to break from the house. The wood inside was old and dry, and through the window they saw the mounting flames.

The inferno spread quickly, creating such an updraft that it sucked the irritating gas from the area surrounding it. With red and tearful eyes, the men gaped as the flames raced through the ancient structure. Their weapons remained poised as they anticipated the suspect's flight from a certain fiery death.

Sheriff Early was on his knees, his own weapon still holstered. "That son of a bitch is still in there. He isn't gonna come out. Somebody go back to the cars and radio for the volunteer fire department."

Someone laughed. "Shit, Sheriff, it's too late for that."

"Do it, dammit. Before the whole mountain goes up with it." It had been a dry fall, and the risk of a forest fire was heavy on Early's mind.

"Yes, sir."

Cal, though, was hypnotized by the raging fiery fury. "Burn, baby, burn," he mumbled.

Whit pulled out of his driveway and hurried toward a prearranged interview with Vanessa Andrews at her home. The quick stop at his home hadn't been planned, but there was no way he was going to walk around all day smelling of sour milk.

Whit had never met Mrs. Andrews until that day. She greeted him at the door.

"So, you're Tressa's father?" She escorted him into the living room.

"Yes, ma'am."

She offered him a seat and then said, "She worships you. She's a mighty fine person, Mr. Pynchon."

"I can return the compliment. Tams is one of my favorite people. I'm looking forward to meeting Vanessa."

"Gracious, they're as different as night and day. You know, Mary was one of Vanessa's best friends. Tams, though, is grieving a lot more than Vanessa. I hope you can catch who-ever did that to Jenny and her mother. It's terrible, sir.''

"We'll find the killer."

At that moment, Vanessa Andrews came sulking down the steps.

"Mr. Pynchon's here," her mother said.

"I saw him pull in. Hiya."

"Hi Vanessa. I was just telling your mother how much I like Tams."

Vanessa collapsed into an armchair. "Everybody likes Tams."

Mattie Andrews excused herself. "I'll let you two talk. You answer his questions, Vanessa."

Mrs. Andrews vanished into the kitchen of the house.

Whit pulled out his notebook. "When was the last time you saw Mary Hairston?"

"I can't remember."

Whit looked up. "You answered so quick . . . you didn't even have time to think. Let's back up and start over. This time, think about it for a few moments."

"I told you—I don't really remember. Sometime the week 'fore last maybe."

"What kind of mood was she in?"

"Her usual."

Whit tapped the pad with his pencil. He wanted to be nice for Tams's sake. It was an example of how a personal in-volvement affected his method of investigation. "Miss An-drews—Vanessa—I didn't know Mary Hairston. How would I know what her usual mood was?"

"Last few weeks, she'd been kinda edgy. I guess she was having some trouble at work."

"Did she tell you about any trouble at work?"

Vanessa fiddled with a cover on the arm of the chair. "She

talked to Tams a lot more'n me. They were close. You oughta talk to Cindy Jackson, too. She was friends with Mary.''

"I'm interviewing you right now. According to your mother, you and Mary were best friends.''

"Mother's wrong a lot nowadays. Hardening of the arteries, I guess.''

Whit flipped the notebook closed. "Vanessa, why do I get the feeling that you don't wanna talk to me?''

She bounced up from the chair. "It's not that I don't want to talk to you. I just don't know anything that's gonna help you.'' She paced the living room.

"Let me be the judge of that. Can you tell me if Mary was seeing anyone?''

Vanessa opened a small bowl and pulled out a piece of peppermint candy. "I haven't seen much of Mary lately. Far as I know, she wasn't seeing nobody.''

"I know she dated Cullen Brown some, the lawyer.''

"That was months ago. They broke off.''

"Brown says she started seeing someone else. You have any idea who that might be?''

"Nope.''

"Do you know who she was seeing before Brown?''

Vanessa pursed her lips in an exaggerated gesture of difficult recollection. "Yep. I sure do.''

Whit waited for her to give a name. When she didn't, he stood, towering over her. "Okay, young lady, I don't have time for your games. Let's go down to the courthouse. We'll talk there.''

Vanessa stiffened. "Do what?''

"Get up. Let's move it.''

"I ain't going nowhere with you.''

Whit leaned down close to her. "Wanna bet?'' His gaze

met hers. For a moment, they joined in a battle of wills. Vanessa lost.

"His name was Lewis Luther. He was a real jerkoff."

The phone rang somewhere in the house.

"Where can I find this Luther?" Whit asked.

Before Vanessa could answer, her mother came into the room. "I'm sorry to bother you, Mr. Pynchon, but there's a gentleman on the phone for you. It's Mr. Danton."

She guided Whit to a wall phone in the kitchen.

"What's up, Tony?"

"I've been tracking you down everywhere. I just got a call from the sheriff's department. They passed a message on from Cal Burton."

"What kinda message?"

"He says he's got Jenny Hairston's killer on Tabernacle Mountain."

Whit's thoughts raced. "Tabernacle Mountain? Did they give you a name?"

"Sure did. He's a probationer—a convicted felon. A man named Lewis Luther."

ELEVEN

A CUSTOMARY SHROUD of noxious smog hung in the valley of the Kanawha River. Smokestacks belching steam and fumes offset the classic form of the state capitol's dome. The majestic building, looking like most capitol buildings except for its tarnished gold dome, sat facing the dark waters of the broad river. In a way, the dingy dome symbolized the state of West Virginia itself. Like the dome, the state was once bright and rich, but the dying demand for dirty coal brought an end to the boom.

Anna viewed the city of Charleston and the capitol from the other side of the river. She had been to the Charleston area only twice before, and both times she had been anxious to escape. The Kanawha River flowed in the general direction of east to west, emptying some sixty miles downstream into the Ohio. Besides serving as the seat of West Virginia's government, Charleston—and the string of smaller communities along the riverbank—hosted an internationally recognized chemical industry, an ironic oasis of semisuccess in a failed political state. The evidence of that industry signaled its presence long before the tall smokestacks became visible. She remembered numerous news stories of residents driven from their homes by leaks of fuming irritants. The news stories had become more frequent after the gaseous massacre at Bhopal, India. The Kanawha Valley, like Bhopal, boasted a huge Union Carbide plant. It made her want to hold her breath.

As she inched up Kanawha Boulevard, she kept her eyes on the street signs. The first clinic she sought was located just off the boulevard. The urban area on the south side of the river, opposite the capitol, wasn't properly Charleston. It was called Kanawha City, and that was given as the address for the clinic Anna sought. When she finally located it, Anna was shocked to see two pro-life protesters planted in the clinic's parking lot. They carried placards that accused the clinic of murder. As Anna was parking the car, she saw the two women—both middle-aged, one short and chubby and the other tall and lanky—move toward her.

"Damn," she mumbled.

She quickly exited her car.

"Are you a patient here?" the stubby chunk of a woman asked.

"That's not any of your business," Anna said.

They actually stepped in front of her as if to block her way to the clinic.

"Think about what you're doing," the other said. "It's a crime."

The short woman was jabbing literature at her. Anna glanced at the pamphlet and saw color photos of bloody flesh. She knocked it away. The paper fluttered to the ground.

"Get out of my way," Anna said.

To her surprise, they stepped aside. Anna moved between them.

"You'll be a murderer!" one was shouting.

"God will punish you," the other cried.

Anna wheeled but continued walking backward. "Screw you both," she shouted back.

Anna then turned and hurried toward the door to the clinic. She opened it and stepped inside. There, she paused to gain her breath and found herself in a sparsely inhabited lobby. Three women glanced at magazines. A man, looking especially uncomfortable, fidgeted in a chair. She saw a window cut in the wall with a woman behind it. The window was covered by very thick glass and a metal speaker through which the patients spoke. The receptionist was smiling at her.

Anna moved toward the friendly face.

"Can I help you?" the receptionist asked.

"Well, yes. I have a problem." Anna was shouting, anxious to be heard on the other side of the barrier.

"Would you like to consult a counselor?" The receptionist's words had been faint, but Anna had also read her lips.

Anna smiled. "It's not that kind of problem. Perhaps I should talk with the head of the clinic."

The smile seemed to fade. "I do need to know your business."

Given the protesters outside the clinic, Anna could understand her concern. "It's not something I want to discuss in the lobby—shouting like this, but I wouldn't mind stepping into your office. I'm not one of those . . . uh . . . activists stationed in your parking lot."

The receptionist pondered the request and studied Anna's face. Anna hesitated to show her press card. In the first place, she wasn't there as a reporter, and she remembered her editor's warning. A second concern was the attitude most people had developed toward reporters.

"It's a serious matter," Anna said, hoping that suggestion would tip the scales in her behalf.

"It's against policy, but come around to the side door. It's out in the hall."

Once she was inside, the receptionist offered Anna a seat.

"Do you really need such caution?" Anna asked.

"A year ago, a woman came in. Then we had our clients come into this office to complete the necessary documentation. Once the woman came in, she started to scream anti-abortion slogans and wrecked the place. She ruined a computer."

"It's an emotional issue," Anna said. "I guess you have to be concerned with security. I just didn't realize that the issue was so controversial in Charleston. I'm from Raven County down in the south end of the state."

"What's the serious matter?" the woman asked.

"Well . . ." Anna took a second to gather her thoughts. "A close friend of mine was recently the victim of a rather serious assault. She's in a coma. As a result of that same assault, her seven-year-old child was killed. Only after the assault did we discover that my friend was pregnant. She's unmarried, and she had in her possession the name of this clinic. She has no other relatives at all."

The woman inched forward with interest. "That's terrible."

"The hospital may be able to keep my friend alive through the term of her pregnancy, but we have no idea who the father may be—or whether he even knows about the pregnancy. In fact, knowing my friend as I do, I suspect she had told no one."

The receptionist made a face of frustration. "It's horrible, but what can we do?"

"I have reason to believe she may have been considering an abortion. She had the number of your clinic in her possession." Anna delved into the small briefcase she carried. "I've brought a photo of her—"

"Even if we knew who she was, we couldn't provide you with that information. It's highly confidential."

"I know that," Anna said, "but this situation is rather unusual. And I know I have no legal standing—"

"There's just no way."

Anna dropped the photo on the desk. "That's the woman. Her name was Mary Hairston."

The receptionist glanced down. Anna focused on the young woman's hooded eyes. Not a hint of familiarity.

"We just can't help," the woman was saying, her attention no longer on the photo.

"Perhaps if I talked to your supervisor or the director of the clinic. Just check with someone before you turn me down."

The receptionist checked the watch on her wrist. "Just a moment." She vanished down a hallway.

Within the suite of the offices of the clinic itself, there hovered the definite odor of a hospital. A table off to her side was cluttered with pamphlets on planned parenthood and birth control. From some cavern deep in the building she could hear the voices of a male, his words heavy with some foreign accent.

An older woman, a traditional nurse's cap placed upon a high bun of silver hair, returned with the receptionist. She came to Anna, offering her hand. "I'm Alma Meade, administrator of the center."

Anna introduced herself. "I'll just take a few moments of your time."

The woman wasn't smiling. "There's no need. We can't help you."

"But you haven't heard—"

"I have. Susan here briefed me on your request. My heart goes out to the poor woman and her child, but medical records are confidential, especially those in a circumstance such as ours. I am fascinated by the prospect that this woman's fetus may be nurtured while she remains comatose, but there's no way I can help you."

"It's crucial," Anna managed to say.

"I repeat. No way. However, if the court were to appoint a committee or guardian to represent the woman, and that individual executed a release, then perhaps we might be able to accommodate."

Anna reached down and retrieved the photo. "Would you look—"

The nurse blocked the photo with her hand. "No, I cannot look at your photograph. Susan here has already told me the woman's name. We simply cannot provide you with any information."

"You can't even tell me if she was here?"

"We cannot."

But Susan, who stood behind the administrator's shoulder, was shaking her head in a slow and deliberate fashion, keeping her eyes on the back of the older woman's head. As far as Susan was concerned, Mary Hairston had not been to the clinic.

As the car started the climb up the mountain, Whit and Tony, his passenger, had lost sight of the billowing cloud of smoke that rose from a point halfway up Tabernacle Mountain.

"The sheriff's department dispatcher didn't say a

damned word about a forest fire," Tony was saying. "Maybe we'd better stop and call somebody."

"It didn't look like a forest fire to me," Whit said.

"What the hell do you know about forest fires?"

Whit braked as he guided his car into a steeply banked curve. He gunned it once his tires were pushing against the slope of the bank. "Let's just get up there and find out what that goddamned Burton has done."

Tony's fingers scraped for a hold on the dash. "Jesus, Whit. Don't kill us in the process."

The tires screeched with agony as they tried to keep hold of the mountain road. The color left Tony's usually swarthy face. "Slow down, Whit!"

By that time, the car was starting up a long straight stretch of road. Whit floored the accelerator.

"Oh, Jesus Christ!" Tony wailed as he saw the road vanish into a horseshoe curve.

"Hang on," Whit said.

"You're never gonna make it!"

But he did. Whit jammed on the brakes just as they reached the curve. The car seemed to slouch down as it shot around the turn.

"If I get out of here, Whit, you're fired."

Whit kept his eyes on the road. "Is that just another empty promise?"

They squealed around two more curves. As they came out of the third one, they both saw a blue light ahead of them. Whit slowed down and pulled in beside a Milbrook PD cruiser that was parked in a picnic area along the mountain road.

"Where's Burton?" Whit asked.

The officer pointed across the highway. "Up that logging trail."

Whit followed the officer's finger and saw a narrow opening in the forest and a road that amounted to little more than a cow path.

"Oh, no," Tony said.

"You can make it," the city cop said. "Hell, a fire truck's gotten up there already."

Tony leaned down so that he could see the officer standing at Whit's window. "Is it a forest fire?"

"Naw. Some old shack's burnt up."

"What about the suspect?" Whit asked.

The officer crossed his arms. "Burton said to send you on up when you got here. He'll fill you in."

Whit rolled up his window and looked at Tony. "That sounds like trouble to me."

"You're not actually going to try to drive this car up that road?"

Whit was turning the vehicle. "Sure am. It's dry and wide enough, and I'll be damned if I'm gonna hike. It doesn't look too rutted. We can make it."

Tony renewed his grasp on the dash. "If you get this damned thing stuck, don't expect me to pay the wrecker bill."

Whit, though, had been right. The logging road was in excellent shape. Other than the whipping branches that smacked back as the car passed, the drive was uneventful. Even with the windows up, the odor of smoke seeped into the car. As they neared the shack, puffs of smoke blew into the face of their vehicle.

"I see the blue lights," Whit said.

Tony saw the huge red bulk of a fire truck. A river of water flowed from a clearing and across the road.

"It's gonna be muddy there," Tony warned.

Whit stopped his car where it was. There was enough

room at that point for him to turn to head back down the trail.

Sheriff Ted Early rushed to meet them as they exited the vehicle. "We got a situation here, Tony." Early chose to ignore Whit. Their differences were harsh and long-standing.

"What about the suspect?"

The question was hardly out of Tony's mouth when an ambulance crew came down from the house. They carried a body bag.

"That's him," Early said.

Tony looked at his investigator, then back to the sheriff. "He's dead?" Tony asked.

Whit was stunned. "They didn't tell us that."

Early shrugged. "We weren't sure about it until we located the body. Hell, he might have slipped out of the back on us or have still been alive in there somehow."

"Gimme details, Early."

The sheriff held up a hand. "This is Burton's case. We simply assisted. I'm gonna let him brief you."

Whit was examining the pile of smoking rubble. The wind had started to blow. Embers, aroused by the breeze, glowed between chunks of debris. "So, where is the bastard?"

"He was right over there." The sheriff pointed toward a fireman who was still using the hose to pour water on the fire.

"Looking for me?" Cal came from behind them.

Whit whirled. "What the hell happened here?"

The detective lieutenant continued to smile. "We caught your friggin' murderer, Pynchon. While you were sitting around with your thumbs up your ass, we were out investigating."

"I assigned the case to Whit," Tony said.

Cal nodded. "Yeah, you did. That was your mistake. Mr. Prosecutor. One of these days, you're gonna put some faith in somebody besides him."

Whit started to challenge the gloating lieutenant, but Tony laid a restraining hand on his shoulder. "Was that a subject named Lewis Luther in the body bag?"

"As far as I know," Cal said.

Whit rolled his eyes. "Just what the hell does that mean?"

"It means, the body looks like a roasted marshmallow. They say them black folks are hung like horses. That body's got a hard-on a foot long. Fire does that, you know—makes a cock hard. Besides, we saw Luther in the shack before the fire, and nobody else. So I'd say, as far as I know, that the hunk of well-done and well-hung meat is Luther."

Tony stepped close to Cal, so close that no one but he, Whit, and Cal Burton could hear his words. "You're an ignorant asshole, Burton. I don't find you funny at all. If this man's death looks in any way to have been unnecessary, I'll prosecute you. You understand me?"

Cal narrowed his eyes. "Yeah, but it was an accident pure and simple. A tear gas canister started the fire."

"What did you have on Luther?" Whit asked.

"I was hoping you'd ask." The Milbrook cop moved over to a cruiser and leaned against the hood. "Mary Hairston had been seeing Luther sometime back. They got in an argument, and Luther roughed her up. We tried to pull him over the other night, and he pulled the rabbit routine and ran. Made 'im look pretty gawddamned guilty to me."

"That's it?" Tony asked.

"Hell, Danton. I didn't come up here to charge him with murder. I had traffic warrants. I just came up to talk to him and serve those pissy-ass warrants. He's the one who decided on a shoot-out, not us."

Whit was shaking his head. "I guess you just happened to have tear gas."

A fireman approached the three men. "I found this." He offered Cal a fire-blackened handgun.

Even at a distance, Whit recognized it. "That's a .38 caliber revolver, Burton. The killer used a .25."

Cal Burton shrugged. "So what? I expected Luther had several weapons. He was on probation for felony assault, by the way."

A surging wind buffeted Anna's small car as it cruised south toward Milbrook. The four-lane highway had been carved out of the mountains of southern West Virginia, and the man-made valleys became a funnel for the wind as it heralded an approaching cold front. As soon as she had escaped the shroud of smog that enveloped the Kanawha Valley, the sky had turned a deep azure, but its beauty was doomed. The wind had come up quickly. Over her right shoulder, she could see the clearly defined line of slate-gray skies that marked the front itself.

She had visited two other abortion clinics. There had been no protesters, but the welcome she had received had been even less enthusiastic than the first. At both, the receptionists had looked at Mary Hairston's photo. There hadn't been the slightest hint of recognition. She had also talked with the directors of both centers. For what it was worth, Anna had the feeling that Mary Hairston had not been to any of the three centers in Charleston.

As she topped a ridge, the imposing double summit of

Tabernacle Mountain sprung into view. The wind seemed
to intensify as it pushed her car toward the passing lane.
A Neil Diamond tape entertained her, but she pushed the
button to eject it. Then she twirled the knob on her radio
until she found the local Milbrook station. Tabernacle
Mountain still separated her from Raven County itself, but
the station's transmitter, located atop the mountain, easily
reached out to Anna.

Anna had pulled into a rest stop to stretch several miles
back. The wind had sliced into her with the chill of winter.
Was it going to snow? She had hoped for a longer Indian
summer, if for no other reason than to keep Whit's mood
at a level above homicidal.

The station played a conservative mix of current soft
rock, country, and oldies. She looked at her watch and
saw that it was 4:56. Just four minutes away from news
time. The weather would follow.

Just a year ago, Anna would have looked forward to the
first snow. There were several ski resorts within an easy
driving distance of Raven County. This year, though, when
she thought of snow, she thought of Whit Pynchon's winter depression.

Sometimes, he's such a child, she thought.

Electronic beeps announced the news.

"This is WKWV news," a deep voice declared. "Raven
County authorities say that the killer of a young Raven
County child is dead."

Anna's fingers fumbled to increase the volume as the
announcer stumbled through a hastily prepared flash.

"As of airtime," the announcer concluded, "authorities are still withholding the identity of the dead suspect.
Details remain sketchy, but it appears the suspect died in
a shoot-out with local police—"

"Damn," Anna exclaimed.

She forgot about the storm that shadowed her. She forgot, too, about Whit Pynchon's depression as she brought the speed of her small car up to 70 m.p.h. Her hands were locked on the steering wheel as she fought the lateral strength of the breeze.

At 5:30 P.M. she hurried into the newsroom of the *Journal*. Harold Jones, a pencil clamped between his teeth, pecked away at his terminal's keyboard. Anna had always found him a pitiful little man, the kind that always had a fresh sweat stain under his arms no matter how cool it was.

She put a hand on his shoulder. "Evening, Harold."

He looked up and smiled in spite of the pencil in his mouth, revealing decay-blackened teeth. "They nailed the no-good bastard."

"I heard on the radio."

The smile on his face faded. "They already have the story?"

Anna nodded. " 'Fraid so, Harold. No big scoops on this one. Sorry, guy. So, who was the killer?"

"A guy by the name of Lewis Luther. He was a former lover of Mary Hairston, or so it appeared."

Anna waited for him to go on. Instead, he turned back to the screen of his terminal.

"Dammit, Harold. At least give me the details."

The obit writer lifted a typed statement from his desk and gave it to Anna. It was a news release from the Milbrook Police Department. "That's all we got."

The release quoted Detective Lieutenant Cal Burton, who outlined the case against Luther and the manner in which the suspect had died. The last paragraph of the release was a final quote from Burton.

Anna read the last paragraph aloud. "The lieutenant said, 'It's unfortunate that a jury won't get a chance at this case.' What a jerky thing to say."

"What's that?" Harold Jones asked, his attention riveted to the words he was typing.

"Nothing. Tell me, Harold, did you ask any questions?"

He stopped his pecking. "Whadaya mean?"

"I mean, how did they get this guy? What about details on the shoot-out? The fire? You could use some background on Luther, too. You don't say anything about his family."

Beads of sweat decorated Harold's balding forehead. "Look, Anna. It's my story now. I've got to get it written."

Anna choked back an angry response and started to leave the building. She almost collided with Will Binder in the front lobby.

"Anna, I'm glad I ran into you, pardon the play on words."

"What is it?" Anna asked. She was in no mood for another dressing-down.

"I've been trying to locate you all day."

"I didn't feel well this morning. I—"

"Not still chasing the Mary Hairston story, I trust."

"Of course not."

"Have you talked with Ms. Jackson?"

"Ms. Jackson?"

"The young friend of Mrs. Hairston who works in composing."

Anna feigned a smack to the forehead. "God, I'm dense. No I haven't. Actually, yesterday was the first time I'd ever met Cindy. I've seen her here, but our paths haven't crossed."

"I see. Well, I told her this morning that my wife and I were talking last night, and she suggested that we cover the cost of the child's funeral."

"That's generous of you, Mr. Binder."

"I should have thought of it yesterday. Sometimes, I'm rather dense, too. I was discussing the matter with my wife. As I said, it was her idea—and a damned good one."

As polished as Will Binder was, he appeared uncomfortable to Anna. "Tams—Tamantha Andrews—will be especially happy. It's a magnificent gesture, Mr. Binder."

"Mary Hairston has been a long and faithful employee of the *Journal*. It's our way of helping."

TWELVE

THE PUNGENT AROMA of Lewis Luther's crispy body hung in Whit's nostrils. The smell of smoke permeated his clothes. For most of his drive home, he had kept his car window rolled down, hoping the icy air might banish both odors. It promised to be a cold night, maybe even snow. What a damned change from midmorning when it had been sunny and warm!

His breath turned to fog as soon as it escaped his mouth. Three blocks from his home, he surrendered to the chill and rolled up his window. The last rays of sun found a small hole in the overcast, creating a purple sunset at the summit of Tabernacle Mountain.

Come next week, daylight-savings time would end. To Whit, that was the true beginning of winter. He despised the early darkness. It made the frigid winter nights seem endless.

Whit tried to think about Lewis Luther. He knew nothing about the man. For that matter, he knew little about Mary Hairston or Jenny Hairston. Maybe Luther was the killer. If it was so, then Whit had nothing else to do but settle back and brave the coming winter.

He didn't see the two figures on his porch steps until he turned into his driveway. There they were, huddled together like refugees—his daughter and Tams. He jerked the car to a stop and jumped out.

"Are you two okay?"

Tressa got to her feet, wrapping her arms around her chest. "We're freezing, Daddy."

"Why on earth are you sitting out here?"

"I forgot my key," Tressa said, her lips trembling.

Tams walked stiff-legged as Whit herded them toward the front door.

"Where's your car?" Whit asked as he fumbled with a key.

"We walked. The car started missing or something. I left it at the service station and we walked over."

He managed to open the door. "Inside . . . both of you . . . before you freeze."

Whit flipped on the lights. Both of the young girls pranced about his living room as they tried to warm themselves.

"I was hoping Anna might be here," Tressa said.

Whit shrugged. "I don't know where she is."

At that moment, they heard a car door slam outside. Seconds later, Anna hurried into the house. "Golly," she said, "that wind is horrible."

She noticed Tams and Tressa. "I was just over at Tams's. Mrs. Andrews is worried sick about you. Where's your car, Tressa?"

"It's broke."

Tams moved in front of Whit. "We heard they found the killer."

Anna and Whit traded glances.

"The Milbrook police were trying to apprehend a suspect for questioning," Whit said. "There was a lot of gunfire and a fire, and the man died."

"Who is it?" Tams asked. "The radio didn't say."

Whit sat down in his recliner. He leaned forward to Tams. "His name was Lewis Luther. Did you know him?"

Tams gasped and swayed a little. Tressa hurried to her and put an arm around her.

"You know him, then," Whit said.

Tams nodded. "He couldn't have done it."

Anna stood behind the two girls. "Why do you say that, Tams?"

"I just know he couldn't have done it."

Whit reached out to take Tams's hand. It felt like ice. "You know he's been in trouble before, don't you?"

"Sure, I do, Mr. Pynchon. He's big, and he's mean, too. Mary dated him. You know that, don't you?"

"Yes, we know that."

"Well, he was mean to her," Tams said.

"Why didn't you tell me about Luther, Tams?"

The young girl still trembled. "I guess I never thought about him. It was so long ago, almost a year maybe. Besides, I just know Luther couldn't have done it."

Whit pulled the distraught young teenager closer. "You keep saying that, Tams. Why couldn't he have done it?"

Tams looked at Whit and then up to Anna. "He was mean, like I said, but there wasn't anyone in this world as crazy about Jenny as Lewis was. Not even me. He called Jenny his little chocolate ball. He was all the time bringing her toys and presents. Sometimes, after he and Mary stopped dating, Lewis would come by Mary's just to say hi to Jenny. Mary let him 'cause she knew how much he loved Jenny. No way he could hurt Jenny."

"Perhaps it was an accident," Tressa said.

Tams turned on her friend. "No way, Tressa! I mean it! Somebody else did it, not Lewis. You can believe it if you want—that he would kill her—but not me . . . not ever."

Anna put her hands on Tams's shoulder and turned her around to face her. "Well, I have some good news for you."

Tams wiped a wayward tear from her face. "Good news?"

Anna made a face. "That was a bad way to say it. I have some news that will make you feel better anyway."

Anna's words even had Whit interested. "Just what have you been up to?"

"I had stopped by Tams's house to tell her the news. By the way, Tams, just as soon as I tell you, you call your mother and tell her you're all right. She's worried to death."

"I will," Tams said. "What's the news?"

"First, Tams, have you seen Cindy Jackson today?"

"No, why?"

"You remember Mr. Binder at the newspaper?"

Tams nodded that she did.

"I saw him late this afternoon. He told me that he—or the newspaper—is going to pay for Jenny's services. He wanted me to tell you. He also wants you to go to the funeral home first thing tomorrow and make the arrangements."

A slight smile formed on Tams's face. "Me? He wants me to? I can handle it?"

"He sure does. And, yes, the arrangements are up to you."

Tressa clapped. "That makes us both feel better. Can I come with you, Tams?"

"I hope you and Anna both will help me."

"You know we will," Anna said.

Whit patted the young black girl on the shoulder. "Go call your mother. Tell her I'll drive you home in just a few minutes."

Tams started toward the phone, but she stopped and turned. "One thing, Mr. Pynchon. Lewis still didn't do it."

Later that night, Anna snuggled against Whit as they sat

on the living room floor. They both wore heavy velour robes and nursed glasses of strong drink.

"Are you closing the case?" she asked.

"I'll leave that up to Tony. I'm sure as hell not satisfied with the evidence against the guy."

"It fits, doesn't it?"

"That doesn't matter. The real question is whether it's the truth. Tams certainly doesn't think so."

Anna shrugged. "She's a kid, Whit. Her emotions are in control."

"Right now, I don't wanna think anymore about it." Whit leaned back against the sofa, his body limp from the three drinks he'd already consumed. "I'm drunk."

"You acted like a real asshole today at lunch," Anna said, her hand stroking his bare thigh.

"Me? You were the one who committed assault with an ice cream cone."

She smiled. "You deserved it."

"Jesus, lady. My testicles just about turned into brass balls. It was cold."

"The least you could have done was—well, forget it. At least the kid will get a decent burial. Seriously, Whit, you need to relax. You've been tight as a drum lately."

"I hate winter."

Anna belly-laughed. "That's obvious. I just wish you wouldn't take it out on the rest of the world. You'd think winter was the product of some conspiracy invented solely to torment Whit Pynchon."

He lifted his head in mock surprise. "You mean it isn't?"

Anna kissed him, pressing her body tightly against his. The embrace lasted for a long time.

"We haven't done this since our trip to the beach," she whispered.

He thought about it. "Are you sure?"

"That's one thing I usually remember."

She saw him smile.

"My God," she exclaimed, "you can swell up like a bantam rooster."

"I simply appreciated the compliment."

He slid a hand inside a robe to cup the firm flesh of a breast. Anna moaned as his fingers caressed the rigid flesh of her nipple.

Whit started to get up. "Let's go to the bedroom."

She pulled him back to the carpet. "No way. Your mood might swing before we get in there."

"Damn, you sure are down on me," Whit said.

She giggled as she pulled open his robe. "Not yet, but I'm gonna be."

The Raven County prosecutor had watched the late news and was turning off the television when his phone rang. Tony's wife was already in bed. He rushed to answer it before it woke her.

"Mr. Danton?" The voice on the other end was male and unfamiliar.

"Yes?"

"This is Harold Jones. I'm a reporter for the *Journal.* We've—"

"Do you know what time it is?" Tony asked.

"I apologize, Mr. Danton, but we've just received information on a story that we want to confirm."

"I'll be in my office tomorrow morning," Tony said.

"Not according to the report I have. I understand you'll be in court on a hearing about Mary Hairston."

Tony clinched his hand around the phone. "I have no comment."

"Won't you at least confirm the hearing?" the reporter asked.

Tony felt his anger rising. "Look, you folks print what you want, but, like I have said, I have no comment."

"Is Mary Hairston pregnant?" Jones asked.

Jesus, Tony thought. *They know it all.*

The reporter read his silence. "I gather that's true," he said.

"Mr. Jones, there is a hearing scheduled for tomorrow morning with regard to Mary Hairston. That's all I have to say."

But Jones wasn't about to let go. "Do you believe that Lewis Luther was the father? Was that behind what happened?"

Tony slammed down the phone. Maybe Whit Pynchon had the right idea about the press after all.

"Stop here," Vanessa Andrews cried.

Lloyd Smith stomped on the brakes of his shiny black Lincoln. The tires squealed. He was taking her home after a movie and a stop at his apartment for a "quickie." Both of them were slightly inebriated.

"What the hell's wrong?" he asked.

"I wanna use that pay phone."

Lloyd frowned. "You what?" The snow flurries had materialized. They were so light, they were barely visible in the car's bright headlights.

"I have a call to make."

"It's after eleven," Lloyd said as she climbed out of the car.

Vanessa ignored him and slammed the door. She hunkered in her heavy coat as she hurried to the phone booth. It was located at the corner of a small parking lot squarely in the middle of Milbrook. Once she was inside the booth and out of the wind, she pulled a small slip of paper and a dime from her coat pocket.

The phone rang three times before it was answered by a male voice. Unlike the previous night, the man on the other end of the line sounded wide awake. If he wasn't, she thought, he's gonna be.

Vanessa muffled the speaker with her hand. "I called last night. Remember?"

"Who is this?"

"I know what you did."

"Dammit, who is this?"

"I'll be back in touch again," Vanessa whispered. "I want fifty thousand dollars."

"Are you some kind of kook?"

"Fifty thousand dollars, or I make a call to the cops."

Vanessa hung up the phone just as Lloyd Smith laid on his horn.

"The Hungers" arrived to haunt Cindy Jackson right after she climbed into her bed. Giant peanut butter cups floated in a tantalizing circle just above her head. A bowl of vanilla ice cream, smothered with thick chocolate and topped with walnuts, clunked down on the table by her bed. From some other place in her small apartment—the kitchen probably— came the whirring sound of a milkshake machine.

"Dammit! Dammit! Dammit!" she cried. "Leave me alone."

But they didn't. The peanut butter cups still drifted above her. The bowl of ice cream rattled on the table, and the milkshake machine increased its churning speed. Resigned to a life of marginal obesity, Cindy threw back her covers and hurried barefoot into her kitchen. First, she went to the refrigerator and opened the freezer. Thick frost covered a gallon carton of ice cream. The minute she lifted it she knew it was too close to empty to satisfy her. The lower portion of her fridge contained nothing of sufficient sweetness to curb her food lust.

Cindy moved to a small metal cabinet where she kept her canned goods. The contents were sparse, and it required no more than a quick look to know that it, too, contained nothing that she wanted.

The clock above the stove told her that it was 12:06 A.M. Not late at all when you considered that the Jiffy Mart stayed open all night. It was intimidatingly late for a walk to it. Cindy's car remained in the shop, waiting not for a part but for Cindy's payday. That was the garage's policy.

''I won't go,'' she said aloud—and knew at once it was a vain effort.

She went to the window and peered down three floors to the complex's parking lot. It was brightly lit, and in the silver glow Cindy smiled at the small flecks of falling snow. She hurried to her bedroom and tossed off the tentlike blouse she always wore to bed. Careful not to look in the mirror at her oversized stomach and hips, she pulled a pair of blue jeans over her legs and a thick sweater over her head. From her closet she withdrew a winter coat.

Midnight or not, she was looking forward to a walk down to the Jiffy Mart during the first snow of the winter.

In some other situation, the man with the blackened face might have been a refugee from a minstrel show. A bright gibbous moon had risen an hour before, and its cold light, peeking through the sporadic snow clouds, caught the white of his eyeballs as he studied the front door. He was just about to turn and seek some less illuminated rear entry when he saw the young black woman approach the exterior door and push it open.

He slipped down behind a bush, trying to decide if the Fates had delivered his quarry to him. She passed within three yards of his place of concealment, and under the moonlight he caught a quick look at her face. Her skin was deep chocolate, and her features blended into the shadows. She appeared bulky enough beneath the heavy coat, but he remained uncertain.

When she was a block away, he made the decision to follow her. It required that he keep to the shadows, dressed as he was in black fatigues and his face smeared with camouflage.

Anna languished in the afterglow of their lovemaking. Whit was stroking the soft skin of her back. It was an interlude of tenderness for which she had been yearning. More than that, it was an opportunity to try to talk to Whit about his surly mood. It was also a chance to tell him about her theory. She decided to start with the latter issue. For the moment, it was the most important.

"I have a confession to make," Anna said.

Whit stretched out on the floor beside her. "This sounds like fun. Is it something pornographic?"

"It's about the Hairston case."

It had been the wrong thing to say. Whit climbed to his feet. "That's the last damned thing I wanna talk about."

Before he could walk away, she grabbed his ankle. "Wait, Whit. It's important."

He almost fell face-first on the floor and whirled to glare down at her.

She released him. "Seriously, Whit, it is important."

He lifted his robe from the floor, put it on, and sat down

on the sofa. "If you want to ruin a pleasant evening, go ahead."

She quickly pulled on her robe and sat beside him on the sofa. "Damn you, Whit. For once, can't you be a little human?"

He saw the sparkling moisture in her eyes and slipped an arm around her shoulder. "I'm sorry. What is it?"

"I think Mary Hairston was trying to get an abortion."

He cocked his head at her. "Why do you say that?"

"When I was at her house, I found the numbers of several abortion clinics circled."

"Abortion clinics? Around here?"

"No, they were in Charleston, but their numbers are listed in our yellow pages."

Whit was genuinely interested. "Why didn't you tell me?"

Anna lowered her head. "I wanted to check it out for myself."

He shook his head. "Yeah, I shoulda known that. So, did you check them out?"

"I drove to Charleston this afternoon. I took a photo of Mary, but none of the clinics would talk to me. I managed to show them the photo, though, and I don't think any of them recognized her."

Whit shrugged. "So, that's that."

"But it's not," Anna countered. "There were dates written down along with the phone numbers. I think one of the clinics is in Roanoke. I think we oughta check down there."

Whit was puzzled. "I admit it's a startling possibility, but what's the significance now?"

"Maybe the father made the arrangements, Whit. Or maybe he even went with her. There were two dates listed. I did a story on abortion clinics. Usually, it requires several visits. I doubt she would have gone by herself."

"What were the dates?"

Anna went to her purse, which rested on the desk in Whit's living room. She pulled her notebook out. "September eighth and fifteenth."

"Obviously she didn't go," Whit said.

"But maybe she did. And maybe that clinic can tell us who was with her? Or who made arrangements for the abortion? It's a lead, isn't it? Maybe it will solve the dilemma over Luther. I can tell it's still bothering you."

"I guess it is."

"So, I'm driving to Roanoke, Virginia, tomorrow," Anna declared.

"Stop by my office first."

"Why?" Anna asked.

"To pick up a mug shot of Lewis Luther. Maybe someone can identify him."

The light, fluffy snow had ended, replaced by shimmering moonlight. The sidewalk on which Cindy walked was damp in spots, but there wasn't a flake of snow to be seen—and certainly no accumulation. The ground and concrete remained much too warm to permit that.

She walked quickly now, her excitement over the snow having yielded to the anxiety she had felt before she saw the flakes. The market was two blocks from her home, and the shortest route to it led through a sparsely developed residential area. Most of the property remained covered with second growth forest and brush—and FOR SALE signs, of course. The properties were likely to remain on the market. No one really wanted to build a nice new house near the complex.

Most of the folks who lived there were nice enough, but Cindy had to admit there were more than a few who weren't nice. Some of that small group drank too much. Others had been arrested for selling dope or breaking and entering. One old man had been sent to prison twice for murder. They had released him when his heart had started to fail. Sick or not, he was given a wide berth by most of the people in the complex. According to rumor, he kept a loaded pistol with him at all times.

The sidewalk on which she walked was new, constructed by the city in the hopes of spurring development in the area. She passed one lot that had been sold. The skeleton of a building rested amid a gaggle of construction equipment. According to the sign on the property, it was destined to be a medical supply house.

Beyond the construction site, she saw the sign and lights from the market. She quickened her pace as an owl hooted in the woods to her left. Across the street, on her right, a light burned in the front window of a small house. The lights from the store and the house made her feel better.

If she had taken the time to look over her shoulder, she would have seen nothing. The dark form gradually closing the distance behind her moved with practiced grace through the darkest shadows of the construction site. Other than the faint crunching of small stones, he moved without any sound. His hands were free, but a large knife, rendered temporarily useless, occupied one of the bellowed pockets of his pants.

Cindy reached the parking lot of the Jiffy Mart and was smiling when she saw Terry behind the counter. She didn't know his last name, but he owned the market and usually worked the late-night shift.

Terry jumped when Cindy shoved open the door.

"You startled me, Miss Jackson. I didn't notice your car lights."

Cindy laughed. "Not any way you could. I walked."

"This time of night? That's not too smart."

"My car's in the garage, and my sweet tooth got the best of me." The aroma of coffee filled the store. It came from a convenient stand located just inside the door. Cindy inhaled deeply, relishing the flavorful aroma. She went straight to the row where the candy was located and decided upon a ten-pack of Reese's Peanut Butter Cups.

"You walked down here for this?" he said.

Cindy felt her face warm. "Oh, I almost forgot. I need some bread, too. Anyway, I couldn't sleep, and I looked out and saw it snowing—"

"Snowing?" He glanced out the front of his store.

"You had to be quick to see it," she joked.

The store owner, though, didn't smile. Instead, he moved from behind the counter and toward the front door.

"What is it?" Cindy asked.

He pressed his face against the glass.

"It was snowing," she said. "Honest."

"I thought I saw something out there—a shadow sorta, go across the parking lot."

Cindy stepped beside him and gazed out at the brightly lit parking lot. "I don't see anything." Still, she trembled a little.

The storekeeper was scratching his head. "I guess I'm the one who's jumpy. That's the biggest reason I work the night shift. Ain't fair to ask an employee to risk his neck for your store."

He started back toward the counter, then stopped to look back outside. "I can swear I saw something."

Cindy clutched her coat tight against her ample bosom. "Stop it. You're scarin' me."

"I'm sorry. Look, Miss Jackson, why don't you let me give the city police a buzz. I expect one of their patrol cars will give you a lift home. I'd be happy to do it myself 'cept my wife's got the car t'night. Hell, she keeps it most nights. She had some kinda silly meeting to go to—''

''Oh, no. I'll be fine.''

''I bet the cops wouldn't mind a bit. They stop in here all the time, spend a long time drinking coffee. There's not much goin' on this time of night. Why don't you let me call 'em anyway?''

''They got better things to do.''

Terry sighed. ''Lookee here, Cindy. Now, I don't mean to frighten you, but I saw somebody out there. Frankly, I'm gonna call 'em anyway—ask 'em to come check my place out. Whoever it was out there may be casing me or something like that.''

He was reaching under the counter. With a quick flick, he withdrew a long pistol. ''Just in case.''

Cindy gaped at the gun. It looked evil. ''You're really trying to scare the bejesus outa me now.''

''I'm gonna give 'em a ring. You stay put.''

''Okay.''

The store owner moved to the back of the store. Cindy inched a little deeper into the store, too—away from the front windows. She kept her eyes on the glass door and the area of the parking lot beyond it. Cindy had seen nothing. Maybe Terry was just a born worrier. It was understandable, having to spend night after night in the lonely store.

He reappeared. ''Got a little problem, Miss Jackson. They're gonna come, but right now they're tied up with a car accident across town. Must be a pretty good one. All their cars are there. They said it might be an hour.''

''An hour! I can't wait that long, Terry.'' She glanced back at the parking lot. ''I'll just go on and walk. I'm sure I'll be okay.''

''Ah, come on, they said it might be an hour. Might just

be a few minutes. Why don't you pour yourself a big cup of coffee on the house and wait? I'd feel a lot better.''

Cindy was tempted—to wait, that is. ''If I drink even a drop of coffee, I'll never get to sleep.''

''A soda pop then—or a milk. I can even warm the milk in the microwave—''

''I appreciate it, but I gotta be at work at seven tomorrow. I'd best go.''

He waited behind the trunk of a huge poplar that grew to the side of the parking lot. Earlier, when the man inside had seen him, he had made the mistake of moving onto the well-lit lot itself in an effort to get a good look at the woman he had followed.

No doubt about it. It was Cindy Jackson.

The front door to the market opened, and she stepped out. The man inside stepped out with her, and the watcher inched back into the shadows.

''I don't think it's a good idea,'' the man in the store was saying.

In the peace of post-midnight, his words were crystal-clear.

''I don't have that far to go. 'Sides, you're the one that oughta be careful. Nobody'd wanna mess with me.''

''Long as I got this''—he brandished the pistol—''I'll be fine.''

She walked down the lot toward the street, passing so close to the black figure that he could hear her breathing. The man in the store stayed outside, the gun held down, watching the young woman.

''I'll stay here until you're outa sight,'' he called after her.

She turned and waved.

A whispered curse came from the shadows.

* * *

Cindy's rate of respiration increased as she hurried back toward her home. All she wanted to do was reach the safety of the complex. The owner of the store had really scared her, as much with his own gun as by the figure he'd said he'd seen.

When she reached the construction site, she looked back over her shoulder. The lights from the store were still visible, but Terry had gone back inside. Her pace quickened.

Suddenly she stopped.

Footsteps! Dear God, I hear footsteps. She didn't bother looking back over her shoulder again. The sounds didn't come from feet pounding concrete. Instead, she had heard the gravelly sound of feet on rough earth.

Her heart started to flutter.

"Who's there?" she asked in a whisper, hoping there was no one to hear anyway.

Silence answered her.

She started walking again, and again she heard the sound. This time she didn't stop. She jammed the bag containing her purchase under her arms and started trotting. Her huge breasts, absent the control of her wire bra, jogged up and down on her chest. She was just beyond the construction site when he stepped out in front of her. She ran right into him. Her hands went out to brace themselves against him. They rammed his face. It felt wet and gooey.

Her eyes jerked upward and locked into his. She prepared to scream and stepped back so she could bring her knee up into his—

The knife flashed just as she hiked her knee. The pain drove into her gut, but her knee made a jarring contact. The man reeled back, but, as he did, Cindy felt the pain slice upward. A warm feeling flooded her pelvis and thighs as he backed away, bent double by the force of her blow.

For just an instant, she thought she was unhurt. Then the pain exploded in her gut. She stared down and saw curls of entrails pouring from her stomach.

"Oh, Jeeees—" She tried to back away from the sight of her guts. They sparkled in the moonlight.

"Damn you!" he was saying, trying to catch his breath.

Blood gushed from the gaping rip of a wound. The stench of her bowels drifted out in wisps of fetid steam. Cindy was backing away, trying to pull the heavy coat around her to keep herself from losing everything. The pain came and went in waves. It wasn't so bad. The nausea was worse—and the weakness that was spreading down into her legs.

She backed into the brush and turned to flee, but something snagged her. She tried to see—

"Oh, Mommy," she wailed. A glistening tube of flesh stretched from the gaping hole in her coat to the small limb of a tree. She reached down to—

Her legs collapsed, and down she went. Her head started to spin. With what strength and presence of mind she had left, she reached down to put herself back together. That was when he came up behind her.

THIRTEEN

THE HALL OUTSIDE THE COURTROOM of Judge David O'Brien was as quiet as it would be all day long. It was 8:15, Thursday morning. Most of the offices in the courthouse wouldn't open for another fifteen minutes. Whit sat on a bench, his attention fixed on the front-page story about the death of Lewis Luther. A sidebar to the story announced the news of the hearing. Whit read it.

"I don't know where they got their information," Whit said to Tony, who sat beside him, "but it's right."

"The hospital might have tipped them, but I'd bet my money on Morley Clarke."

Whit folded the paper and dropped it beside him on the bench. "What's Clarke got to do with this?"

"That's who the judge ended up appointing to represent Mary Hairston."

"He's a bumbling fool," Whit said.

"Yeah. That's probably why O'Brien gave him the case. He appointed Cullen Brown in the first place. I told you that, didn't I?"

Whit nodded. "He's still high on my list of suspects."

"I thought he had an alibi."

"Of sorts. I've checked with the doctor he went out with Tuesday night. Just as he said, he was in depositions most of the next day, but there were still chunks of time unaccounted for. We've got such a large bracket for the time of the murder—all day Wednesday up into Thursday morning.''

Tony didn't like to think of trying a fellow attorney for murder. He brought the subject back to attorney Morley Clarke. "Anyway, poor Mary Hairston is now being represented by Raven County's worst lawyer.''

An unenthusiastic bailiff opened the courtroom door from the inside and peered out. "The judge is ready," he announced.

"So is the State," Tony told the officer, "but Mrs. Hairston's lawyer and the lawyer for the hospital aren't here.''

The bailiff checked his watch. "Judge O'Brien isn't going to like the delay.''

Tony held up his hands. "I'm here. What can I say?''

They heard footsteps. A young man neither of them knew reached the top of the steps and came straight toward them. He introduced himself as Harold Jones.

"You're the one who called me last night," Tony said. It was an accusation.

"Was the story correct?" the reporter asked.

"No comment," Tony said. "I will say this to you, Mr. Jones. I don't appreciate midnight phone calls. No matter what you ask at that time of the night, you're not going to get your answers.''

"You're a public official," the young newsman countered.

"See why I hate the bastards?" Whit said.

Harold Jones, his face red, started to answer Whit, but at that moment Morley Clarke, waddling under his obesity, appeared at the top of the steps. He stopped to get his breath. Jones hurried down the hall toward him. Tony got to his feet. "Let's go eavesdrop.''

By the time they caught up, the reporter was making notes

on what Clarke, still winded by the weight he carried, was saying. "I'm proud to represent a woman seeking the right to die with dignity."

"Oh, my God," Tony said under his breath. "The fat son of a bitch doesn't even know which side he's on. I gotta talk to him."

"No problem," Whit said.

Tony tried to stop Whit, but it was too late.

Whit's hand latched onto Morley Clarke's arm. "Come on, fella. The judge is in a hurry."

"Take your hands off me!" Clarke bellowed.

Tony intervened. "Come on, Morley. Let me talk to you a sec before we get into the hearing."

"Just as soon as this thug of yours gets his hands off me."

Whit let go and turned on the reporter who was behind them. "This conversation's private," Whit said.

"But I was talking to Mr. Clarke."

"The press conference is over, kid."

Tony had pulled Mary Hairston's appointed attorney several yards down the hall. The two lawyers were engaged in an animated conversation.

"You can't do this," the reporter was telling Whit.

"Do what?" Whit asked.

"Interfere with me! I was talking to Mr. Clarke."

At that point, the lawyers ended their conversation. Clarke headed for the courtroom door. Jones headed him off. "Mr. Clarke, I had some more questions—"

Clarke brushed the reporter aside. "I have nothing else to say."

Tony motioned for Whit, and they followed Clarke into the courtroom.

"Did you get through to him?" Whit asked.

Tony shook his head. "The dumb son of a bitch still wants

to talk about death with dignity, but I think I at least convinced him to let me do the talking.''

Ben Shanklin, attorney for the hospital, appeared a few moments later, and the bailiff went to notify the judge. He mounted the bench at once.

''I have a jury trial continuing this morning,'' O'Brien told them. ''Let's get on with this.''

Tony didn't give Clarke a chance. ''Your Honor, the State of West Virginia asks to intervene on behalf of the unborn child. After giving the matter some thought, it's possible that the interests of this unborn fetus and the interests of the comatose mother might at some point become in conflict—''

O'Brien held up his hand. ''Hold on a minute, Tony. How can that happen?''

The prosecutor hadn't come prepared to make such an argument, but the attitude of Morley Clarke had made it necessary. ''Your Honor, a situation might exist where a decision must be made with regard to the life of the mother versus the life of the unborn child. In most cases, medical authorities would save the mother. In this case, given the mother's medical condition, the alternative decision might be more appropriate.''

O'Brien shook his head. ''You're bent on making this thing complicated, Tony.''

Shanklin interjected an objection. ''The Court has appointed Mr. Clarke to represent both the mother and the fetus. I see no reason to turn this proceeding into a three-ring circus—two rings is more than enough.''

Tony nudged Whit in the ribs. ''Does that make you the clown, Ben?''

O'Brien's gavel wasn't that handy, so he snapped his fingers. ''Tony, I don't have time for your comedy this morning.''

"I was just carrying Ben's metaphor to its ultimate and logical conclusion."

O'Brien's brow knitted. "That's the end of it, Tony. No more."

"Yes, Your Honor."

The judge looked to Mr. Clarke. "As attorney for Mrs. Hairston, Morley, what do you have to say?"

Clarke grunted as he stood. "Nothing, Your Honor. If Mr. Danton wants to intervene, I have no objections."

"I need to buy some time," Tony whispered to Whit.

"You've got O'Brien pissed already."

The judge pondered Tony's request. "The Court will permit the State to intervene on behalf of the fetus. Mr. Clarke, you will then represent the interests of the mother."

Tony stood again. "If it pleases, Your Honor, I was talking with Mr. Clarke prior to the hearing. To be frank, we're all plowing some new legal grounds in this case. As you know, Mr. Clarke wasn't notified of his appointment until very late yesterday. Rather then rush into a hearing, why not postpone this matter for a week or so until—"

"I object! I object!" Shanklin shouted.

O'Brien, who had found his gavel under the file, hammered it on the surface of the bench. "Mr. Shanklin! Lower your voice!"

Shanklin was red-faced. "My client needs to have this matter resolved as soon as possible."

"Why the rush to commit murder?" Tony asked.

Shanklin shook his finger at Tony. "That's just the kind of inflammatory nonsense the hospital fears. You tried to sensationalize this yesterday, and you're engaging in the same demagoguery today."

Harold Jones sat in the empty courtroom, his pencil hurrying to make notes on the drama. O'Brien, for the moment, was ignoring the war of words as he watched the reporter write.

"Gentlemen," O'Brien said, "let's continue this discussion in my chambers."

Jones looked up and found the judge smiling at him as the lawyers filtered back toward the sanctity of the judge's chambers.

O'Brien waited for them to be seated around his desk. "That's a reporter out there, gentlemen. I'm not going to provide him with any unnecessary color to this story."

Tony started to say something, but O'Brien stopped him. "You oughta know better, Tony. This case will end up on the network news if we're not careful."

"That may be, Your Honor, but Mary Hairston has a right to have that child. The legal issues in this case are complicated. I need time to research the issues. So does Morley."

"That's right, Judge," Clarke said. "Fact, I had no idea what I was gettin' into. Reckon you might find someone else to handle this case? I'm a little out of my depth."

O'Brien slowly shook his head. "It's your baby, Clarke."

Tony laughed. "Good pun, Dave."

Shanklin started to say something, but O'Brien closed him off. "I'm going to postpone the case for a week, Ben. I know you object, but I also know that I haven't given Morley here much time to prepare."

"Will the injunction remain in effect?" Tony asked.

"It will," O'Brien said. "And I want all of you to remember two things. First, I don't find anything funny about this case. Let's can the jokes. Second, it doesn't take any soothsayer to know that the courtroom will be filled with the press next week. And I'll have to conduct that hearing in a public forum. So, all of you had best be prepared."

* * *

It took Anna two hours to drive from Milbrook to Roanoke, just as it took two hours to drive from Milbrook to Charleston. The drive into Virginia, though, was a pleasure. In spite of the snow flurries the night before, the morning had dawned chilly but sunny. Forecasters predicted that the temperature would rebound to the fifties in Milbrook. In Roanoke, ninety miles southeast of Milbrook, they promised temperatures in the sixties. It amazed Anna how much difference a few thousand feet of altitude could make.

She arrived in Roanoke at 10:30 and stopped for a brunch at the restaurant of a Holiday Inn. After she had ordered, she asked the waitress if she would bring a phone book. She found only one clinic listed in the yellow pages. It was a place to start, and, if there were other clinics, then perhaps the staff at the first would be familiar with them. Anna had accompanied Whit to his office and collected a mug shot of Lewis Luther. She carried it in her purse.

According to the waitress, the clinic's address wasn't far from the Holiday Inn. Anna wouldn't have to deal with the clutter of the main downtown area. By 11:30, she was sitting in the clinic's lobby, waiting to be ushered in to the office of the clinic administrator. Within a few moments, a tall and stately woman, looking to be in her fifties, came out to greet Anna.

"I'm Jane Rich." She offered Anna her hand.

Anna introduced herself and said, "I'm here to inquire about a woman from West Virginia who may have come down here for your services."

The woman's smile turned to a frown. "I'm sure you understand that we can't release medical information—"

"I've heard that already. This is very important. If you would just let me explain . . ."

Anna fully expected to be turned away. Instead, the woman smiled. "Come into my office. We'll talk."

She was led into the rear of the clinic and a small but brightly decorated office. The administrator poured a cup of coffee for Anna. "I'm certain you can understand the reason behind our policy," she said as she gave Anna the coffee.

"But the woman I want to ask about is in a coma," Anna said. "All I want to do is try to help her."

"A coma?"

"Can I explain?"

Jane Rich sat down behind her desk. "Yes, please."

She told the woman the entire story, and the clinic administrator listened with almost passionate interest. When she was finished, the administrator was wiping away a tear.

"I'm moved, Ms. Tyree."

"Will you help?"

"If I can. We receive many referrals from West Virginia."

Tom Bukowsky hadn't seen Will Binder lose his temper for many years. The last time was in Nam when one of Binder's subordinates had lit a cigarette one dark night and drawn enemy fire. No one had been injured, but Will had browbeaten the young man until he cried. At that moment, Bukowsky was on the receiving end of Binder's fury; there was no danger, though, of the editor shedding any tears.

"Why in the hell didn't you consult me about that story on Mary Hairston?"

Bukowsky wasn't a young wet-nosed recruit. Furthermore, he believed that his news judgment had been sound. "I don't consult you on news decisions, Will."

"My wife read Jones's story this morning and cried. We didn't need to print that Mary Hairston's pregnant, for God's sakes."

"It's news, dammit. In fact, it's probably going to be national news if the hospital tries to keep her alive until the baby's born."

"That's nonsense," the publisher said.

"It's been done before."

"When?"

"I don't know yet, but Jones is researching it. I remember reading stories about it, though."

Binder rose from his desk and began to pace. "If he comes up with it, I wanna see it. Until then, as far as I'm concerned, Tom, we're through exploiting that poor woman's misery. It's finished, Tom. The murderer is dead."

The editor couldn't believe what he was hearing. "Jesus fucking Christ, Will. The real drama in this case is still to come. Murders happen all the time. This is much bigger than that. Look at the issue, for God's sakes. The hospital apparently wants to remove her from life support. The state's attorney is saying he might charge the hospital with murder if they do that. They're talking about keeping a woman in a coma for months to keep a fetus alive. It's a chance for award-winning journalism."

"It's sensationalism, Tom. Yellow journalism. The case on Mary Hairston is closed, goddammit."

"Will, think about it, man! Think what you're saying."

Will wheeled on his old friend. "Dammit, Tom. You don't have to live with my wife! She's been on my back for years, wanting a kid. She's too damned sensitive about these kinda things, but I have to live with her. I've told you how it's going to be."

The editor was silent for a moment. When he spoke, it was without emotion. "Do you think your wife won't hear or read any more about it if we stonewall it?"

"Back off, Tom!" Binder's face was livid. "I don't have

to justify a fucking thing to you. Maybe she will read about it somewhere else, or even see it on the national news, but at least I won't get the blame for it. I don't want to be a part of it, Tom. From now on, the *Journal* lets the woman live— or die—in peace.''

''The marine I served with in Nam wouldn't let a woman browbeat him.''

''That guy's long dead, Tom.''

Jane Rich studied the photos of Mary Hairston and Lewis Luther. ''I don't think either one of them has been in here. I might not have seen the man, but I interview every woman who comes in for a termination of pregnancy.''

''Every one of them?'' Anna asked.

''Every one of them. It's a part of our policy. If I'm unavailable, on a trip or something, we schedule accordingly.''

Anna sighed. ''Are there other clinics in Roanoke?''

''We're the only one. There were several others, but they've relocated or closed.''

Anna gathered up the photos. ''Well, I appreciate your kindness. It's been rather difficult. Most clinics in Charleston wouldn't even give me the time of day.''

Jane nodded. ''Everyone's so afraid of lawsuits. And, as you know, what we do ranks as one of the great emotional issues of our time. The pro-lifers are waging guerrilla warfare against us. Some of them would love to get their hands on the names of some of our clients. A few are no more than terrorists.''

''I know,'' Anna said.

The woman leaned across her desk. ''I might be able to help.''

Anna's eyes brightened. ''How?''

''It's possible that she visited clinics in Winston-Salem or

Greensboro or maybe even Charlotte. If you want me to make some inquiries with the directors of those facilities, I'd be more than willing to try. I know most of them, and I'm sure they would be candid with me once they knew the circumstances.''

"Would you really do that?"

"Of course. I think your cause is worthwhile, but it's possible she made an appointment and never showed. It happens very, very often. After all, it's rather obvious that she didn't go through with the procedure.''

"That's true," Anna said. "Maybe I'm just spitting in the wind.''

Jane Rich reached over to pat Anna's hand. "I'll make a few calls and be in touch with you.''

Vanessa found her sister sitting in the living room of the Andrews home. Her eyes were wet and reddened. The morning newspaper rested on the floor at her feet.

"Your Mary wasn't the saint you thought she was, little sister.''

"Shut up, Vanessa."

"I'm surprised she didn't tell you."

"She didn't tell you, either.''

"Wanna bet?" Vanessa purred.

"Did she? Did you know it?"

Vanessa winked at her sister. "You'll never know.''

Tams looked up. "Maybe she told me, too.''

"Yeah. Sure."

"The wake's tonight, Vanessa. You are going, aren't you?''

Vanessa went to the television and flipped it on. It was almost time for *General Hospital*. "I've got a date tonight.''

"Vanessa! Mary was your best friend.''

The screen popped into focus. "Hush, now. I wanna watch my soap."

Tams ran from the room, leaving Vanessa to watch her program. Her mind, though, wasn't on *General Hospital*. She had remained awake most of the night trying to devise some foolproof plan by which she could safely collect her fifty thousand dollars. There was no doubt in her mind that he would pay the money if he had it. If she reached the conclusion that he couldn't really raise that much, she'd settle for less—but no less than twenty-five thousand.

Vanessa was so absorbed in her thoughts that she didn't notice her mother walk into the living room. Mattie Andrews picked up the television's remote control and turned it off.

"Hey!" Vanessa cried.

Her mother sat down beside her. "Girl, you and I are gonna have a talk."

Vanessa grabbed for the control. "After my program."

"Now!"

"Oh, Mother!"

"What's got into you? Tams says you're not going to the funeral home tonight."

"I have a date."

"So, call it off."

"No way, Momma. I'll go to the funeral tomorrow. I always intended to go to the funeral. I was just ribbing Tams. She's such a baby."

"And you oughta be old enough to know better than to torment her about Mary. I'm surprised at you. I can remember when you and Mary were like two sisters."

Vanessa lowered her head. "I'm sorry about Mary, Momma. You know that."

Mattie Andrews shook her head. "Girl, I don't know anything anymore—not about you."

* * *

In spite of the snow's flirtation the night before, the afternoon had turned warm again, especially for Todd Branscom, who was mixing concrete for a small air conditioner pad at the construction site near the housing complex. The rest of the crew was working on the other side of the project. It was late afternoon, almost quitting time, thank God. Branscom had stripped his shirt after lunch, and his sweat was starting to smell. He was looking forward to a hot shower and a six-pack of ice-cold beer.

As he counted shovels of sand for the mix, he caught sight of the dog out of the corner of his eye. Since it was so late in the day, the animal didn't even merit a turn of his head. The neighborhood was alive with them, family pets and mangy strays. The construction crew spent a small part of each workday driving them off the construction site.

Todd started mixing the soupy liquid in the wheelbarrow. The gentle breeze, tinged with the coolness of the fall, dried some of the sweat on his back. He stood to give it more surface. It was then that he noticed the stink.

"Damn," he muttered, looking back toward the brush that ringed the sides of the site.

The dog, a black and white pet judging by the heavy collar around its neck, ripped and tore at something long and limp. Todd squinted at it. "What the hell you got?"

The animal lifted its head, and its dark eyes conveyed a message of defiance.

Todd moved closer. Whatever it was, its surface was covered with bits of leaves and dirt.

The dog growled.

"You little asshole." Todd picked up a shovel full of sand and slung it at the animal. It flinched, squinted its eyes, backed up, and ran off.

It left its meal in the weeds. Todd moved closer and used the shovel to prod the object of the dog's interest. The smell worsened. He worked the shovel underneath the strange-looking debris and lifted it closer. That's when he saw the web of blood vessels that laced its surface.

"What the fuck?"

Todd hadn't had much education, but whatever it was, it came from something dead—and something pretty damned big. He looked back over his shoulder to see where the rest of the crew were working. They were out of his line of sight. With the piece of meat cradled in the shovel, he took it around for them to see.

Once he was out of the side, the dog pushed its head back out of the brush. It carried more of the delicacy in its mouth, this time a piece almost twice as long as the piece confiscated by the workman. Seeing that the man was gone, it darted across the street to the yard of a small house, a good portion of Cindy Jackson's intestines trailing behind it.

FOURTEEN

"I'M PROUD OF YOU," Anna told Whit.

They were in his car and on their way to the Milbrook Funeral Home.

"I absolutely, positively dread this," he said. His left hand held the steering wheel. The fingers of his right hand fiddled with the collar of his shirt. "And this tie is too gawddamned tight. There's nothing more useless than a tie. What the hell does it do? It just hangs there like an impotent dick."

Anna laughed. "No one made you wear one. It was your choice. I think it's touching."

"Touching?"

"Beneath that tough exterior beats the heart of a man who cares a great deal for his daughter."

Whit offered no response.

"Does Tony think Luther's the killer?"

Whit gave up on the tie and concentrated on his driving. "You know, he really hasn't said. I would take that to mean that he thinks Luther's the guilty party."

"How about you?"

"I'm undecided—no more certain of anything than I was last night."

"Have you thought about what Tams said?"

Whit's hand returned to the knot of his tie. He unloosened it. "The hell with this."

"Answer me," Anna said.

"People kill people they love all the time, Anna. I have my doubts that Lewis Luther's the culprit, but it's not because of what Tams said. It probably doesn't matter."

They had reached the funeral home. Tressa's car was one of the few in the lot. Whit pulled beside the Toyota.

"Why do you say it doesn't matter?" Anna asked.

"Police close cases all the time on flimsier evidence. Hell, sometimes the arrest of one serial killer will close murder cases from one coast to the other."

Whit started to exit the vehicle, but Anna stopped him. "What's that got to do with this case?"

"I don't know. I'm just nervous, I guess. Come on, let's get this over with."

She didn't offer to move. "Just a minute, fella. You aren't going to run in, say hi, and dart out again, are you?"

Whit made a face. "I'll stay as long as I can stand it. If you wanna stay longer, I'm sure Tressa will give you a ride home."

Anna had told Whit about the offer to help that came from the administrator of the Roanoke clinic. He hadn't been encouraged, but by then his mood had slipped back into a kind of quiet funk.

"Try to be decent," Anna said to him as they entered the mortuary.

"These places smell like death."

"Those are flowers."

"Dead ones," Whit said.

The lobby was empty, but the name of Jennifer Hairston decorated a small black sign standing in front of an open door. Anna guided Whit toward the door. It opened into a medium-size room. The casket, surrounded by several baskets of flowers, filled the far end of the room. Tressa and Tams stood at the casket talking with several elderly black women.

Anna leaned close to Whit as they approached the casket. "You should be proud of her."

"I am."

Tressa rushed to her father. "Daddy, I'm glad you came."

Whit hugged his daughter. She then hugged Anna. "I bet you made him come."

Anna smiled. "No, I didn't. I didn't make him wear that tie, either."

Whit had an arm around Tams. She started to lead him toward the closed casket. He balked. Anna and Tressa fell in behind them and pushed him forward. The two black women moved to the visitors' register, signed it, and left the room.

Tams stepped right to the casket. She reached out and touched the blanket of yellow roses that covered the metal coffin. Whit, his face slack with discomfort, took a place beside her.

"I wanted to see her," Tams said, "but the funeral man said that he couldn't do that."

"It's for the best," Whit said.

Tams slipped her hand in his. "It's a beautiful casket, isn't it?"

The young girl was right. The surface was burnished copper, and rich woodgrain covered the sides. The handles were simple but stylish.

"Did you pick it out?" Whit asked.

"Tressa and I did. We both liked it. We also picked out a dress for Jenny. She was so pretty."

Anna was standing behind Whit. She put a hand on his shoulder and felt him slump a little.

"I just wanted to say good-bye," Tams said. Tears were flowing from both eyes.

"I'm sure Jenny knows you're here," Anna said.

Whit turned away. He swiped at a lonely tear on his own cheek. He couldn't help but think how he would feel if it were Tressa inside that sterile metal tube.

A group of three people came into the room. Tams recovered quickly. She went to greet them and brought them by Whit and Anna. They were employees who worked at the *Journal.* Anna nodded to them as Tams chatted.

"This is barbaric," Whit said. "Visitation tonight, and a funeral tomorrow. One would be enough."

"Like I told you, it purges the grief," Anna said.

"Or magnifies it."

Several other people came into the room, still more *Journal* employees. Tressa slipped over to Anna and her father. "I'm glad people are coming. Tams was afraid no one would show up."

Anna was staring at a tall, striking blonde who had just stepped in the door. She was accompanied by Jack Arnold, the *Journal* business manager. "That can't be that foppish bastard's wife," Anna said to Whit.

"If it is, I'm damned impressed."

Anna pinched him.

"They're coming straight over here," Anna said.

Whit watched them approach. The man looked the same as he had when Whit had talked with him. He wore a three-piece pinstripe, the vest of which was stretched like a drumhead over his gut. In the subdued light of the mortuary, his stained skin took on a jaundiced appearance. The top of his bald head gleamed with the ever-present sweat.

The woman, on the other hand, belonged on the big screen. Her pale blond hair appeared totally natural. Not one dark root to be seen. Her skin was fair but not so white that it appeared washed out. As she neared him, he saw her dark green eyes.

"You're Miss Tyree?" she asked.

Anna ignored Jack Arnold. "Yes, I'm Anna Tyree."

"I'm Katherine Binder."

Anna and Whit traded looks of startled surprise.

The woman was still talking. "Will couldn't make it tonight, but Mr. Arnold kindly agreed to bring me by so we might pay our respects."

"That's very kind," Anna said.

"Frankly, Miss Tyree, I was appalled by the coverage that the *Journal* saw fit to publish this morning. I understand you're a reporter—"

"But that wasn't my story," Anna said, glaring at Jack Arnold.

"I'm well aware of that," the wife of the publisher said. "Perhaps it should have been. I suspect the entire matter would have been handled with more taste. I don't visit the newspaper very often, but I have wanted to meet you. I think you're one of the best reporters William has."

"An opinion not shared by everyone," Anna said.

Jack Arnold rolled his eyes and managed then to slip away from the two women.

"Are those the two young ladies that William told me about?"

Anna called Tams and Tressa to her and introduced them to Mrs. Binder.

"Call me Kathy," the woman said.

"I was wanting to thank Mr. Binder for what he did," Tams said.

"I'll tell him, but it was something we both wanted to do."

Anna turned to Whit. "Mrs. Binder, this is Whit Pynchon. He's investigating the case." She held her breath.

"I thought the case was solved," Kathy Binder said as she shook Whit's hand.

"So it seems," Whit said.

The woman was quick. She read the uncertainty in Whit's face. "Do I detect some doubt on your part?"

"Without a confession or a jury verdict, I always have a doubt."

"A reasonable one?" the publisher's wife asked.

Whit just shrugged. "If you will excuse me, Anna, I'm going to slip outside for a smoke."

Kathy Binder wagged a finger at him. "That's a nasty habit—"

Anna quickly steered the woman out of Whit's path. "He tends to become violent in defense of his right to smoke."

The two women moved off to a corner to chat. Whit slipped from the room. There were ashtrays on tables in the lobby. Whit pulled out a cigarette and settled into one of the chairs.

Just as he started to light it, Tony Danton walked into the funeral. "Damn, I never thought I'd see you here. I was just at your place."

"What's up?"

"Another murder."

Whit sighed and lit the cigarette. "When it rains, it pours, Tony."

"We're not sure yet, but this one might be related to this case."

Whit's interest was piqued. "Who is it?"

"A young black woman named Cynthia Jackson. She apparently worked with the Hairston woman at the paper."

"Then it's got to be related," Whit said.

"Maybe . . . maybe not. She walked to a convenience store last night around midnight. She never made it back home. The city boys found her body about an hour ago in a wooded section near the southside housing project."

"What prompted them to look?"

"A goddamn dog—a family pet—drug her guts into a house nearby."

Whit grimaced.

"She's pretty badly mutilated. It took better than an hour to come up with her identity."

Whit stood. "I'll drive over there. Will you see that Anna gets home?"

"I'm going with you."

Whit went in to find Anna. She was still talking with the wife of the publisher. Jack Arnold, appearing to be suffering from crotch itch from the look on his face, stood behind his boss's wife.

Whit ignored him. "Something's come up, Anna. I have to go."

"Is it the Hairston matter?" she asked.

Whit smiled. "Ask me no questions—can you get a lift home?"

Mrs. Binder jumped into the conversation. "We'd be happy to drop her off."

Whit looked to Arnold for confirmation.

The man was nodding.

Whit started to turn.

"Does it have anything to do with your case?" Katherine Binder asked.

Whit glanced at Anna, who was bracing for what she anticipated to be a sarcastic, probably embarrassing reply.

"I really don't know," Whit said.

Anna sagged with relief as he walked away.

Vanessa had planned to have the Andrews house all to herself that night. She expected her mother to go with Tams to the funeral home. Right after supper, though, her mother had gotten one of her headaches. So much for being alone. At that moment, her mother was lying on the bed in her room, a cool washrag draped over her eyes.

There was a phone by her mother's bed. Mattie Andrews wasn't likely to pick it up, but Vanessa didn't want to take the chance. She went to the door of her mother's room and eased it open.

"Feeling any better, Momma?"

Her mother slipped the washrag from her face. "Not a bit, Vanessa. Would you freshen this for me?" She offered the washrag.

"Sure."

Vanessa moved to the bed. The phone rested on a nightstand beside. She reached out for the washrag and fumbled with it. It fell to the floor.

"I swear," Vanessa said, bending down to retrieve the damp cloth. In the process, she quickly unhooked the modular phone plug from the wall jack.

"Be back in a sec, Momma."

She went to the bathroom, soaked the rag in cold water, and returned it to her mother. "I'm going down and watch *The Cosby Show*. You need anything, you call me."

Mrs. Andrews eyed her daughter. "You wantin' something, child?"

"Oh, Momma!"

"I'm just not used to all this kind treatment."

Downstairs, Vanessa went to the wall phone in the kitchen. She dialed the number. It rang a dozen times. Vanessa was ready to slam the phone down when a winded voice answered.

"What took you so long?" Vanessa demanded to know.

"Who is this?"

"We talked last night."

There was a loud gasp, then utter silence on the other end.

"You gonna get me the money?" Vanessa asked. She intentionally made her voice sound illiterate.

"I don't think I can raise that much."

"Who you jiving, mister?"

"Listen, can't we talk about this or something? You've got this all wrong." There was utter desperation in his voice.

"Sure, I do, hon. Sure, I do. Lookee here, it's gonna cost you fifty grand to keep this mouth hushed. I'm gonna call you tomorrow at four P.M. at a phone booth on the parking lot downtown. Know where I mean?"

"I think so."

"You'd best know!"

"Yeah, I know."

"Okay, you be there at the booth at four."

"Why can't we meet and talk—"

"Look, fool, you best have fifty grand by tomorrow. I'll tell you tomorrow where to leave the money."

"How do I know that'll be the end of it?"

Vanessa laughed. She loved the sense of power she felt. "Did I say it was gonna be the end of it? You played, buster; now you gotta pay. Think of it as child support."

The moon hadn't come up yet, and the hand-held flashlights carried by the Milbrook officer did little to push back the darkness in the bramble-clogged woods. Whit and Tony stood at the edge of the shallow grave.

"How the hell did they find it?" Whit asked of Chief Tom Wampler.

"Good police work," the chief snapped.

Whit belly laughed.

Tony stepped in to forestall another confrontation between the two men. "From what I gather, they just followed the trail of blood and guts. One of the chief's men here stepped into the hole and fell. She was just covered with leaves. Besides, it was daylight then."

Wampler changed the subject. "We might as well call off the search. I think we've found as much of her as we're gonna."

The body of Cindy Jackson occupied a black plastic bag that had already been carried back to an ambulance waiting on the streets. The bits of her that had been found near the murder scene had been slipped into the bag with her.

"The medical examiner isn't going to like it if something turns up missing," Whit said.

"Christ a'mighty!" Wampler said. "God knows how much the friggin' dogs have eaten."

"By the way," Whit said, "where's Burton? I can't say I miss his charming presence, but I'm surprised he's not here."

"We tried to reach him, but, with the Hairston thing wrapped up, he took a few days off. That okay with you, Pynchon?"

Whit chuckled. "Hell, he can retire for all I care. 'Fact, I wish—"

Tony drowned out Whit's comment. "Maybe the Hairston case isn't wrapped up, not after this."

"Luther coulda killed her—"

"No fucking way!" Whit interjected. "No goddamn fuckin' way. We got a witness that saw her alive long after Burton fried Luther."

"Oh, yeah," Wampler said. "That's right. Well, there's still nothing to tie her killin' to the Hairston thing. She just picked a bad time to go for a stroll."

Tony shook his head. "That's putting it mildly. Listen, Chief, go back and tell those ambulance drivers to take her straight to Charleston tonight. I'll call the State Medical Examiner to let him know it's on the way. I want a report quick, especially regarding the time and cause of her death."

"So, I can call off the search?"

"For tonight," Tony said. "But I want your boys back at first light. I don't want any more of Cynthia Jackson's insides carried into the house of some unsuspecting citizen."

"One more thing," Whit said as the chief turned to go deliver the message. "You might tell Burton that this is my case, too. I don't want him sticking his nose into it."

Wampler brandished his flashlight at Whit. "You best remember he pulled your goddamn nuts outa the fire on your Hairston thing."

"I wonder," Whit said as the chief vanished into the forest darkness.

Cal Burton ordered another round for the sparse clientele in the small bar.

The bartender passed out the drinks and brought Cal the double. "You celebrating something, Cal?"

The Milbrook detective raised his glass. "Fucking right, Bert."

"Easy, Cal. Not so loud. There's a woman or two in here."

Cal popped his hand over his mouth. "Oops! Sorry, Bert. Don't wanna run off any of your whores."

Bert sighed. If you operated a bar in the corporate limits of Milbrook, you put up with Det. Lt. Cal Burton. "Come on, Cal. Just don't be so loud, man."

"Okay . . . okay. Hey, I am celebrating something. Have a drink with me."

Bert kept a bottle for just such times. It contained diluted Coke. "Lemme get some of my brand," he said.

"Get it, man."

Bert poured himself a drink from the unlabeled bottle. "What are we drinking to?"

"To me," Cal shouted. He turned to the small crowd. "Drink to me, people."

Everyone did, including Cal. He emptied his glass.

"Gimme some of your brand, Bert."

The bartender slid the bottle down under the counter. "Here, lemme give you yours. Ain't healthy to mix bourbon and brandy. That's what I drink, Cal."

"So, I wanna taste your brandy."

"Naw. Stick to your bourbon. It's on the house."

Cal slammed a fist down on the bar. "I said I wanna taste your brand. Whatsa matter? I'm not good enough to drink your fuckin' special stock."

Bert pulled the bottle from under the counter and filled Cal's glass.

"Drink with me," the cop commanded.

"Sure, Cal."

The bartender filled his own glass.

"To me, Bert. Nobody fucks with me."

Cal lifted the glass to his lips. Bert waited. The amber liquid vanished, and a surprised smile formed on the cop's face.

"Pussy," Cal whispered.

Bert smiled. "I don't drink booze, Cal. That's what I like—Coke and water."

The cop started to laugh. "I just wanted ya to know, Bert.

Nobody fucks with Cal. Not even you. Set 'em up again. All these are on the house.''

Mary Hairston had been moved from the critical care unit that morning to a telemetry area of the hospital where her heartbeat could be monitored by radio signals. It was standard operating procedure in cases where the patient was expected to be maintained for a long period of time on life support. There was no reason for the patient to continue to occupy one of the precious-few critical care beds.

At midnight the halls of the hospital were usually silent. Not so that night. Just down the hall from the nurses' station the voice of an aging male patient bellowed out obscenities.

The two nurses at the station suppressed their rage. "The old bastard'll work himself loose in a few minutes," one nurse said to the other.

"Think I'd get caught if I slipped him a shot of Thorazine?" the other asked.

"With our luck, he'd die."

"Probably, but I don't think I can stand a whole shift of that. Why the hell didn't they put him in psychiatric?"

The elder nurse pointed to the monitor. "He's got a bad ticker."

"Let's go scare him, then."

"Shame on you."

A call button sounded. It was from a room down the hall. One of the nurses pressed a button that opened an intercom into the room. "Can I help you?"

"I can't sleep with all that shouting," a woman's voice said.

"I'm sorry, ma'am. I'll be glad to come close your door."

"Can't you shut him up?"

"We've tried."

"Do you know what I'm paying—?"

The nurse flipped off the speaker. "Jesus!"

It wasn't the first complaint.

The two nurses were busy recording patient charges on the appropriate charts. Neither of them saw a door open down the hall. It led to a seldom-used staircase down to the first floor. A shadowy figure hurried through the door and down the hall where it entered a men's bathroom across the hall from the old man's room.

The crazed shouting continued.

"I better go check on his restraints," one of the nurses was saying.

The other was watching his monitor. "Look at that. He's hollering and pulling on those restraints, and his heart rate's still under a hundred. There's nothing wrong with him."

"Tell that to the doctor."

"This is terrible."

"When I get back, you can take your break."

The nurse entered and found him wrestling with the cloth restraints. He reeked of body filth. The nurse took a deep breath before bending over him.

"Now, Mr. Billings, you're just going to have to relax."

"Fuck you! I wanna go home! You got no right tying me down like this. I ain't no criminal!"

The nurse ignored him and cinched the cloth restraints a little tighter.

"You're a goddamned cold-assed whore!"

The nurse leaned down with her lips close to his ear. "Screw you!"

And she was gone.

The figure inside the men's bathroom cracked the door. He watched as one nurse went on a break, leaving the other alone on the floor. He slipped out of the bathroom and into the room of the old man.

"Who are you?"

The figure wore a wide-brimmed hat that concealed his face. Black fatigues, covered by a black raincoat, gave him the appearance of death, which he was. He put a finger to his lip and started to unloosen the man's restraints. The old man smiled.

A few seconds later, the old man rushed from his room and ran right by the nurses' station. His hospital gown came off, flapping over his head and then settling to the floor in his wake.

"Hey," cried the lone nurse. She saw the thin buttocks vanish around the corner. She placed a quick call to the snack bar to summon an orderly and then went after the naked escapee.

The trespasser hurried into Mary Hairston's room. He stood over her bed and studied her passive face. The swelling was still there around her eyes. He reached down and lifted her cool hand. She didn't so much as twitch. He leaned down and placed his lips near her ear.

"I'm sorry, but it's got to remain our secret—no matter how many must die."

He heard voices.

Johnny Stamper had taken the desperate call from the nurse in telemetry. The other orderlies gathered in the snack bar had kidded him about his luck, and he'd vowed to get even. Then he'd gulped his soft drink and hurried to the service elevator. It was closer to the snack bar than the lobby elevators.

When he pushed the button, it opened immediately. The ride upward took just a few seconds. When the door opened this time, Johnny found himself facing a man wearing a black hat and an overcoat.

''Who the hell are you?''

It was the last thing Johnny ever said. The last thing he saw was the look of panicked surprise on the man's face. Then, the edge of the man's hand exploded against his Adam's apple.

The young orderly crumpled to the floor of the elevator, his last gasps of breath whistling through the crushed piping of his throat.

FIFTEEN

WHIT FOUND TONY in the second-floor waiting room. He and a city officer were interviewing a nurse.

"What happened?" Whit asked.

The prosecutor left the cop with the nurse. "Somebody tried to kill Mary Hairston. On the way out, the assailant added one more to the list—a hospital orderly."

"How?" Whit asked, too stunned by the ever-increasing death toll to ask anything more pertinent.

"The hospital pathologist's examining his body now."

The one A.M. phone call to Whit had come from the Milbrook PD. There had been no explanation—simply an urgent message from Tony Danton. Whit was to come at once to the second floor of the hospital. He'd hauled his tired body from bed and complied.

"Did he get into the critical care unit?" Whit asked. That seemed incredible. Even family had a hard time getting a clearance to enter the CCU.

"The hospital moved her out of CCU this morning—uh, I mean, yesterday morning."

"You're kidding me?"

"Nope. The administrator says it's standard procedure in cases like hers. They kept her on the respirator, though."

Whit shook his head. "Wait a minute, Tony. That means

the killer had to know it. Hell, we didn't even know it. That should narrow the field.''

"That's what I thought. Apparently the hospital's been besieged by calls from reporters. Did you watch the news tonight on television?''

"No, why?''

"It was on television—that she was no longer in the critical care unit.''

Whit threw up his hands. "The damned press again.''

"Anyway, whoever it was created a diversion. They had an old man here who was crazy as a bedbug. The hospital had him restrained in a room not far from Mary Hairston's. Our would-be killer let him loose. While they were trying to round him up, the culprit slipped into the room and pulled a tube loose from the respirator. It was probably supposed to look like an accident. The orderly was found in the elevator. Apparently he must have run right into the killer.''

"But Mary Hairston didn't die?''

"Not quite. As soon as her heartbeat dropped to a certain level, an alarm sounded on a monitor. A nurse heard it and managed to get into the room soon enough to save her. I'm told, though, that it might have deprived the fetus of oxygen long enough to have done some damage to it.''

Whit ran his hands through his hair. "Jesus Christ.''

Tony looked over his shoulder and lowered his voice. "I don't believe a damn word of it. I think they're just wanting an excuse to pull the plug. I get the impression that the administrator wasn't a damned bit pleased with the nurse who reinserted the ventilator tube.''

"Where's the old man? He had to get a look at our man.''

Whit could see from Tony's face that the news in that regard wasn't good, either. "They took him to CCU. It seems he had some kind of heart attack. It's not serious, but they won't let us talk to him."

"The hell with them," Whit said. "I'll go talk to him."

Tony stopped Whit. "If the guy dies after you do that, you might get your ass sued off."

"Fuck it," Whit said. "I'm tired of getting jacked around on this case."

"Let's wait, Whit. From what I'm told, the old man's so crazy that it's not worth the risk."

"So, what do we do? Why did you bother to wake me up if there's nothing to do?"

"Go down to the ER entrance. It's the only way to enter the hospital this time of night. Maybe someone saw something."

Whit sighed. "Whatever you say, Tony. You do know what this means, don't you?"

"What's that?"

"Luther's not the killer."

"Yeah. So it appears."

"It also means that asshole Burton caused the death of an innocent man."

Tony nodded his agreement to that conclusion, too. "I can't figure why anyone would want to kill Mary Hairston. What the hell can she do to hurt anyone?"

"Maybe it's the baby he's worried about," Whit said. "Think about it. I'll go down and talk to the people at the emergency room entrance."

A skeleton clerical crew occupied a small suite of offices near the emergency room entrance. The emergency room itself was located off the side of the door. If its staff weren't out in the lobby, they would have no way of seeing people who entered or left the hospital.

So Whit concentrated on the three women in the admissions area. All three had come to work at eleven P.M. That was the time the shift changed.

"There's all kinds of people in and out that door between ten-thirty and eleven-thirty," the supervisor of the admissions crew explained. "Besides, every door in the hospital is open until nine P.M. Someone could have come in before then and just hung around. Even after nine, you can go out any door you like."

"Great security," Whit had said.

He went into the emergency room itself. It had been a busy night since eleven P.M. They had all heard about the incident on the second floor and the sudden death of Orderly Stamper, but no one had noticed anything out of the ordinary.

Whit met Tony coming off the elevator. "It was a waste of time."

"I'll have a guard on her door from now on," Tony said, as the two men left the hospital.

"I've got one other idea. I'm gonna pay a visit to a lawyer."

"A lawyer?"

"Cullen Brown. Let's see what he's up to at two-thirty in the morning."

"Be my guest," Tony said. "By the way, the orderly's windpipe was crushed, apparently by a blow."

"One blow?"

Tony shrugged. "I don't know. He's on his way up to the medical examiner, too. It's gonna be a busy night there."

The lawyer was at his door almost at once. The curtain parted as Cullen Brown peered out to see who was coming to call at 2:42 A.M. The front porch light came on, and the front door swung open.

"What the hell do you want at this hour?" he demanded of Whit.

Whit looked the man over. His long coal-black hair was mussed. The pajamas he wore were crumpled.

"I just wondered if you had been home all night?"

Brown's eyes flamed. "Get the hell out of here."

"Someone made an attempt on Mary Hairston's life tonight. Whoever it was killed a hospital employee in the process."

Cullen Brown's anger evaporated. "At the hospital?"

"They disconnected her from the life support system."

Brown opened the screen door for Whit. "And you think it was me?"

Whit stepped into the small house. "I thought maybe I'd better check."

"Do you want to go check my bed? It's probably still warm, and I don't think I've had a wet dream. Not yet anyway. I'm all alone, so I don't have anyone who can alibi for me."

Whit looked back out the door at Brown's car. It was parked in the short driveway. "I'd rather check under the hood of your car to see if it's still warm."

"I swear to God," Brown said.

"Do I have your consent?"

Brown cast a suspicious eye at the investigator. "I'm surprised you haven't checked it already."

"I'm a little rusty on my search and seizure, Counselor, so I didn't take the chance. I wouldn't want to mess all over your rights."

Brown ran a hand through his hair. The effort gave it some sense of order. "I guess you know that you haven't the slightest probable cause for a search warrant."

Whit nodded. "Yeah, I know that. I thought maybe you'd like to be eliminated as a suspect."

Brown managed a weary laugh. "Come on, Pynchon. Even if you find that motor block stone-cold, I'm still going to be a suspect. If you aren't thinking it already, you'll soon wonder if I used a taxi or if I walked. The hospital's not that far from here. Face it, Pynchon. You suffer from a bad case of nigger suspicion."

"It'd be easy enough to check out the taxis, Counselor. I was more interested in whether you own a bicycle or something of that sort."

Brown shook his head. "You're something else, Pynchon. Shit, go check the car. I need to go back to bed. I have to be in court first thing in the morning."

"So, you consent to a search?"

"Hell, yes. You want it in writing?"

Whit pulled a white sheet of paper from his jacket. "As a matter of fact, I do. In case you haven't seen one of these, it's a 'consent to search' form.

For an instant, Whit thought that Brown was going to attack. His body went rigid. His jaws bulged as he clenched them.

"Danton's going to hear about this," the lawyer said through his clamped teeth.

"First thing in the morning, friend. When I left him a few minutes ago, I promised him a report."

The lawyer snatched the form from Whit's hand.

"Before you sign that, Counselor, I want to advise you of one thing. If that engine block is warm, I'm going to come back in here and place you under arrest for suspicion of attempted murder. Then I'm going to take you to the courthouse and try to arrange a lineup."

"A lineup? You have a witness?"

"Of sorts." It wasn't entirely a lie. There was the old man in the hospital CCU. Besides, under present court rulings, there was nothing wrong with obtaining a confession by trickery or deception.

Cullen Brown marched over to a large desk in what appeared to have been a dining room at some point in the house's past. It had been converted into a home office. In his rage, he knocked over a cup filled with pens and pencils.

"Dammit to hell," he mumbled, retrieving one from the floor. With a flourish he signed his name on the form.

He paused, however, before he returned it to Whit. "Now I have a cautionary word for you, Pynchon. You go ahead and check under the hood of that car. You'll find the engine cold. After that, if you so much as look at me again, I'll file one hell of a lawsuit alleging police harassment. I might not win, but I can guarantee you that I'll keep you in court as much as I can."

He handed Whit the form. "Go ahead and search the garage, too. The door's unlocked. You won't find any bicycles or scooters."

"I'd planned to," Whit said as he moved toward the front door. He stopped before he went out. "For what it might be worth to you, Counselor, I hope that engine's cold. I'd bet you're a pretty decent lawyer. Too bad you didn't feel like you could represent Mary Hairston. She needs somebody with your passion."

"Spare me your compliments, Pynchon."

The engine in Cullen Brown's car was cold. Whit found no bicycles in or around the garage. As soon as he closed the door on his own car, the lights in Cullen Brown's house flicked off.

Vanna White must have been poured into the red low-cut

dress she was wearing on that morning's *Wheel of Fortune*. Next to *General Hospital*, it was Vanessa's favorite daytime show. It's what she wanted to do with the money she was about to collect. With fifty thousand dollars, she could go to Hollywood and take poise and acting classes. Vanessa knew her body was just as good as Vanna's. Sometimes, as she lay in bed waiting on sleep, she imagined herself in a white, slinky dress that contrasted with her deep-bronze skin. Her long well-manicured fingernails flipped the dream letters over with much more class than did Vanna.

The phone rang. Vanessa kept her seat. She heard her mother answer it and start talking. Her complete attention returned to *Wheel of Fortune*.

A few minutes later her mother came into the living room. ''I got more bad news, hon.''

Vanessa kept her eyes on the TV. ''What this time?''

''Cindy's dead.''

That turned Vanessa's head. ''Cindy? Cindy Jackson?''

''That was her stepmother that called. Cindy must have gone for a walk to the store late last night. She got mugged or something.''

''You're kidding?''

''I don't joke about death, child.''

''No, I mean about walking to the store. I always told Cindy that her appetite was gonna kill her.''

''Vanessa! You shame me, girl!'' There were tears in Mattie Andrews's eyes.

''I didn't mean nothing by it, Momma.''

''You best get that dress of yours down here so I can wash it,'' her mother commanded.

Vanessa turned. ''What dress?''

''That nice black dress. That's what you're gonna wear to Jenny's funeral, isn't it?''

"I forgot about it."

Mrs. Andrews put her hands on her hips. "Shame on you, young lady."

"I don't feel too good today, Momma. I think I'm gonna stay home. It's about my time of the month." At that moment, someone on *Wheel of Fortune* emitted a shriek of joy. Vanessa jerked back around to see a young, fat girl hugging Pat Sajak.

Her mother's hand rapped the back of her head.

"Momma!"

"You get off your lazy ass and get upstairs and get that dress so I can wash it! Now! You're taking me to that funeral."

Vanessa was on her feet, backing away, her hand on her head. "Momma! You hit me!"

"I'm gonna do worse than that."

Vanessa's pride was harmed more than her head. "You are not! I'm not going to that funeral."

Mattie Andrews aimed a stern finger at her daughter.

"That's okay by me, child, but I want the keys to my car. You won't be using it anymore."

"Come on, Momma—"

"Don't 'come on' me. Hand 'em over! Now!"

"They're upstairs."

"Then march right up there and get 'em."

Vanessa was trembling with rage. "This ain't fair!"

"It's just the start, girl. From now on, you're gonna pay me room and board. Fifty dollars a week—"

"I'm taking care of you, Momma!"

"Pardon my French, but like hell you are! You're leechin' off me, girl. I don't need your kind of taking care of. If you don't like the rent, then you can just hustle your lazy behind outa my house. Me and Tams don't need you."

Vanessa's eyes narrowed. "I just might do that."

"Fine, girl. Don't let the door smack you in the butt on your way out. Now, get up there and get me those keys. I mean it."

Vanessa pouted. "Okay. I'll go to the funeral."

"No way, child. It's gonna take more'n that. It's time you faced up to a few things."

"What do you want outa me, Momma?"

Mattie Andrews went to the television and turned it off. "That's the first thing I want. A little peace and quiet. That darned thing blares all day long. I think that's what gave me a headache yesterday."

She then went to the couch and sat down. Vanessa glared down at her.

"Come Monday morning, Vanessa, I want you out looking for a job. Ain't no reason why you can't work."

Vanessa's mind was working fast and furious. "Okay, Momma, if you say so."

"I mean it, girl!"

"I know, Momma. I'll do it. Monday morning."

"And you're gonna have to start taking care of a few of the chores in this house."

"Okay, Momma."

Mrs. Andrews cocked her head at her daughter. "Vanessa, you're full of it. You're standing there lying through your teeth."

"No, I'm not."

Her mother stood. "We'll see what we see. Now, get up there and fetch that dress."

"Right now, Momma."

Once she was out of her mother's hearing, she started mumbling. "You'll be sorry. I'm gonna be gone tomorrow . . . maybe even tonight. You'll be sorry."

"What's that you're saying?" her mother shouted.

"Nothing, Momma."

"They're going to can you if you don't start doing some work," Whit said to Anna. They were in his car on the way to Milbrook High School. The morning had dawned under a gunmetal overcast, but temperatures were on the rebound. The weather report called for a clearing trend after lunch—just in time for Jenny's funeral, Anna hoped.

"I took a few days off. The publisher wanted me to oversee the arrangements for Jenny."

"Which Tressa and Tams seem to have handled rather well—so far as funerals go."

They had just left the hospital. Mary Hairston's condition was listed as unchanged. According to the physician attending her, the brief interruption in the life support appeared to have caused no serious damage. Dr. Fragliano, the obstetrician, wouldn't venture any opinion on the welfare of the unborn child she was carrying.

"We plan to perform some tests the first of the week," he had said. "That should provide some indication."

Even Anna had noticed his lack of enthusiasm. "Do you think Mary Hairston would be better off someplace like Duke or the University of Virginia in Charlottesville?"

It was late morning, and the traffic on the main street of Milbrook was light. Most of the people in the town were at their jobs. Nonetheless, Whit drove at a leisurely pace. He was still fuzzy-headed from his lack of sleep.

"I doubt they would accept her case."

"I'd think it would be a medical challenge. Damn! I wish I were still on the story. I might be able to create some interest in her."

Whit chuckled. "According to Judge O'Brien, the hearing

next week will draw all the press attention anyone wants. He's downright gun-shy about it."

"But why? You'd think he would welcome something different."

"No way. O'Brien's on the verge of retirement. He's the type who prefers the wham-bam cases—the ones that don't aggravate his hemorrhoids."

He had told Anna about Cindy Jackson the night before, and to his surprise she had asked very few questions. The sudden escalation of violence seemed to have numbed her.

A traffic light caught Whit. Anna stared out the window at the empty storefronts along Main Street. Dust clouded their plate-glass windows. Finger-written messages decorated the dusty surfaces. Anna saw that a boy named Kenny, at the time he passed the window of a relocated hardware store, had loved Mary. It was one of the few messages that wasn't X-rated.

"I have a confession, Whit."

The light changed, and Whit eased through it. "What's that?"

"I'd love to leave this place. I have this abiding urge to pack up and go, just like that. I'm starting to have nothing but bad memories."

Whit glanced over at her. She wore a light blue sweater and jeans. A windbreaker was draped over the seat.

"Alone?" he asked.

Anna turned her face to him. She reached over and touched his thigh. "Of course not."

He pulled the car into the crowded parking lot of the high school. "Times have really changed, Anna. When I went to school, none of the kids had a car to bring to school."

"When you went to school, they rode horses," she quipped.

"Anna!"

She snickered. "I'm sorry. I forgot how sensitive you are about your age."

He found a narrow opening between two cars and started to work his own vehicle into the space. "I'm not sensitive about my age."

"Yeah, sure."

The attempt on Mary Hairston's life and the quick and efficient murder of the orderly had reopened the investigation. Whit was now more convinced than ever that the woman's pregnancy was the key to the case. He was equally convinced that Cindy Jackson had died at the hands of the same person. He had never really questioned Tamantha Andrews. That was the reason for a visit to the school. They both would see Tams later that day, but Whit wanted a chance to talk with her before the funeral.

The secretary at the school used the public address system to summon Tams to the office. When the young girl arrived, her eyes were openly concerned.

"Has something happened to Mary?" Tams asked as soon as she saw Whit and Anna together.

Anna put an arm around her shoulder. "No. There are just some questions we need to ask."

The secretary offered them the use of a conference room in the school's administrative office area. It was a sparsely furnished room, the walls of which were covered with artwork done by present and former students.

The three of them sat down around a small circular table.

Whit inched close to the teenage girl. "Tams, I need to know some things. I don't know why I didn't think of asking you sooner since you were—are—so close to Mary." It was difficult for him to think of her as still alive.

"Okay."

"Did Mary ever go out of town for a day?"

"Or even a few days?" Anna added.

Tams pondered the question. "Yes, two days."

"She was gone two days?" Whit asked.

"No, I mean I sat with Jenny after school on two days, two separate days. Lemme think. It was last month, September."

"I knew it," Anna said.

Whit shushed her and then said to Tams, "I want you to think very hard. Do you remember what those days were?"

"Not right off."

"Don't be so quick to answer," Anna advised. "Think about it."

"All I can remember is that they were about a week apart. Mary said she was going out of town to do some shopping. She didn't get back home till very late on both days."

"Who went with her?"

"She didn't say."

"But someone did go with her?" Anna asked.

Tams's pretty, smooth skin knitted into a baffled frown. "I don't know. She didn't say. I guess I assumed someone did."

"Do you know who it might have been?" Whit asked.

"Maybe my sister. I know it wasn't poor Cindy. Mary liked Cindy, but she got on her nerves."

"Your sister?" Anna asked. "You mean Vanessa."

"Uh huh."

"Why do you say that?" Anna asked. "I know they were good friends at one time, but I got the impression they weren't too close now."

"I really don't know that she did go, but they were still good friends. You sure wouldn't know it now—not the way Vanessa's been acting."

"But you didn't know if Mrs. Hairston was seeing anyone?" This time the question came from Whit.

Tams shook her head.

"Maybe she mentioned a man's name. Think hard," Anna urged.

"I don't think she was. She always talked about that lawyer and Luther. If she was dating somebody else, she musta been keeping it quiet. I guess I know why now."

Anna took Tams's hand. "Don't think harshly of her, Tams. Those things happen to very good people."

"I know that. I just wish she would have told me."

Although most of Anna's day-to-day wardrobe was at Whit's, some of the more esoteric garments remained at Anna's town house. Whit dropped Anna off there so she could start dressing for the funeral.

Her phone was ringing as she stepped through the door. She rushed to answer it.

"Is this Anna Tyree?" The voice belonged to a woman.

"Yes, it is."

"Anna, this is Jane Rich at the Roanoke Women's Center."

"Oh, hi, Jane."

"I might have something for you."

"Seriously?" Anna's breath stopped.

"I called several clinics, including one in Charlotte, North Carolina. The director there remembers a patient meeting the description of the woman you were asking about."

"When was this?"

"Back in mid-September."

"That's when she would have been there. What does she remember?"

There was a pause on the other end. "That's the bad news.

As soon as I outlined the circumstances to her, she dried up. Her attitude shocked me. In fact, she even went so far as to say that she had been wrong—that it couldn't have been the person you were looking for."

"Oh, I see."

"But I don't think that's true, Anna. The woman just became frightened."

"Why?"

"As I told you, the fanaticism of the pro-lifers has made most of us more than just a little paranoid."

The director of the Roanoke abortion center provided Anna with the address of the Charlotte facility as well as the name of the director.

"I wish there were more I could do than just thank you," Anna said.

"There is. Nail the bastard who did it."

Anna pushed down the button to get another dial tone. She was going to call Whit at the courthouse, but she realized that he hadn't had time to get there yet. Instead, she grabbed the windbreaker and started back out the door. She decided to stop by the courthouse on her way to Charlotte.

Her phone rang again before she reached the door. On the chance that it was Jane Rich again, or maybe even Whit, she returned to answer it. The voice on the other end belonged to neither Jane nor Whit. It was the *Journal* editor, Tom Bukowsky.

"Anna, you're back on the Hairston story. Binder made the decision himself. He wants you to cover the funeral this afternoon."

Just my damned luck, Anna thought. "What about Harold Jones?"

"He screwed up."

"Gee, Tom. I can't make it to the funeral."

"Hon, this isn't a request. It's a job requirement, an assignment made by Will Binder himself."

"I'll be working on the Hairston story, Tom, but not at the funeral."

"There's one thing you don't do to Will Binder. You don't disobey one of his orders. You're expected to be at the funeral."

Anna smiled. "Let someone else cover the funeral. Maybe just send a photographer. If my lead turns out, I think Will Binder will be very happy with the result."

"Anna, I think I've made myself clear. You're to take over the story, and the first thing you're to do is cover the funeral. If you're not there, don't bother coming back."

SIXTEEN

CAL BURTON WAS MISERABLE. His stomach blazed from acid indigestion. The walls of his office wanted to wobble whenever he moved his head. A sharp, throbbing pain hammered away at each temple. The hangover had been bad enough before he arrived at the city police station. He'd planned to be off that day. If someone had told him that he could feel any worse than he had when he'd woken up, he'd have at the very least called them a liar.

But they would have been right. The summons came from the chief himself with a brief explanation. Someone had tried to kill Mary Hairston the night before. As far as the chief was concerned, that meant Lewis Luther hadn't been the perp after all. Cal had tried to dispute the assumption, but his efforts were useless. Even Cal had to admit that Luther appeared to be innocent—at least when it came to the Hairston case. Not that Cal cared that Luther was dead. There were probably plenty of other criminal transactions committed by him. If he hadn't been guilty of the Hairston crime, he had probably been guilty of something, and given Luther's record, it had probably been something serious.

Cal's inner anguish originated from his failure to clip Pynchon's wings. When you mixed equal parts of a hangover and

243

Cal's disappointment, it produced a sodden, painful rage within the small lieutenant.

The detective rested his swirling head on the desk. Seconds later the intercom buzzed. The sound sent a shock wave through the suffering officer. He fumbled to answer it.

"Jesus, whadaya want?"

"Whit Pynchon is asking to see you."

"Tell him to go to hell."

"But—"

Cal shut off the speaker and rested his head on his desk. He didn't need a dose of Pynchon's crowing—not the way he felt. How long had it been since he'd had such a hangover? A decade at least.

The door to his office burst open. For a split second the noise didn't register.

"You mourning Lewis Luther?" a loud voice asked.

Cal was looking up, but the hands were on his shoulders before he even saw the angry face of Whit Pynchon.

"What the hell—"

Cal was hoisted out of his seat and across his desk. The hot bile surged into his throat. He started to cough, choking on the burning effluvium from his stomach. As Whit pulled Cal over the cluttered desk, arrest reports and mold-filled Styrofoam coffee cups scattered on the floor. When his feet came up, the detective's heels caught his desk chair and turned it over.

"You stink, Burton."

But Cal was coughing so hard he couldn't answer.

Whit shrank from the stench of soured booze. "An innocent man's dead because of you. Our body count has tripled!"

"Put me down," Cal managed to say. There was no indignant anger in his voice. Instead, he was pleading.

Whit complied. The cop smelled so bad, Whit no longer could suffer it. Cal's torso draped down on his desk. "Jesus, Pynchon. You're crazy."

Whit loomed over him, his face twisted by anger and revulsion. He watched as Cal managed to right himself. The ashen-faced detective used his shirt-sleeve to wipe his mouth.

"The prosecutor sent me here to give you a message," Whit said. "He's seriously considering presenting the death of Lewis Luther to a grand jury. If he decides to do so, Burton, then he's going to recommend that you—and perhaps others—be indicted for involuntary manslaughter."

Cal's eyes focused on Whit for the first time. "That's bullshit, Pynchon. We had legitimate warrants on the guy. The bastard fired on us."

"I'm not here to debate the point. I'm just carrying a message. I hope you get a chance to plead your case to a jury."

Cal eased off his desk. "Get the hell outa my office."

"I'm not through. You're to stay the hell away from the case. You understand?"

Cal's stomach threatened to erupt again. He started toward the door, his hand over his mouth. Whit's hand reached out to grip his arm.

"I want an answer."

Cal Burton nodded. It was the best he could do at the moment.

Anna found Tony Danton at his desk, his small frame almost hidden behind a stack of law books.

"Where's Whit?" she asked, breathless from her excitement.

Tony looked up over the stack of books. "Hi, Anna."

"I need to see Whit."

"I sent him over to the Milbrook Police Department. After I thought about it, it was probably a mistake. He may be in jail by now."

"In jail?"

"I had a message for Burton. Your face is flushed, Anna. What's wrong?"

Anna had no idea how much Whit had told Tony. She doubted that he would be very happy to know that she was pursuing an investigation of sorts on her own. "I just need to talk to Whit."

"Barring disaster, he should be back before long," Tony said. "Nothing's wrong, I hope. It's not Tressa—"

"Oh, no. She's fine."

They both heard his voice all the way down the long hall that ran the length of the prosecutor's suite of offices. He had said something to the office's receptionist. Anna rushed out to meet him. Tony followed her.

"Anna?" Whit was shocked to see her rushing toward him.

"Jane Rich called me. She's the woman at the Roanoke abortion clinic, and she said that Mary Hairston—well, a woman fitting her—"

Whit put his strong hands on her shoulders. "Christ, Anna. Slow down."

Tony stood behind her, his expression twisted by confusion.

Whit guided her into his office. Tony stood at the door.

"Now." Whit said, "Slow and easy, tell me what it is."

"There's an abortion clinic in Charlotte, North Carolina, that may have seen Mary Hairston."

"What's all this about? Do I have a surprise coming?" Tony asked.

"I'll explain in a minute," Whit said. He turned back to Anna. "Are you sure?"

"According to Jane—"

"Who's Jane?" Whit asked.

"That's the lady in Roanoke who agreed to help me."

"I remember. Go on."

"Anyway, she talked with the director of the Charlotte clinic and that lady said they had a client who matched the description."

"What else?"

"That's all. After Jane explained the situation, the woman wouldn't say any more. I know it was Mary Hairston, Whit. I was wanting to go down this afternoon."

Whit took her hand. "It's a three-and-a-half-hour drive to Charlotte."

"It doesn't matter. I've been ordered to cover Jenny Hairston's funeral this afternoon."

"Ordered?" Whit asked.

"Binder has put me back on the story. What should I do, Whit?"

Tony moved into Whit's office. "Will one of you tell me what the hell is going on? I am the goddamned prosecutor around here."

"Remember when Anna went into Mary Hairston's house?"

Tony smiled. "Yeah, the night she committed burglary."

"I did not!" Anna said.

Whit put a hand on her shoulder. "When she was inside, Tony, she discovered evidence that Mary Hairston was planning on an abortion. She's been checking with various clinics in the region."

"So, what's the significance?"

"Don't you see?" Anna said. "There's a chance they know who the father is. Maybe even the man was with Mary."

Tony paced the perimeter of Whit's small office. "That's highly unlikely."

"It's worth pursuing," Whit said. "I'm going to Charlotte."

"But what about the funeral?" Anna asked.

"Tams and Tressa will understand."

"You really think it's a lead?" Tony asked.

"It's worth a trip down there."

"I'll go with you," Tony said.

"What about the reports from the medical examiner?"

"I'll phone him from Charlotte."

The weather forecasters were wrong in their prediction for a clearing trend by midafternoon. Throughout the early afternoon, an upper-level low-pressure system deepened. The clouds over the mid-Appalachians thickened and lowered. It started to drizzle just as graveside services for Jenny started. Vanessa and her mother stood behind a group of employees from the *Journal*. The two women tried to share an umbrella, but it was too small to cover them both.

"I'm going back to the car and wait," Vanessa said.

Given her daughter's recent mood, Mrs. Andrews thought herself fortunate to be at the graveside rites at all. "Suit yourself," she said.

As Vanessa hurried back to the car, Mrs. Andrews slipped around the group of mourners and moved behind Tams. As a group of Jenny's classmates sang "Jesus Loves Me" she rested her hands on her daughter's shoulders. From the spasmodic vibrations telegraphed through her palms, Mattie Andrews knew her daughter was crying.

She leaned down. "Be strong, child."

Anna stood on the other side of the grave. She was with Will and Katherine Binder. Anna had brought Tams and Tressa to the services, but the mortician had quickly whisked the two girls to seats reserved for the family beneath a canvas shelter. It was an honor for Tams.

When Binder had noticed Anna, he had motioned to her. She reached his side just as the minister started the services.

"I'd like to talk with you for a few moments after the service," he'd whispered.

She waited for the audience.

Interstate 77 threaded its way due south along the spine of the Appalachians toward North Carolina. A few miles before it reached the Tarheel State, the highway took a precipitous drop off Fancy Gap Mountain, descending five miles to the Piedmont of North Carolina. From there, it leveled out as it passed through Statesville, then along the banks of Lake Norman, and eventually cut a wide path through the middle of Charlotte, North Carolina's largest city.

The gray rainclouds had ended with the mountains. By the time Whit and Tony reached Lake Norman, the skies above were blue and almost cloudless.

Whit had turned off the car's heater miles back. He now rolled down his car window for a moment. The air that rushed in wasn't warm, but it wasn't rain-chilled, either. "See why I want to move south. It gets even nicer closer to the coast."

"It rains here, too—and snows some," Tony said.

"Admit it, though. It beats the hell outa West Virginia."

"You're obsessive."

They passed under Interstate 85. "Charlotte's just ahead," Whit noted. "Do we have any idea where this clinic is located?"

Tony checked the notes Anna had given him. "Somewhere on Independence Boulevard."

"You can turn onto Independence from I-77, but do I turn east or west?"

"Hell, Whit. I don't know."

"Charlotte's a big town. It could take us all day to find this place."

Tony read off the street number.

Whit threw up his hand in a gesture of frustration. "Hell, we'll just turn off west. If it's wrong, we'll go back the other way and hope the place doesn't close before we find it."

The traffic on the interstate was heavy enough, but, as soon as they maneuvered the tricky turn onto Independence Boulevard, it became slow and exasperating. Tony tried to read some street numbers, but most of the retail businesses located along the divided four-lane were situated several hundred yards back from the highway.

"This is goddamned impossible," Tony said.

"There's a service station. I need gas. Maybe I can get directions."

As it turned out, the area they sought was located east of I-77. Whit had made the wrong turn. Thirty minutes later, they pulled into the parking lot of a nondescript brick structure with a small sign that identified it as the Central Carolina Family Planning Clinic.

"I was expecting something a little larger," Whit said as he and Tony headed for the front door. "This place looks like a dentist's office."

"I'll refrain from any jokes, my friend."

A receptionist, a petite black woman, told them that Mrs. Stupalsky, the clinic director, had left for the weekend.

Whit pulled out his ID. "We need to see her. It's of vital importance."

The woman was unimpressed. "I'm sorry, sir. As I said, she has left for the weekend."

"Is she still in town?" Tony asked.

"I'm sure I really wouldn't know."

"By the way, what was her name?" Whit asked. "The name you mentioned doesn't sound right."

"Mrs. Stupalsky. Miriam Stupalsky."

Whit pulled a notebook from the pocket of his corduroy sportscoat. He feigned shock. "She's not the person we need to see anyway. Is this the Charlotte Center for Women's Studies?"

The receptionist looked first at Whit, then at Tony. "No, it's the Central Carolina Family Planning Clinic. I've never heard of the Center for Women's Studies."

Whit threw up his hands. "Wrong place!"

Tony gaped. "Dammit, Whit—"

"Come on, Tony. The guy must have misunderstood when we asked for directions."

"Whit!"

He hustled his boss out the door.

"What the hell was that all about?"

"I didn't want her calling the lady. With a name like Stupalsky, we can probably find her ourselves. That woman in there isn't about to give us her home address, and I didn't want her tipping the lady that she has visitors on the way."

"But what if she has an unlisted phone?"

"Then, I can always come back and beat the address out of the receptionist. Right?"

The minister ended the prayer with a throaty "Amen." He approached Tams and squeezed her hand. "My child, God will remember the love you felt for this child. People do not need to be of the same blood to be family."

He went on to Tressa. Mattie Andrews inched around to face her daughter, staying under cover of the shelter. The intensity of the rain had increased during the service, and a breeze was now beginning to push the drops under the canvas cover.

Tams stood and hugged her mother. "I'll miss her."

The mourners were moving quickly to their cars.

"She's in God's hands, child."

Tams buried her head in the ample bosom of her mother. "It seems so wrong to do this without Mary here. I almost feel guilty."

"Come on, child. Ride home with Vanessa and me."

Anna and the Binders moved to them, waiting. Tams pulled away and looked around. "Where is Vanessa?"

Her mother sighed. "She went back to the car."

Tears streamed down Tams's face. "It shoulda been her, not Mary."

Mrs. Andrews gasped. "Tams! Don't say such things."

"I don't care, Momma."

Kathy Binder leaned down to Tams. "Tamantha, people deal with grief in many different ways. I understand your sister was a close friend of Mary Hairston's. Maybe she's behaving as she is because of her grief. Some people can't show it with tears. They think others will consider them weak. Give her a chance."

Tams started again to thank Mrs. Binder. The publisher used the opportunity to pull Anna a few yards away. "I'm sorry that I insisted on your presence today, but I may be out of town tomorrow. I wanted to touch base with you."

"That's all right, Mr. Binder." What the hell else could she say?

"We now have two of our employees dead, and I gather

there may be a connection. Can you shed any light on it yet?''

"Did you know about the attempt on Mary Hairston's life and the murder of an orderly late last night?''

Binder's eyes widened. "No, I didn't.''

"After that happened, Whit—uh, the police think it's all tied in.''

Binder managed a tired smile. "By 'police' I gather you mean Pynchon?''

"Yes, sir.''

"Does he have any leads at all?''

"Actually, I think he's developed one pretty good lead. That's where he's gone now and why he's not at the funeral.''

Binder lifted his eyebrows. "Care to share it with me?''

If it hadn't meant revealing that Anna had continued her own inquiry into the case, she probably would have. However, to avoid implicating herself, she said, "As soon he shares it with me.''

"I gather he's a pretty stubborn man, Miss Tyree.''

"That's an understatement.''

He placed a hand on her shoulder. "As soon as you do find out something, please call me. I'll be home tonight, sometime after six, and the number's in the book. With two of my employees victims of this killer, you might say I have developed a personal interest.''

"I will, sir.''

"And if there's anything I can do to help, call me, too.''

"I promise.''

SEVENTEEN

THE CHARLOTTE AREA PHONE DIRECTORY listed two Stupalskys. The first, M. E. Stupalsky, lived at 1900 Shadow Lane. The second, F. A. Stupalsky, was simply listed as Lake Norman, which was located north of Charlotte.

"I'm betting on M. E. Stupalsky," Whit said. "Besides, it's obviously the closest."

Tony nodded his agreement. "Sounds reasonable to me. Now, how the hell do we find Shadow Lane?"

They were standing in the office of a small service station. Whit had asked the manager of the business for a phone book. The man, red-faced and bloated, hadn't been too anxious to cooperate. He didn't have time to help folks who weren't buying something from him.

Before he asked about Shadow Lane, Whit gathered up several cans of soda and a handful of peanut butter crackers. He took them to the cash register. There, he asked for a carton of cigarettes. North Carolina was the heart of tobacoo country, and cigarettes were much cheaper then in West Virginia.

"By the way," he said as he handed the man a twenty-dollar bill, "do you know where Shadow Lane is?"

"Never heard of it."

"You can keep the change."

The man glanced up at Whit. "I still never heard of Shadow Lane. There's been so many new subdivisions goin' in 'round here. Used to be, I knew my way 'round this town as good as anyone. Not anymore. Town's gone to hell with all this success, too."

"How do I find the police department?"

"Looks like it's coming to you," the manager said. He nodded toward something in front of his station.

Whit glanced out the front window of the station and saw a police cruiser pulling into the station.

"That's the first thing that's gone right today."

Whit hurried out to the cruiser. The officer inside glared as he rolled down his window. He was alone in the vehicle. Whit pulled out his ID and flashed it. The officer's face turned friendly.

"You're mighty far from home."

"Sure am," Whit said. "I'm down here looking for a witness in a case. It's crucial that I interview her. I think the person I'm looking for might live on Shadow Lane. Can you tell me how to find it?"

The officer rubbed his chin. "Shadow Lane? Hang on a sec."

He fumbled around in a case that he used as an armrest in the front seat. From it he pulled a worn city map. Tony had come up behind Whit. "Can he help us?"

"He's looking."

"Here it is." The officer got out of the cruiser. "I stop in here for coffee at the beginning of my shift. Old Jeb in there makes a good cup."

The cop spread the map out on the hood and spent several minutes showing Whit, who was making notes, how to find Shadow Lane.

"You gotta watch all these little subdivisions, though. Once you get inside them, they all look the same."

"Since I don't know what I'm looking for, that shouldn't be a problem."

Tony watched the bumper-to-bumper traffic that flowed in all four lanes of Independence Boulevard. He had no faith whatsoever. There was no way they were ever going to find Miriam Stupalsky in the mass of humanity that constituted Charlotte, North Carolina.

The cop ended his explanation. "Think you can find it?"

"I can try." Whit said.

"I gotta go handle traffic downtown," the cop said. "Any other time of the day I'd be glad to lead you there."

"You've been a big help."

Once they were back inside the car, Whit dropped his forehead on the steering wheel. "Jesus, Tony. I'll never find the place."

Tony looked at the time. "It's four. We can take all night if we need to, but, first, let's find a phone so I can call the M.E."

Whit lifted his head and gazed out at the late-afternoon traffic on the thoroughfare. "Rush hour gives me the hee-bie-jeebies."

"I'll drive."

Whit managed a chuckle. "That would give me the willies. The heebie-jeebies are nothing compared to the willies. There's a pay phone right over there." He pointed to it on the far side of the station at which they were parked.

"Want me to call now?"

"Yeah, I need a little break."

They both climbed wearily from the car. Whit leaned up against the front fender while Tony went to place the call. The prosecutor was back much too quickly. "Barucha's on his way home, dammit. The assistant gave me his number. We'll call later."

"Our luck's not worth a damn today. Let's go find this lady."

Tressa left the graveside services with Anna. As Tams was helping her mother across the uneven lawn toward the car where Vanessa waited, the owner of the funeral home approached them.

"Could you stop by the funeral home and pick up the deed to the cemetery plot?"

"Me?" Tams asked.

"It's in your name, young lady."

"My name?"

"That's how Will Binder wanted it."

Tams nodded that they would. She told Vanessa about it as they climbed into her mother's car.

Vanessa was livid. "I gotta git home!"

"It won't take a minute to pick up the things," Mrs. Andrews said. "Besides, it's my car. It goes where I say it goes."

"Shit." The epithet was spoken under Vanessa's breath, but Mattie Andrews heard it. Her mother's pocketbook caught Vanessa on the side of her head. Through surprise rather than pain, Vanessa jerked her head to the left, away from the blow. Her head clunked hard against the window.

"Dammit, Momma."

A second thrust of the purse missed Vanessa's head by inches.

"Stop it!" Vanessa shrieked.

"I've had a gullet full of your sass," her mother said.

"If I was able, I'd give you a proper thrashing. You're a misery to be around."

Vanessa's bickering ended. They drove in silence to the funeral home. Tams, more than a little shaken by the violent confrontation between her mother and older sister, hurried inside, collected the documents and mementos, and hurried back. She could feel the hot eyes of her sister as she brushed by the driver's door.

It was a little past four when they finally pulled to a stop in front of the Andrews house. Vanessa bounded from the car and took the steps two at a time. Tams and her mother followed at a slower pace. The rain had stopped for the moment, and a bright sun shone through a small gap in the rapidly moving clouds.

"I don't know what's gotten into her," Mrs. Andrews said again as Tams helped her up the steps.

"She's gonna hear it from me," Tams said.

"You'll be wasting precious breath."

Vanessa was nowhere to be seen when they stepped into the house.

"I'm going upstairs, Momma."

"I don't want you two fighting."

Tams had started up the stairs. "Us fighting? What about you two in the car?"

Mrs. Andrews set her jaw. "I lost my head."

Tams reached the top of the steps. She heard her sister's voice. It was coming from her mother's room. Tams slipped down the hallway. The floor of the old house creaked under her weight. Tams cringed.

She inched up to the door. It was ajar a few inches. She pressed tightly against the wall as she tried to catch her sister's words.

Though Vanessa spoke in a coarse whisper, Tams easily

understood her words, spoken—Tams assumed—into the phone by her mother's bed.

"Leave the money—fifty thousand dollars—on Jenny Hairston's grave," she was saying.

Tams covered her hand with her mouth.

"Put it in a plastic bag. Do it at nine tonight."

Vanessa had stopped talking, apparently listening to the response.

"You listen to me. I'm not alone in this. If you mess with me tonight, my partner knows enough to put you away."

Another moment of silence. Tams tried to quell the trembling of her body. Her knees were knocking together. Surely, Vanessa could hear them.

But her sister was talking again. "That's a cheap way outa several murder raps, asshole. I oughta make it a hundred grand."

Tams was breathing fast now. Her stomach threatened nausea. She couldn't believe what she was hearing. Her sister knew who the killer was—maybe had known the whole time.

Vanessa wasn't in any hurry to get off the phone. Didn't she think anyone could hear? Or did she even care?

"You got it? Fifty grand—nine P.M.—in a plastic bag—on Jenny's grave. Don't mess up."

Tams heard the phone come to rest in its cradle. She darted down the hall and vanished into her bedroom, slamming the door behind her. Then she collapsed onto her bed, burying her head in the hefty pillows.

She gurgled into the downy softness as she heard her sister coming down the hall. Vanessa was humming! Tams wanted to rush out of her door and throw herself at her sister. She wanted to beat her with her fists, kick her, scratch and bite her. Instead, her fingers clutched the silky material of her bedspread as her sister tripped down the steps.

Tams eased off her bed and went to the door. She peered out, then crept back down the hall toward her mother's bedroom and the phone.

"Shadow Lane!" Tony cried.

Whit followed his finger and saw the sign. "Now which way?"

The street ran to the right and to the left of the intersection at which they were stopped. Behind them, an impatient commuter honked a horn. Whit shot a finger back over his seat and then glanced into the rearview mirror. A woman was returning the gesture.

"So much for the innocence of southern belles," he said. "Eenie . . . meenie—"

"Dammit, Whit, you're holding up traffic."

He turned left.

They had explored most of residential Charlotte, or so it seemed. Up one street and down another. Whit was sick of sleek homes framed by tall loblolly pines. Almost every one of the homes was surrounded, too, by rhododendron and other shrubs. For a while, the search had been pleasant as they both appreciated the efforts that had gone into landscaping many of the residences. After a while, they grew weary. Whit's legs threatened to cramp. His buttocks were seared by sweat. Tony complained of an aching in his neck and shoulders.

"If we don't find it soon," Whit was saying, "I'm gonna have to stop. Maybe we can grab a bite to eat."

But Tony wasn't impressed with the idea. "Once it gets dark, we'll be totally lost. You can eat later."

And Tony was right.

"I saw a house number. It said 1826."

"Find another," Whit urged. "Which way are they running?"

Because of a sloping hillside, the homes had moved closer to the street. "There's another. It's 1830."

"Mrs. Stupalsky should be a block ahead."

The setting sun glared straight into their eyes. Whit dropped a visor in front of his face. "You watch for the house. I'll watch the road."

They passed a huge playground and swimming pool that seemed to run a whole block itself.

"There it is! 1900 Shadow Lane."

Whit slammed on the brakes. The car stopped in the middle of the roadway.

"Some house," Whit said.

The two-story Tudor sprawled over a huge lot. A forest of pine and oak rose behind it.

"It's a friggin' mansion."

"There must be a lotta money in killing babies."

"You're a goddamned misanthrope, my friend."

"Well, look at the goddamned house. It's as big as a damned hotel, Tony."

A large round tower sat in the center of the structure and provided a focus to its architecture.

"Maybe her husband's a doctor," Tony said. "I always say we couldn't be too smart or we'd be doctors."

"Probably delivers babies. That way they cover all the bases."

Tony laughed and cuffed him on the shoulder. They were both so tired, they were punchy. Whit pulled his car into the wide driveway that sloped down toward the house.

"Wanna bet they've got a butler who answers the door?"

he said as they ambled up the walk toward the massive
front door.

He was wrong. A middle-aged woman, buxom and just
a few pounds shy of obese, greeted them.

"May I help you?"

Whit pulled out his identification. "Mrs. Stupalsky, my
name's Whit Pynchon. I'm with the office of the Prosecutor of Raven County, West Virginia. The gentleman with
me is Tony Danton. He is the prosecutor."

The woman wore her sparkling gray hair high on her
head. Her pale face was heavily made-up. She squinted at
his badge.

"Did you say West Virginia?"

"I did."

The woman was skeptical. "What do you want with
me?" She spoke through a small crack in the door.

"A few moments of your time. May we come in?"

The woman was flustered. "What's this about?"

Tony jumped into the conversation. He had the notes
from Anna. "I believe a woman by the name of Jane Rich
from the Roanoke center called you."

That struck a familiar chord. "Oh, yes. Ooooooh . . . I
told her I was wrong. I'm sorry you people drove so far.
Now, if you'll excuse me—"

She started to close the door, but Whit laid a hand
against it. "Mrs. Stupalsky, if you don't think we can
subpoena you here in North Carolina, you're wrong. We
can and will. You can make it a darned sight easier by
talking to us now."

The woman's deep blue eyes measured Whit. After a
few seconds, she opened the door. "Come in."

The interior of the home awed them both. A circular
staircase filled the Tudor column. Three steps led down

into a living room with a cathedral ceiling. A huge fire-place filled one wall of the room. The furnishing was white French provincial.

"Mrs. Stupalsky, your home is very attractive," Tony said.

The woman, despite her displeasure, was gracious. "It was my husband's pride and joy. He passed away two years ago. I plan to put it on the market soon."

"Sell it?" Tony asked.

"It's much too big for one person."

Tony saw a wall covered with plaques. He stepped over to them. Many of them had been bestowed upon Henry A. Stupalsky, but here were also a large number bearing the name of Miriam Stupalsky. Several recognized the woman for her work with the American Cancer Society. Others were related to family planning.

"You're very active," Tony said.

"I stay busy to avoid the loneliness. Please, have a seat."

Whit's buttocks were numb from the hours spent in the car. "I'd rather stand, Mrs. Stupalsky. It's been a long drive."

"And a wasted one, I'm afraid." The woman eased down into a chair. "As I told Jane, I'm afraid I was mis-taken. She shouldn't have called you. I asked her to forget my error."

Whit leaned against the doorframe. "We have to be sure, ma'am. I've brought photos of the woman we're in-quiring about."

Obviously Miriam Stupalsky was a woman who handled herself well. "I really wouldn't care to see them—I'm sorry, I didn't catch your name."

"Pynchon . . . Whit Pynchon."

"You see, Mr. Pynchon, the work we do at the center is strictly confidential. Even if this woman had been a patient at the center, I couldn't divulge any information about her case. That would be most unethical."

Tony sat on a sofa across from the woman. "Did Jane tell you about the case?"

"No, not really. It doesn't matter—"

"Oh, but it does!" Whit said. He left his position against the doorframe and sat beside Tony. "This afternoon, a seven-year-old girl was buried in a lonely grave at the base of a rather lonely mountain. From what you've said, you know something about loneliness—about grief, too. Here's the grief, lady. Someone put a bullet in her brain. That same 'someone' tried to put a bullet in her mother's brain. He—or she—didn't succeed. The bullet lodged in her skull. That same individual has killed at least one more time—and maybe two—in two days. We're talking about a war, lady, and right now you're our only weapon."

Mrs. Stupalsky closed her eyes. "It sounds awful."

"It *was* awful," Whit said. "That woman walked around her house for several days with that bullet in her head. The child was there, too, becoming more putrid every day. They couldn't even open her casket. You know something, Mrs. Stupalsky? That poor woman bathed the body of that child every day."

Tony saw the discomfort on the woman's face. "Whit! Take it easy!"

He shushed Tony with a wave of his hand. "Mrs. Stupalsky wants to talk about ethics. I want her to hear about Mary Hairston. Do you know that Mary Hairston's still alive? She's on a life support system. She's carrying a baby, too. Last night, someone tried to murder her and the baby. He waltzed into her hospital room and yanked the tube loose, Mrs. Stupalsky. On his way out, he took the life of an orderly. Now, I ask you, what does your policy have to do with all this? How can you sit there, so prim and proper, and say to us that you don't care about Mary Hairston, her dead child, and her yet-to-be born child?''

"I care, Mr. Pynchon. However, as I told Jane, I think I was wrong.''

Whit pulled a photo from his pocket. "Fine! Maybe you were. All I want you to do is look at this photo.''

The woman lowered her head. "I can't do it.''

Tony ached for the woman. He saw and appreciated her pain. "Like Whit told you, it won't be hard to force you to testify in a West Virginia court, Mrs. Stupalsky. If it eases your conscience, I am serving as Mary Hairston's guardian at this point. I didn't have time to prepare documentation, but in that capacity I would have a right to access her medical information. If you cooperate with us now, we'll try to keep you out of it. I can't make any guarantees other than to say I'll do my best.''

Mrs. Stupalsky wrung her fingers. "Is that possible?'' she asked, her question directed toward Whit.

"He's the boss man," Whit said of Tony. "It's up to him. I can tell you this: He's a man of his word. If he says he'll try to keep your name out of it, then he will.''

Tony stood and went to the agonized woman. He stopped in front of her. "You don't know either of us, Mrs. Stupalsky, and you have no basis to trust us. Just trust in your own sense of decency. You know it's the right thing to do.''

The woman thought about it for several silent minutes.

Finally, she reached out her hand. "Let me see the photo."

Tams's fingers trembled as she dialed Tony Danton's home phone. Tressa had told her that the Raven County Prosecutor had gone somewhere with Mr. Pynchon, but she was hoping they were back. She had already tried Whit Pynchon's number and received no answer. Danton's phone rang five times.

"Answer," Tams whined. "Please answer."

Someone did—a woman."

"Is Mr. Danton there?"

"Who's calling please?"

"This is Tamantha Andrews."

"I'm sorry," the woman said, "but Tony's not home right now. I don't expect him back for a while."

"Do you know where he is?"

"Who did you say this was?" the woman asked.

Tams answered with a question of her own. "Is this Mrs. Danton?"

"Yes, it is."

"I'm a friend of Tressa's."

"Tressa?"

"Mr. Pynchon's daughter."

"Oh, yes. Mr. Pynchon." To Tams it sounded as if Mrs. Danton hadn't much use for Tressa's dad.

"I need to get in touch with Mr. Danton. I have some information about the murder of Jenny Hairston."

"Oh, dear. I see. He's out of town. He's with Mr. Pynchon. I really don't know when to expect him."

"When he gets back, will you tell him to call me? Please?"

* * *

"Hold on a second," Mrs. Danton said. "Let me find something to write down your number."

Tams heard the phone clunk down.

"Hurry," she said. "Please hurry."

She was afraid that Vanessa would walk in to her mother's bedroom.

"I have some paper," Mrs. Danton said when she came back on the phone.

Tams gave her the number. "It's urgent."

"I'll give him the message."

Tams hung up the phone, picked it up again, and started to dial the number of Tressa's mother.

"Tams!" It was Vanessa, calling her.

She hung up the phone.

"I'm here!"

"Dinner's ready."

"Just a sec."

She lifted the phone and dialed the number again. Mrs. Pynchon answered the phone.

"This is Tams, Mrs. Pynchon. Is Tressa there?"

"Tressa's never here. You should know that better than anyone."

"I thought maybe she might be home."

"Not tonight. You might try her father's number."

"I know she's not there."

"Oh, I see. Well, Whitley probably took her to dinner somewhere."

Tams started to tell Mrs. Pynchon that Whit was out of town, but she thought better of it.

"Tams! Come eat!" It was Vanessa again. Was she coming after her?

"If she comes home, Mrs. Pynchon, have her call me?"

"I will—"

The door to Mattie Andrews's bedroom opened. Tams slammed down the phone as Vanessa stuck her head in the door.

"What are you up to?"

"I'm trying to call Tressa." Tams's hands quivered as her sister glared at her.

"Come on and eat before Momma has a fit."

"I'm coming."

Vanessa waited for her to move. "You've got a funny look on your face. What have you been up to?"

"Calling Tressa; I told you."

"Move it. Momma's in a bad enough mood anyway."

Her older sister followed Tams down the steps. Tams dreaded having to sit at the same table with her.

EIGHTEEN

MIRIAM STUPALSKY NEEDED little more than a glance at the photo of Mary Hairston. She was nodding. "That's the woman who came to our clinic. No way would I forget her, but I need to call the clinic for the precise dates."

"Won't it be closed?" Tony asked.

"No, the clinic stays open until seven on Monday, Wednesday, and Friday for those women who work."

"That's a compliment to your sense of public spirit," Tony said, anxious to make the woman feel better.

"Our purpose is to serve," Mrs. Stupalsky said. "Before my husband died, I was chairman of the center's board. After he passed away, the director's position became open. I took it. I believe very strongly in the center. That's why this breach of faith is so difficult for me."

"You're doing the right thing," Tony said. "Trust me, it's no breach of duty."

Whit was growing edgy. "I don't mean to rush you, ma'am, but we have a long drive back to Milbrook."

"Of course. I apologize for being so long-winded."

But Tony said, "Just ignore him, and take all the time you need."

"If you'll excuse me, I'll make the call from my study." The woman rose to leave. Whit stood, too.

She noticed the look of concern on his face. "You needn't fear, Mr. Pynchon. I've decided to cooperate. I just prefer to obtain these details in the privacy of my study. Make yourself at home."

Once Mrs. Stupalsky was out of the room, Tony said to Whit, "You treat everyone as if they were goddamned criminals."

"Most of the people you and I deal with are just that."

"In this case, she's not. I have a lotta respect for the lady. Besides, if she clams up, we get nothing out of her until we get her back in West Virginia. We can bluff all we want, but you seem to have forgotten just how much damned bullshit I have to go through to bring back a witness from another state."

"In other words, don't rock the boat."

"You got it, Whit. I'll handle it from here."

Whit paced nervously as several more minutes went by. Eventually Mrs. Stupalsky reappeared with a yellow legal pad in her hand. "Now, what do you wish to know?"

Whit withdrew his own notebook. "Just give us a chronological explanation. I'll interrupt with questions when I have them."

"The young woman—she identified herself as Mary Smith—appeared at the clinic on September eighth. During that visit her pregnancy was confirmed, and she was counseled."

"Meaning?" Whit asked.

Mrs. Stupalsky carefully phrased her answer. "I discussed with her the import of her pregnancy. Actually, counseling is more of a tool I use to determine that the woman is capable of making an adult decision about abortion. I want to be sure that the woman is making the decision on her own—of her own free will and not as a result of coercion."

"Much like a confession," Whit observed.

"I assume," the clinic director said, obviously not impressed with Whit's analogy.

"What opinion did you reach with regard to Mary Hairston?" Tony asked.

"I received contradictory signals. Quite apparently, Mrs. Hairston was a thoughtful, intelligent young woman. At the same time, I observed certain indications that led me to believe that she wasn't entirely in favor of a termination of her pregnancy."

Whit leaned forward. "How do you mean?"

"She kept using 'we' instead of 'I.' I've found that the use of the editorial 'we' indicates something less than certainty on the part of the person using it. Usually it means that she's being pressured."

Whit knitted his eyebrows. "Anything else? That might have indicated some uncertainty?"

"Oh, yes. When I pressured her, she told me that, and I quote, 'it's for the best.' That's another signal. Mrs. Hairston wasn't saying to me that she—Mary Smith as she identified herself—wanted her pregnancy terminated."

Tony was looking at his watch. "Mrs. Stupalsky, may I make a call? It's long-distance, but I'll use my credit card."

Whit gave Tony a puzzled look.

"Barucha," Tony said, then added for Mrs. Stupalsky's benefit. "He's our state coroner. I'm trying to reach him to get a critical report."

"Surely." She directed him to a phone in the study.

"Was she alone?" Whit continued.

"Actually she wasn't."

Whit leaned forward, his interest obvious. The clinic director continued to talk. "She was accompanied by a young black woman, slim and very pretty, with a rather flip attitude about it all. Frankly, I wasn't much impressed by her companion. She was taking the whole thing as a joke.''

"Did Mrs. Hairston call her by name?"

"Not in my presence."

"Can you give us a more precise description?" Whit asked.

"Not really. She wasn't present when I interviewed Mrs. Hairston. The best I can tell you is that she was tall—maybe five-foot-ten-inches, that she weighed maybe a hundred and twenty pounds. She had a good figure. Oh, she was black with rather light skin . . .''

"Vanessa Andrews!" Whit exclaimed.

Moments later, Tony returned from the phone. "That's strange," he said.

"What is it?"

Tony glanced at Mrs. Stupalsky. "I'll spare the lady the details. Cynthia Jackson died from blood loss, but Barucha found traces of face black on her body."

"Face black?" Whit wasn't familiar with the term.

"You know, the stuff quarterbacks put under their eyes to knock the glare of the sun?"

Whit was nodding. "Or that people use when they don't want light glaring on their face at night."

"Exactly," Tony said. "Barucha said it's also called camouflage."

Anna and Tressa sat in a steak house waiting for their dinner to be delivered.

"He should have been at the funeral," Tressa said.

No one had offered her a detailed explanation yet for her father's strange absence. "They came up with a lead on the case, Tressa. It required immediate attention."

"Couldn't someone else have gone?"

The restaurant was crowded, as it always was on a Friday night, and the tables were placed close together. When Anna spoke, it was in a hushed whisper.

"It's important enough that only Whit could handle it. You want the killer caught as much as anyone."

"Of course I do," Tressa said, "but the funeral services were important, too. I mean, Daddy could have stayed. I can't believe they both had to go."

"As I said, their trip may be very important."

"I hope so."

The waitress delivered their salads. Anna was famished, but Tressa picked at hers.

"Aren't you hungry?" Anna asked.

"I was thinking about Mrs. Hairston. What's going to happen to her?"

Anna stopped eating. Her face became solemn. "You know as well as I do that there's little hope of her recovery. The only thing we can hope to do is save the baby—and that may be asking too much."

"And what happens to the child? It'll be born into a world where no one wants it or cares about it."

Anna marveled at the young woman. "Tressa, you have a wisdom most adults lack. That, I suspect, is going to be the crux of the whole issue."

"If I was old enough, I'd take the child."

"I know you would."

A devious smile crept over Tressa's face. "What we need to do, Anna, is get you and Whit married. You could start married life with a little one."

Anna almost spewed her wine all over the table. Once she had recovered, she started to laugh. "Whit Pynchon is the only child I can handle right now."

* * *

The light filtering into the Stupalsky home was beginning to fade. Mrs. Stupalsky broke her narration to turn on several lights.

"Let's see," she said as she perused her notes. "Mrs. Hairston returned to the clinic a week later—on September fifteenth. At that time, she was scheduled for the actual procedure. I still had my reservations, though, and planned to spend a long time counseling her."

"Was she alone?" Whit asked.

"No, but I'll get to that in a minute."

Whit kept his eyes on his wristwatch. He wanted to be on the road home. He wanted to talk to Vanessa Andrews. "Mrs. Stupalsky—"

"Mr. Pynchon, you've intruded into my home. You've virtually intimidated me into a violation of a matter of conscience. The least you can do is to permit me to tell this story in my own fashion."

Whit sighed. "I apologize. Go on."

Tony was grinning at Whit, gloating over the fact that the woman had so promptly put him in his place.

"Anyway, she arrived at the center in the company of a man. She informed me that he was the father."

"Describe him," Whit said.

"Mr. Pynchon!"

"Mrs. Stupalsky, do you realize that this man is probably the individual who killed her daughter and all but killed her, not to mention—"

"I don't think so," she interrupted. "He wasn't the type, but you're diverting me."

Whit rose to his feet and began to pace. "For God's sakes, tell it your own way."

"I intend to."

Tony, too, was anxious, but he also admired the woman's determination.

"As I was saying," the clinic director said, "I had both of them in my office. It was obvious that Mrs. Hairston was very upset. Further, the gentleman was pushing a little. Actually, I suspect he was pushing a lot outside of my presence. He was pushing a little even while I was there. I probed and prodded. The young woman said very little, but the man kept explaining that the abortion was her idea, not his. As Shakespeare said, he protested too much."

Mrs. Stupalsky paused. Both of the men were hanging on her words. Time seemed to become suspended as the speaker gathered her thoughts.

"We were in my office, and Mrs. Hairston suddenly stands. 'I'm not going to do it,' she declares. The man argues with her.

" 'I've made up my mind,' she says.

"He's at first angry—very, very angry, but then he takes her hand. He tells her, 'If that's what you want, then I'm behind you.'

"And then they leave."

Whit couldn't stand it any longer. "Tell me about the man!"

"That's one reason I remembered her," Mrs. Stupalsky said. "Now, I'm no prude. Heaven knows, I'm no prude—"

"The man, Mrs. Stupalsky?" Whit pulled out a photo of Lewis Luther. "Was that the man?"

The director took a single look at the photo. "Heavens, no! As I was saying, I'm no prude, but this is still the South. The man was white. More than that, he was so Aryan. Tall and strikingly blond, just about one of the most handsome men I've ever seen."

Whit looked at his boss. "Will Binder? It couldn't be."

* * *

Throughout the early evening, Tams had slipped off to one
of the three phones in the Andrews home. She had called
Whit Pynchon's home three times. No one had answered.
She had also tried to call Tony Danton again. No one had
answered there, either—not even his wife.

Vanessa had spent the evening in the living room, glued
to the television as she watched *Wheel of Fortune* and, after
that, *Jeopardy!* Mrs. Andrews kept to the kitchen, busy making a batch of brownies for them.

Brownies. Tams felt her world being torn apart, and she
was helpless to do anything about it. If she confronted Vanessa, then it might blow any chance of getting the killer. If
she allowed her older sister to carry out her plan, what then?

Tams dared not tell her mother.

She stayed in her room as much as she could, sneaking
out every so often to try to reach someone—Tressa, Whit
Pynchon, Anna, or Tony Danton. No one was where he or
she was supposed to be.

Tams lay on her bed. She was chilling as she pondered her
alternatives.

The idea came to her about eight P.M.—an hour before the
money was to be left on Jenny's grave. As she perfected her
plan, she cried. How could Vanessa be so cold and cruel?
Her sister was a criminal.

"Are you sure you don't want me to take you to your
mother's?" Anna asked as she pulled to a stop in front of
Whit's house.

"I wanna wait on Daddy if it's okay."

"It's fine, Tressa. It's just such a miserable night. He might
be late."

Anna was right. The rain had started again. With it came a low, thick fog that hugged the ground. The drifting mist consumed the lights from Anna's car. They scurried into the house to escape the icy drizzle and clinging fog.

"Are you worried about them?" Tressa asked as Anna hurried to turn on the lights.

"It's just getting so foggy."

"You still haven't told me where they went, Anna."

Anna sighed. Given the treacherous weather, she didn't want to worry Tressa. On the other hand, she thought of the young woman as an adult. She had a right to know that at least.

"Charlotte, North Carolina," she told Tressa.

"Why on earth did they go there?"

"I'll let Whit explain it when he gets back. It probably was a wasted trip."

"I thought you said it was important."

Anna felt the pressure of Tressa's questions. "It might be, Tressa, but—"

The shrill cry of the phone broke into her explanation. Tressa answered it.

"Thank God!" Tams cried. "I've been looking for you all night. Where were you?"

"Anna took me to dinner. I was kinda down—"

"Vanessa knows who the killer is."

"What?"

"She's going to meet him, I think. She's blackmailing him, Tressa."

Tams spoke in a low, excited whisper.

"Slow down, Tams."

"I don't have time to talk. She's getting ready to leave. I'm gonna hide in the backseat."

"Tams! Where—"

"I gotta go!"

"Tamantha!"

The phone went dead.

NINETEEN

TAMS STOOD AT THE PHONE at the foot of the steps. Upstairs, she could hear the sound of water running. Vanessa was in the bathroom, brushing her teeth. Tams had already started for the front door when she remembered she hadn't told Tressa where Vanessa was going. She went back and picked up the phone. Her heart throbbed in her chest. Her hands were icy. Just as she started to dial the number the sound of running water ended.

"Oh, shit," she said under her breath.

Her eyes fell upon a notepad and pencil by the phone. Quickly, she jotted the words JENNY'S GRAVE.

The soft thumping of her sister's feet sent Tams rushing out the front door. As soon as the cold drizzle struck her, she realized she had forgotten her coat. No time to go back after it.

The many years of going up and down the long string of steps served Tams well as she tripped down them through the thick fog. The car was parked at the bottom of the steps. She opened the back door and dived into the narrow space between the front and rear seats. Already she was shivering from the dampness.

"Damn," she whispered, having forgotten to close the door. She reared up and pulled it closed.

As she scrunched down on the floorboard she saw the porch light go on. An eternity later there was a flash of yellow light as the front door opened.

Please, God. Don't let her see me.

The fog was so thick that Tams never saw her sister. Her heart leapt into her throat as the driver's door creaked. Her sister slid into the car. Tams felt the car sink as her sister sat down and slammed the door.

Tams knew she'd been caught when her sister cried, "Fuck it!"

The door snapped open.

"Damnation," Vanessa was saying.

Tams held her breath.

What would she say? How would she explain? *I just wanted to get out of the house, Vanessa. Honest!* It sounded like the lie that it was. She held her breath, waiting for the back door to fly open.

But the back door didn't open. The front door closed and then there was only the sound of footsteps as her sister climbed back up the steps.

What now?

What if they noticed she wasn't in the house?

And Tams needed to pee—*of all things!* The realization struck in a moment of sheer panic. The pain in her stomach exploded into life. *Not now! For God's sakes, not now!*

More footsteps . . . getting louder. Vanessa was coming back. Tams locked her leg muscles together, trying to forestall the flow of urine from her bladder. She chilled, and her teeth chattered so loudly that she knew Vanessa could hear them.

The door opened.

Tams heard the jingle of keys. Vanessa had forgotten the

keys. She always forgot the keys. Tams almost laughed aloud. Instead, she felt the warm flow of her urine.

Whit's vehicle crept up the steep incline of Fancy Gap Mountain. He continually flipped his lights from bright to dim and back as he sought to see something of the road ahead of him. Only the white line immediately ahead of his right front fender was visible in the cottony fog that hugged the mountain.

"Keep your eyes on the edge," Whit told Tony.

"You're driving blind, Whit."

"So, what the hell do I do? If I stop, a goddamned truck'll run up my ass."

Twice, Whit had almost done exactly that himself. The red eyeballs of the trucks' taillights had suddenly appeared a few yards in front of him. Both times he had swerved out into the passing lane to avoid rear-ending the vehicles.

"Slow down," Tony urged.

"If I go any slower, you could get out and walk ahead of me."

Tony's fear was palpable. "When we get to the top, let's pull into one of those motels."

"We gotta get back."

Whit was right. They had a cold-blooded murderer who could kill again at any moment. Tony and Whit both had decided not to phone their evidence back to Raven County. Neither wanted the case against Will Binder muffed by some foul-up by the Milbrook Police Department.

"The fog may not be so bad once we reach the top." Whit's fists had a white-knuckled hold on the steering wheel. His neck throbbed with tension.

"I can't believe it," Tony said. It was probably the twentieth time he had said it since they left the home of Miriam Stupalsky.

"It all fits," Whit said. "The bastard was playing around with Mary Hairston. She got knocked up. As long as she was gonna have an abortion, everything was cool. Then she changed her mind. Given Binder's distinctive appearance, he's scared to death the baby will give him away."

Tony had thought about that. "I wonder what the kid will look like."

"Dead, maybe—if we don't get back."

"I just—"

"Can't believe it," Whit said in unison with Tony.

The red glare popped into view ahead of them.

"Oh, sweet Jesus," Whit cried.

Tony threw up his hands to cover his face.

Tams's call left Tressa shaken. She quickly repeated Tams's words to Anna.

"How did she find out?" Anna asked.

"I don't know! What are we gonna do?"

"Call her back. Quickly Tressa!"

Tressa redialed Tams's number. She got Mrs. Andrews.

"Where's Tams?" Tressa asked.

"Up in her room, I think."

"Oh, please check. I hope so." Tressa was suddenly relieved. Maybe it was all a joke—or a mistake. If it was a joke, she'd kill Tams.

"Mrs. Andrews thinks Tams is in her room," Tressa told Anna.

"Thank God."

Tressa heard Mrs. Andrews calling Tams. "Tams! Tamantha! Answer me, girl!"

Mrs. Andrews picked up the phone. "Hold on a second, Tressa. I'll go up and see what's going on."

Before Tressa could stop her, the phone was laid down. "Come on," Tressa urged, knowing no one could hear her.

Anna paced the living room, her mind racing.

Several moments later, Mrs. Andrews picked up the phone. "She's gone, Tressa! She's not here."

"Is Vanessa gone?"

"She was going out tonight. She left a few minutes ago."

"Oh, no," Tressa said.

"What's wrong? Tams didn't say she was going anywhere." Then Mrs. Andrews noticed the scribbling on the pad. "Wait a minute. There's something written on the pad. It says JENNY'S GRAVE. That wasn't there this afternoon. I know it wasn't."

"Tams has gone to Jenny's grave," Tressa said aloud—for Anna's benefit.

"Oh, lordy. On a night like this?"

"She went with Vanessa."

Mrs. Andrews laughed in a knowing way. "Oh, I don't think so. That doesn't make no sense, not unless Vanessa maybe got to feeling bad. Come to think of it, she's been actin' mighty funny t'night."

"I'll go there and look for her, Mrs. Andrews."

"What on earth—?"

Tressa didn't mean to hang up on Mrs. Andrews, but she didn't have time to say anything else.

"You're not going anywhere," Anna was quick to say.

"But Anna—"

"No, Tressa! I want you to stay here and wait on your father. Tell him what's happened."

Anna was picking up the phone book.

"What are you going to do? Call the police?"

Anna shook her head. "No way. Your father's taught me better than that."

"Are you going to the cemetery?"

"Yes, but I'm taking help." Her fingers were perusing the phone book. She dropped it and dialed a number.

"Who are you calling?"

"Will Binder. He said if I needed anything, to call him. I'm taking him at his word."

Katherine Binder answered. "Hi, Anna. He's just on his way out the door."

"Can you stop him?"

"I'll try."

Moments later, the agitated voice of Will Binder came on the line. "What is it, Anna? I'm in a bit of a hurry."

"I need some help," she said. "It might be a matter of life and death."

The fog didn't bother Vanessa. She had fifty thousand dollars on her mind. She drove slowly, though. No sense messing things up by having a wreck. Actually, Vanessa thought the fog was a bit of good luck. It would make it easier to slip in and get the money.

Traffic was nonexistent as Vanessa headed her car out of Milbrook and into the foothills of Tabernacle Mountain. Mountain View Gardens was two miles outside of the Milbrook city limits, and the fog wasn't quite so thick once she was climbing toward it.

The wind picked up just as Vanessa turned into the entrance to the cemetery. The fog swirled and thinned and was suddenly gone. The headlights of her car settled upon a heavy metal chain and a padlock that dangled from the rusty iron gates.

"Motherfucker," Vanessa said. She hadn't expected the

cemetery to be closed. It simply hadn't occurred to her. What the hell would someone want to steal in a graveyard?

Fifty thousand dollars maybe?

Large drops of rain splattered on her windshield. She didn't relish the idea of slogging through the muddy grass, but she wasn't about to leave the money. Vanessa pulled the car as deep into shadows as she could. The gates were designed to prevent cars from entering the graveyard, but to either side of the stone columns there were no fences. Vanessa took a deep breath and stepped into the grass. She hurried around the outer corner of the stone columns and was at once walking across graves.

Behind her, the rear door of her car clicked open. Tams eased herself out of the car. Though the fog was being dissipated by the rising winds in the area of the cemetery, the rainclouds remained low and thick. Reflected light was caught in their humid underbellies and sent back to earth. The dismal foggy night had suddenly turned brightly eerie, so bright that Tams, still clinging to the shadows of the stone columns, could see her sister tripping across the graves toward a small knoll. Jenny's grave was just over the crest of that knoll.

Tams waited a few seconds and then she, too, entered the graveyard.

A mixture of pride and curiosity brought Cal Burton back to the Milbrook Police Department that night. He'd gone home not long after his humiliation at the hands of Whit Pynchon. There, in the sanctuary of his small apartment, the detective lieutenant had collapsed into his bed where he'd slept the afternoon away.

If Cal hadn't been so hung-over that morning, Pynchon would have paid dearly for his transgression. In fact, Pyn-

chon would still pay for it. He'd had enough of Whit Pynchon!

Did anyone else know what had taken place in Cal's office?
He didn't remember anyone else being present, but then he
didn't remember much more than the rough hands of Whit
Pynchon. That was the main reason for his stop at the station—to see if he was the departmental laughingstock.

The dispatcher at the console wasn't surprised to see Cal.
Nor was he surprised to see the lieutenant wearing jeans and
a plaid flannel shirt beneath the expensive leather coat. Cal,
unmarried, often spent evenings at the department.

"Kinda murky out there, huh, Lieutenant?"

"So thick you could cut it with a knife. The wind's picking
up, though. It'll be gone before long. I guess we've had our
ration of accidents."

The comment prompted an immediate snicker from the
young, sandy-haired dispatcher. "Guess who drove right into
a friggin' phone pole?"

"Who?"

"Chief Wampler."

"You're kiddin'?"

"Nope, wrapped his grill right around it. Leastways that's
what 320 says. He answered the call."

"The chief hurt?"

"Naw. Just pissed."

"What else is going on?"

"Other than accidents, not a damned thing."

Cal plopped down in a rickety folding chair positioned in
front of the Teletype. If the youthful dispatcher had any ink-
ling of Cal's earlier humiliation, he gave no evidence of it.

"Want some coffee, Lieutenant?"

"Sure . . . hot and black. Same way I like my women."

* * *

Will Binder had immediately agreed to meet Anna at the cemetery gate.

"I'm going, too," Tressa said.

"No, you're not. You're going to stay right here and wait for your father. Tell him what happened."

Anna was pulling her coat on.

"Please, Anna—"

"No!" She hurried to the door.

"I think we oughta call the police."

"Mr. Binder will be there, Tressa. I suspect he can take care of himself."

"You're being silly, Anna."

Anna had the door open. She turned to the young girl. "Trust me, Tressa. Just wait for your father."

She slammed the door behind her. Tressa looked over to the phone. Some compelling voice told her to phone the police, but she had heard her father say too many times about how useless they generally were. Maybe Anna was right? Maybe she and the newspaper owner could handle it? And maybe, too, Tams was just imagining things?

The fog's density had lessened as Anna's car pulled into the wide entrance to the cemetery. Mrs. Andrews's car was there. Anna had turned off her lights just before she reached the cemetery. She decided to wait just a few minutes for Will Binder. If he didn't show up soon, she was going on into the cemetery by herself.

Wisps of fog, carried on the arms of the breeze that blew out of the west, rushed in front of her windshield. She tapped her fingers on the steering wheel. It took only a few minutes for her anxiety to force her out of the car. She eased the door open quietly and stepped out. The wind tousled her auburn hair.

She moved toward the far side of the gate, her attention riveted on the murky darkness beyond it. The hand caught her shoulder from behind. It wrapped around her to smother her mouth. Her stomach knotted with fear as she was wheeled around. The face of Will Binder was pressed closed to hers. He had the forefinger of his other hand to his lips, indicating she was to be silent.

Anna slumped with relief as he released her.

"You scared the hell outa me," she whispered, her knees still trembling.

"I didn't want you making any noise. Did the younger Andrews girl hear enough to know the killer's identity?"

"I don't think so," Anna said. "It's all been so confusing—"

"Let's try to slip in unseen."

Anna noticed his dark clothing. "You sure came dressed for it."

Binder looked down at the dark fatigues. "I know. I guess luck was with me tonight when I dressed."

"What do we do?"

"Let's move toward the child's grave. Stay low and quiet. With the grass as wet as it is, we should be able to move in without making much noise."

"After you," Anna said.

Binder put a hand on her back. "No, you go first. I'll follow."

"Are you armed?" Anna asked.

"Armed? With a gun, you mean?"

"Of course that's what I mean."

"I'm afraid not," Binder said. "I'm not much good with firearms."

Anna couldn't believe it. "What are we going to do if we run into the killer?"

"I'll think of something. Come on, let's move."

As she moved into the waiting darkness of the cemetery, Anna was beginning to think that she should have called the police. The publisher of her newspaper wasn't going to be much help at all.

"I can't see where I'm stepping," she complained.

"This is nothing," Binder whispered. "Your eyes will adjust. In Vietnam, when it was dark, it was pitch-black. Your eyes never adjusted. I walked into many a tree face-first."

Vanessa listened as well as looked. The wind made the only sounds she heard—the rustling of the flowers piled atop Jenny's grave, the clicking of denuded tree limbs, the swishing of fallen leaves. She moved to the grave. Her stomach rumbled, a result of her anxiety. *Where the hell is he? Where's the fuckin' bag of money?* If the bastard thought he was going to screw with her, he was wrong. The night air smelled of rain tinged with perfume from the still-fresh flowers at her feet. In a few days, the flowers would wilt and yellow, but for the moment they served to conceal the ugly mud of the fresh grave.

"Please let him show," she said aloud, a dark sort of prayer certainly not meant to be heard by a gracious God.

Jenny's grave was located on a small knoll that overlooked the front portion of the cemetery. Vanessa, her anxious fury mounting, turned to gaze down on the burial ground. The fog was almost gone. Drops of the recent rain twinkled on the grass. She had expected to find the money waiting for her. She'd planned to snatch it and get the hell away. What to do now?

She tensed. Had something moved?

Vanessa dropped to a crouch as her eyes tried to sift human

movement from the natural motion created by the breeze.
Fear quickened her breath.

There!

Something had moved.

It was Tams. She had darted from a grave marker to the
cover of a huge pine. Beneath its canopy, she slipped to
where she could gaze up at Jenny's grave. Tams didn't know
whether the silhouette she saw hunkered down near the grave
was Vanessa or not. It was too dark, too far away. Water
dripped down on her from the mass of thick pine boughs.
The sharp needles reached down to prick her face. She was
trying to devise a plan when the cold palm covered her mouth.

TWENTY

WHIT SLUMPED WITH RELIEF as he turned off the ignition of his car. It was safely parked in his driveway. He had just dropped Tony off at the courthouse and was to return there to meet him after he'd freshened up.

Tressa bounded out on the front porch.

He gingerly eased out of the car. "God, I'm exhausted." It was an understatement. His head throbbed. Already the muscles of his neck had started to draw and tighten from the strain. Cramps in his calves and toes came in unpredictable waves.

Even though he had managed to squeal to a stop before striking the rear end of the car ahead of him on Fancy Gap Mountain, the brush with tragedy had been so close that his knees remained weak. Once he and Tony had recovered, it was only a few hundred yards to the summit of the mountain. There, the fog had vanished until they had reached the West Virginia state line. Even then the breeze was quickly blowing away the mist.

As Tressa was coming down the steps, Whit used the time to stretch. His muscles screamed with pain. He did a deep knee bend and groaned as his knees popped. The big toe on his left foot locked under a muscle spasm. "Jeez! My legs and toes are tied in knots."

"Oh, Dad! I thought you'd never get here!"

He saw the panic on her face. "What's wrong?"

"It's Vanessa—" Her words came out in an incoherent rush. "She knows the killer . . . I mean, knows who he is. I think she was—whatcha call it—I mean, she was black-mailing him."

"Slow down, Tressa. Where's Anna?"

"She's gone after Tams."

"And where's Tams?"

"She followed Vanessa. Vanessa was going to meet the killer."

"What?"

"They're at the cemetery."

"The cemetery?"

"Where they buried Jenny."

Whit grasped his daughter's shoulders. "Okay, take a deep breath, and tell it to me slow."

Tressa took several deep breaths—then told him about Tams's call.

"And Anna went after her?" Whit asked, incredulous. "Alone?"

"No, she called her boss—Mr. Binder."

"Binder!"

"He said he'd go. I told Anna she ought to call the police—"

"You go call the police now, Tressa. I'm going to the cemetery."

"But I wanna go—"

"Dammit, girl! Binder's the killer. Go call the city police and tell them to come to the cemetery. I'm gone."

"Mr. Binder?"

"Do what I said, Tressa!" He was sinking into his car, the misery of his tired body now forgotten.

* * *

"You're hurting her," Anna said.

At the sound of Anna Tyree's voice, Tams stopped squirming.

"Don't cry out," Will Binder told the young girl. He eased his hands off her mouth, obviously poised to cover it again if she screamed—or started to say something he didn't want her to say.

"What are you doing here?" Tams asked, still quaking with fear.

"I was there when you called Tressa," Anna explained. "I called Mr. Binder, and he agreed to help."

"Where's your sister?" Binder asked.

"Up there." Tams pointed to the grave.

"I don't see her," Binder said.

"She's up there. I think she heard something and slumped down. It's either her or the killer."

Binder started to move out from under the pine.

"What are you going to do?" Anna asked.

"You stay put, both of you. I'll crawl up and see what's going on."

He scurried on all fours, like a mutant black crab, into the wet grass, and vanished in the darkness.

"What did you hear on the phone?" Anna asked.

"I just heard Vanessa tell whoever it was to meet her here with fifty thousand dollars."

Even in the subdued light, Anna saw the tears streaming down the young girl's face.

"How could she do it?" Tams was saying. "She and Mary were friends."

"I don't know, honey." Anna's shifted her attention to the knoll on which Jenny was buried. "I saw someone move."

"I'm scared," Tams whispered.

"Take it easy," Anna said. "You stay here. I'm gonna slip up there, too."

"I'm coming, too."

"No—"

"I'm coming!" Tams said. Anna knew there was no way she was going to make her remain under the pine.

Vanessa's leg muscles were starting to protest as she maintained her crouch. She had seen no other movements. The night was still, deathly still. "Where are you?" she muttered. "Damn you! Where are you?"

She slowly rose. Behind her, the shadow shot from behind a wide headstone. His feet moved soundlessly across the wet grass, just as they had many years ago in the jungles and rice paddies outside Saigon. In his right hand, Will Binder carried a compact 9-mm automatic. His left arm locked around her throat. The gun jammed into a crack between her ribs. "Make a sound, and you're dead."

Vanessa's involuntary scream was cut off by the muscled arm that clamped down on her throat. Her legs thrashed. Her hands came up to lock on the powerful forearms.

His hot breath chilled her neck. "You're outa your league, cunt."

"My little sister," Vanessa gasped. "She knows, too."

Binder laughed. "No problem," he said.

With a lightning-quick move he slipped the small pistol in the wide bellows pocket of the camouflage pants he wore. The dark grease, quickly smeared on his pale face, was transferred to Vanessa's face as their cheeks brushed. A black handkerchief was tied on his head, concealing his bright blond hair. From one of his steel-plated jungle boots, he pulled a long knife made of nonglossy black metal—the same knife that had disemboweled Cindy Jackson.

"She does!" Vanessa hissed.

"What she knows won't matter," Binder said.

"I swear to God—"

It was a bad time for a sacrilege. The black blade circled her throat. It left a red ribbon that soon gaped open all the way down to her spinal cord. She hissed and gurgled as her blood—and life—gushed out over a spray of white chrysanthemums.

Anna and Tams were closer than Binder thought. In fact, they had heard the commotion and had dropped to their knees. Above them, the low clouds had taken on a reddish, angry glow. The rain had ended for the moment, and the wind was turning cold. The strange brightness that had illuminated the cemetery was retreating, and the shadows were spreading. The multisized headstones rose like a defending army.

Anna had crept forward; Tams followed.

Anna saw them first and gasped. She whipped a hand out to stop Tams from going closer. The man—neither Anna nor Tams recognized the black-faced man in the dark—had Vanessa in his grip. For a second, everything looked all right—for just a second. Then Vanessa's head had reared back. Gleaming blood shot out from her throat. Tams had choked back a cry. Anna had grabbed the young girl as they watched her sister's body flopping on top of the flowers. Tams started to gag.

In the horror of the moment, the killer vanished.

Tams was crying, still gagging and fighting Anna, trying to reach her sister.

"Be still!" Anna commanded. Where the hell was Binder? Maybe he had run into the killer. "Let's get out of here!"

"Noooo!" Tams shrieked.

Anna didn't even pause to think. In spite of her awkward position, she brought her hand hard against Tams's face. "You have to be quiet!"

The blow stunned the girl. Tears poured from her eyes. Anna pushed her back toward the pine. Several yards away, the figure of Will Binder clutched the wet ground as he crept after them.

Once under the cover of the pine, Anna allowed herself time to think. Perhaps the killer had done his awful deed and then fled. In fact, that seemed the most likely scenario. She had no idea where Binder was—probably dead, she thought.

"Listen, Tams. I'm sorry I had to hit you. I'm sorry, too, about your sister, but we have to try to get out of here."

"He killed her, Anna."

Anna wrapped an arm around the young girl and hugged her. "I know it, but you need to remember that he'll do the same thing to us."

"Who was it?"

"I don't know. It looked like a black man."

Anna heard him first. "Shhh!" she said to Tams, pulling her down tight against the prickly bed of pine needles.

Tams heard it, too. Something—someone—was moving toward them.

"Anna?" The voice was male.

"It's Binder," Anna whispered.

"We're over here." Anna said, this time in a hoarse and loud whisper.

His body rolled under the canopy of the pine. At first, he had the back of his head to them, and it was so dark beneath the pine. When he turned to face them, Anna saw the grease—the handkerchief over his head . . . the bloody knife clasped between his grinning lips.

* * *

Whit wheeled in beside Anna's car and was out of his and moving around the front gate when he remembered he didn't have his gun. There had been no reason to wear it to North Carolina, and he'd left the house in such a rush. Too late to worry about it now.

A few drops of rain pelted his face as he paused just inside the cemetery to listen. At first there was nothing, but then he heard the soft scream. His body went rigid. His hand, out of conditioned reflex, reached for the pistol that wasn't there.

Will Binder's fingers twisted the soft flesh of Tams's throat. The girl's pitiful cry of agony escaped from the palm of his other hand as it tried to smother her mouth. His knife had fallen away into the darkness when he reached for the young girl.

"Scream again," Binder growled, "and I'll rip out your fucking throat."

"You?" Anna said, speechless at the revelation.

"You be still, too. I can kill her with the flick of a wrist."

Anna believed him. Besides, she didn't know the knife was lost to him.

Binder had seen the glare from a car as it pulled into the cemetery entrance. Its lights had been clearly visible over Anna's shoulder. His brain pondered the dilemma as his free hand pulled the pistol from his pocket. If he had still held the knife, he would have slit the squirming little bitch's throat. The gun was too loud. Will Binder wanted more than anything to escape. If he couldn't, well, that would be that. With his gun hand, he probed the thick bed of pine needles, searching for the bloody blade. It eluded him.

The girl continued to twist and contort. He jabbed her stomach with the barrel of the gun. She moaned.

"Be still, dammit."

Anna put out a hand to comfort her.

"Back!" Binder ordered.

Motivated by fear rather than reason, Tams continued to resist. His strong fingers dug out a wedge of her flesh and twisted again, this time so hard that her skin popped like an oversize blood blister. The warm fluid soaked his fingers.

Anna gasped as she saw him increase the pressure. Tams whined and then went slack in his grasp. The pain had made her pass out. That had been Binder's intent. It was a trick he'd learned in commando training. The teenage girl had withstood more pain than had seasoned North Vietnam regulars.

"Why?" Anna was asking. "Surely it wasn't worth—"

"Shut up, bitch." Even though more than a decade had passed, Binder had retained his night vision. Now that his captive was momentarily still, he took the opportunity to scan the terrain between the gate and the incline of the knoll on which he was concealed. His eyes immediately discerned the movement. Someone was approaching, trying to move unseen from marker to marker. The wind turned silent, and Binder could hear the swishing sounds of the intruder's feet on the wet grass.

Anna had heard it, too. She turned. The blow then came unseen, exploding against the back of her head. She slumped.

The black girl stirred. Binder's fingers went to work again on a new pinch of flesh. His broad, trained hand closed off her wailing.

Whit darted from one headstone to another. The pain in his neck and head were gone as he slipped on his stomach across an open space of ground. The dampness penetrated his pants and jacket. As he scrambled toward the cover of a life-size statue of Christ, his elbow cracked down hard on a ground-level metal grave marker. It sent arrows of hot, searing pain all the way up to his chin.

"Jesus," he whispered, knowing for certain he had cracked a bone.

The pain was so intense, he didn't hear the sirens for a moment. When the sound finally did register, he wasn't sure they were headed in his direction.

The shooting pain turned to a nerve-racking throb accompanied by pins and needles. Whit lifted his head and tried to determine which way to go. He could see the pile of fresh flowers. Straight up the incline, he decided, straight toward what he hoped was Jenny Hairston's grave.

Will Binder heard the same sirens. They were coming closer. He also heard the raspy breathing of the man who had just scrambled up the knoll and wasn't more than a dozen feet away. It was the sound of a smoker's lungs. Binder knew it well. In the humid night jungles of Nam the smokers in his intelligence unit had been considered a high risk. Both of his hostages remained unconscious. Anna was still, but the young black girl was beginning to stir.

His night-sharp eyes tracked the nearby movement of the man. He suspected that it was the investigator Pynchon, but he couldn't tell, not yet anyway. It didn't matter. The man was going to die no matter who it was, but he had to move quickly. The sirens were so close; Will Binder hadn't done all this to end up in some filthy prison. His hold on Tams eased as he tried to sight the gun on the shadow as it moved closer to him.

Anna had come awake, and her hand was discreetly on the move, fluttering in the wet needles surrounding her. She wanted to find a rock, anything. Insect legs itched across her face. She squelched any vocal cry, but her body trembled. She held her breath, waiting to die.

But Binder's attention was elsewhere. A few seconds later, her fingers reached out again and touched the icy blade of Will Binder's knife. Her eyes were open wide, full of terror and pain. She traced the blade until her fingers touched the soft rubber handle. They wrapped around it.

Binder loomed over her, both of his hands clamped on the small gun as he steadied it. She felt the heat of his body and smelled his sweat. Her hand rocketed up. The blade sliced across Binder's arm. He cried out in shock and pain. With lightning speed, his strong hands had her. The back of her skull cracked against the coarse trunk of the pine tree. Anna crumpled.

With blood pouring from his arm, Binder stood and fired at the shadow of the man who stalked him. The muzzle flash was followed by a shower of sparks as the bullet whined off the stone behind which Whit Pynchon had dived as soon as he heard Binder's cry.

Blood trickled down Tams's neck. Her fingers found the deep wound just as the rough fingers clutched her. She shrieked.

"It's okay. It's me. Whit."

Tams opened her eyes. She could barely make out his features. Darkness and blood both obscured her vision.

"Mr. Pynchon?"

"Come on, Tams. We're still in danger."

"He's got Anna."

"I know. He took her over that way. I wanna get you back down the hill."

"No! Go after him. I'll be okay."

Whit hesitated. "You're sure?"

"Uh huh."

"Okay." Whit started to move out from under the tree.

"Mr. Pynchon—"

He looked back. "Yeah?"

"It's Mr. Binder—"

"I know that, too."

"He killed my sister."

Whit didn't know that.

"I'll get him."

The sirens were at the gate. Whit eased out from beneath the tree and almost at once saw Binder. He was crouching behind a headstone with Anna in his grasp. A gun was pointed to her head.

"One wrong move, Pynchon, and she's dead."

"What do you want?"

"Out of here, and you're gonna help me."

Whit could see Anna's eyes. They glimmered with a watery fear. Blood—he wasn't sure whose—stained her rigid face.

Headlight beams were filling a portion of the cemetery with light.

"It's a lost cause, Binder. I couldn't help you if I wanted to."

Binder laughed and cinched his hand tighter around Anna's throat.

"Oh, yeah, you can help me. You're gonna go down there and tell the bastards that I have her. If they come for me, she dies—and some of them, too."

"Don't," Anna managed to say.

Binder's arm wrenched. She grimaced in pain.

"Okay . . . okay," Whit said. "I'll go down."

"Move slow and easy."

But Whit hesitated. "One question. Why the Jackson girl? The rest of it I think I understand."

Binder managed a shrug. "I thought she was the one blackmailing me. Turns out I was wrong, huh?"

"I bet you didn't lose any sleep over it."

"Move it, fucker!"

Whit started to ease down the gentle slope. He could hear car doors opening and slamming shut, men's voices, too. But as soon as he got several feet away from Binder, he darted behind a large headstone.

Behind him, Binder rasped, "Pynchon! Dammit, where are you?"

Whit made a wide circle.

Binder was on the verge of sheer panic by the time Whit came up behind him. He heard Whit's approach and whirled just in time to get off a shot. It whizzed by Whit's ear. Anna wrenched from Binder's grasp just as Whit's head pounded into the man's midsection, driving the air from his lungs. Binder, though, had been trained in hand-to-hand combat, and Whit's arm, the one he had cracked on the ground-level marker, was almost useless. As much from sheer reaction as willful intent, Binder brought his knee into Whit's crotch. The force of the blow was enough off center that it only stunned Whit. The maneuver had been designed—and executed—to cripple him permanently.

Headlights saved the investigator. The police cruisers exploded through the gate. Spotlights flared. Binder lunged for cover, leaving Whit writhing in the grass. Anna crawled to him. They both heard the newspaper publisher eject one clip and load another.

The police cruisers screeched to a stop on the road at the bottom of the knoll. Binder watched as men poured from the vehicles. He took careful aim and fired. A cop shrieked in pain and fell to the ground.

Whit shoved Anna behind a stone bench.

"Keep down out of the line of fire."

Whit watched as the cops, mostly deputies, sought cover. The gunfire was sporadic and ineffectual. Clearly, they hadn't pinpointed Will Binder's location. Whit didn't dare show himself, knowing that any movement would draw the cops' fire. He thought about Tams and hoped she stayed well hidden under the pine.

Cal Burton had been at the station when Tressa Pynchon's call came in. At first, he disregarded her story, but within moments he was on the phone to the sheriff's department. Though it was out of his jurisdiction, he drove the cruiser that broke through the gate.

At that moment, he was inching up the knoll on his gut, his .357 in his hand. The deputies remained concealed behind the safety of their vehicles. High atop the knoll, Cal saw the muzzle flash. He came to his knees and fired his revolver. The bullet thumped against the grave marker from which the muzzle fire had come.

Cal was ready to drop to his belly when the 9-mm bullet smacked into his forehead. He never heard the sound of the explosion. The flash of the gun was reflected in vacant eyes. He hung there for a moment, all sensation gone as the blood pumped from the small hole over his heavy brow. Then he dropped face-first into the grass.

"I'm gonna try to get him," Whit said to Anna.

"Dammit, Whit! Stay here. They can do it." Her hand wrapped around his wrist.

He pulled free. Occasional fire whined by him as he

hugged the ground. He managed to crawl to a point where he could see Binder. The man's back was leaning against the stone, his face turned away from the assault. At that moment in time, Whit would have traded at least one arm for a handgun.

Whit's eyes opened wide as he saw the publisher slip the barrel of the automatic into his mouth.

Maybe Whit could have stopped him. He didn't bother to try. The blast drove Binder's head back against the stone. His tall body slumped into a pile.

"It's over," Whit screamed.

"Who's that?" someone shouted.

"Me! Whit Pynchon! Come up! The man's dead."

"You stay put, Pynchon."

But Anna was on her feet, running toward Whit.

"Up there! Look out!" an officer screeched, pointing toward Anna's moving shadow.

Whit rocketed to his feet and dived for Anna. They crashed to the ground just as a bullet passed over their heads.

"Dammit!" Whit shouted. "I said it's over. There's a woman and kid up here you're shooting at."

Seconds later, a flashlight illuminated Whit and Anna. Another officer was aiming his light on the swollen, contorted face of Will Binder.

"Who the hell is it?" the deputy asked.

"It's the owner of the paper. That's your killer," Whit said as he helped Anna to her feet. Tams came dashing from her place of concealment under the pine. Whit stopped her before she reached his body.

"He killed Jenny Hairston," Tams cried.

One of the cops was reaching out to check Tams's wounds.

"And he did this to me," she told him. Blood still seeped from the nasty lacerations on her throat.

"Jesus," someone said. "There's another body over here."

"That's Vanessa. He killed her." Tams started to cry.

Sheriff Ted Early, accompanied by another deputy, approached Whit. The deputy put his jacket around Tams. "Come on, kid. Let's get you to the hospital."

"Go with her," Whit said to Anna. She nodded and led Tams down the hill.

"What a mess," Early sighed.

"Glad to see you, Sheriff."

"You can thank your daughter—and maybe even Cal Burton, too."

"Burton?"

"Yeah, he believed her story."

"That's surprising," Whit said. With that off his mind, he turned his attention to Ted Early. "Any of your men hurt?"

"Cole Surface was grazed by a bullet. He'll want a Purple Heart," Early said. "One fatality—the crazy bastard put a bullet in Cal Burton's head. Just a lucky shot, I guess."

Whit turned from the sheriff. "I'd call it providential justice."

EPILOGUE

THE PHYSICIAN SQUIRMED in the creaking chair that was Judge O'Brien's witness stand.

Danton pressed his question. "Dr. Fragliano, I asked if you have determined the sex of the unborn child?"

The physician looked to Ben Shanklin for assistance. The hospital's attorney gazed down at a legal pad scribbled full of notes and did not offer a saving objection.

O'Brien grew impatient. "Answer his question, Doctor."

The courtroom waited. Whit and Anna sat on the row of benches immediately behind the counsel table occupied by Tony Danton. Tams and Tressa sat another row back. The courtroom was full. The fate of Mary Hairston's child had become a regional, if not national, interest.

The physician shrugged. "To the best of our ability, we have."

"So, tell us," Danton said with a practiced flourish. "Is it a boy or a girl?"

"We believe it to be a male fetus."

"Thank you, Doctor. No more questions."

Shanklin had no questions, either. The doctor sighed with relief and hurried from the courtroom. Tony moved to a position squarely in front of O'Brien's bench.

"There you have it, Your Honor. Both the State of West Virginia and counsel for Mary Hairston respectfully submit that Mary Hairston be given a chance to have her child. It's obvious she wanted it. You heard evidence that she reached the door of an abortion clinic and changed her mind. Her own life's been taken away from her, but she has a chance to reach beyond death—to transcend it. If God sees fit to intervene, then so be it, but surely we have no right to do so—not when the mother of that male child has given clear, convincing evidence that she wanted to bring it into the world."

Tony started to say something else. Instead, he returned to the counsel table. "I won't prolong this. There's nothing else for me to say, Your Honor. Mary Hairston said it all when she walked away from that Charlotte, North Carolina, clinic—with her child."

O'Brien looked down at Morley Clarke.

"I have nothing," he said, surprising no one.

The judge then turned to Shanklin. "Does counsel for the hospital wish to offer any argument?"

Shanklin rose. "Of course, Your Honor." He walked slowly toward center stage, his leather heels clicking on the hardwood floor.

"I doubt that this courtroom has ever hosted so many newspeople," he said. "Take note of that, Your Honor. They're here because this case is news, and what makes news, I ask? Something abnormal. I urge Your Honor to consider the future of this child. Assuming it's born healthy, and as the doctors have said, there's some doubt about that—but, assuming that, it has no one to provide it with a home. It will come into this world a freak, an anomaly. We all know that the State and private homes exist for parentless children, but are these homes capable of isolating this child from the peculiarity of its circum-stances?''

Shanklin turned to look at the crowd. His eyes drifted to Tony Danton. ''The prosecutor here hasn't offered to give it a home.''

Tony jumped to his feet. ''I object!''

''Sustained!'' O'Brien, too, was angry. ''Mr. Shanklin, that's an inappropriate argument.''

''I apologize, Your Honor. In truth, the odds are very much against this child. Its life after birth notwithstand-ing, it runs a very good chance of being handicapped in some way at birth. I have as much respect for human life as any person, and so does the hospital that I represent, but it's the opinion of my client that the interest of Mary Hairston and the child would be best served by discontin-uing life support. Who knows? Mary Hairston may go on breathing without it. She may go on to bear this child. Or she may not. We think that decision should be left to an authority mightier than any we have created. Thank you.''

The judge lowered his head. An anxious hush settled over the courtroom. After a few moments, Judge David O'Brien raised it. Tears glistened in his aging eyes. ''In all my years on the bench, I don't think I've faced a more difficult decision. There's no precedent to which I can look. I myself have five young grandchildren. All of them have two loving parents. In this circumstance, I am being asked to decide the life of a child—to decide whether it should be allowed to be born into a world in which he— or she—will have no parents. In every way, it will stand apart from other children. This child, for most of its young life, will be considered special—''

''It is special!'' a feminine voice cried from the rear of the courtroom.

Heads turned. Judge O'Brien rapped his gavel. The cry had come from Kathy Binder. She stood in the open door.

"I don't know who you are," the judge was saying, "but one more outburst—"

Tony rushed up to the bench. "Judge, that's Mrs. William Binder."

The attractive blonde was coming down the aisle. "I wish to say something, Your Honor."

The judge looked at Morley Clarke. "No objection," Clarke said.

Ben Shanklin didn't know what to say. "Uh . . . I . . . under the circumstances, we have no objection."

Mrs. Binder stood before the judge's bench.

"Proceed with what you want to say," O'Brien told her.

"My husband apparently fathered that child," the tall woman said. "I don't know what made my husband do the terrible things he did. He wasn't that kind of a man. I was married to him for nearly a decade, and this is a side of him that I never, ever knew could exist. Perhaps he carried some deep scar from his years in Vietnam. I can't atone for his crimes, but there is one thing I can do—one thing I want more than anything to do. I want to raise Mary Hairston's child."

The crowd in the courtroom was silent. Tony put a hand on the woman's shoulder. "You don't have to do this, Mrs. Binder."

She jerked away from him. Tears streamed down her cheeks. "I know that, Mr. Danton. I'm not making some offer born out of guilt. I've always wanted children. Will never did. He actually feared little children. Maybe that was a part of it, too. I know this. I want that child. It's a part of Will, and, no matter what he did, I still love him."

The crowd was aroused. Several flashbulbs exploded.

Some of the defiance vanished from her voice. "My attorney has advised me that the court is highly unlikely to grant custody to me since my husband—"

Her sentence died. She wiped a tear from her face and said, "If you don't see fit to grant my request, then rest assured that I will see to the child's financial needs."

Judge O'Brien pounded his gavel until he achieved some semblance of order. He then ordered the attorneys and Mrs. Binder into his chambers.

Anna had clasped Whit's hand so hard it was white. He eased it free of her grip. "Talk about courtroom drama," he said.

Anna was drying her eyes. "She's some lady. I talked with her yesterday. She's got a lot of plans for the *Journal*."

"And now she has someone to pass it on to." Whit said.

Anna gasped. "I never thought of that. Mary Hairston's child owning the *Journal*. Why do you think he killed Jenny, Whit? That's one thing I can't understand."

"We'll never know. I'd say he went to the house expecting Mary Hairston to be alone. Maybe he shot Mary, and the child came down from the bedroom. He was probably just trying to get rid of all the witnesses."

Tams and Tressa were beside themselves with anxiety. They weren't alone. Most of those in the courtroom milled about, discussing this latest development, waiting for it to become resolved.

"Will they let her do it?" Tams was asking of Whit.

Tressa paced around the counsel table. "They have to. They just have to."

Forty-five minutes later, Judge David O'Brien walked

out onto the bench. The attorney for the hospital returned to his table. Tony and Mrs. Binder didn't reappear. The judge rapped his gavel once. All eyes came to rest upon him.

"This court will take the request of Mrs. Binder under advisement. Given her guarantee of financial support, I order that the hospital do all within its power to preserve the life of the fetus. A decision on final placement can await the medical outcome." He hammered his gavel again and vanished before the storm.

Whit and Anna reached a door in back of the courtroom before the stampede of newsmen. The bailiff let them through, then started turning away the reporters. In the suite of offices that constituted the judge's chambers, they found Tony chatting with an elated Kathy Binder.

"We'll just have to wait and see," Tony said. "The judge agreed to consider it."

"And that suits the hospital?" Anna asked.

The new owner of the *Journal* laughed, wiping away her tears of happiness. "They know I can pay the bill."

Tony took Kathy's hand. "You do know there's some chance the child won't make it. Or that it might be born with some handicap."

The woman was still smiling. "I have faith. Something good has to come out of this nightmare."

Whit stood back from the discussion as Kathy Binder starting talking to Anna about a promotion to the position of editor.

"What about Bukowsky?" Anna was asking.

"I had a talk with him before I came here. That's why I was late. He wants to retire. And I fired Jack Arnold."

Anna looked to Whit and saw him staring out the window. She knew what he was thinking. It was snowing outside, the first real snow of the season.

She went to him. "What do you think?"

"About what?"

"About me being editor of the *Journal*?"

Whit sighed. "I guess one happy ending is the best anyone could expect."

ABOUT THE AUTHOR

DAVE PEDNEAU is a former reporter, columnist, and magistrate court judge. His novels include *A.P.B.*, *Dead Witness*, and *Presumption of Innocence*. He lives in southern West Virginia with his wife and daughter.

Attention Mystery and Suspense Fans

Do you want to complete your collection of mystery and suspense stories by some of your favorite authors? John D. MacDonald, Helen MacInnes, Dick Francis, Amanda Cross, Ruth Rendell, Alistar MacLean, Erle Stanley Gardner, Cornell Woolrich, among many others, are included in Ballantine/Fawcett's new Mystery Brochure.

For your FREE Mystery Brochure, fill in the coupon below and mail it to: